DEATH RIDE

DEATH RIDE

Nick Oldham

**SEVERN
HOUSE**

First world edition published in Great Britain and the USA in 2023
by Severn House, an imprint of Canongate Books Ltd,
14 High Street, Edinburgh EH1 1TE.

Trade paperback edition first published in Great Britain and the USA in 2023
by Severn House, an imprint of Canongate Books Ltd.

severnhouse.com

British Library Cataloguing-in-Publication Data
A CIP catalogue record for this title is available from the British Library.

ISBN-13: 978-1-4483-0695-4 (cased)
ISBN-13: 978-1-4483-0698-5 (trade paper)
ISBN-13: 978-1-4483-0699-2 (e-book)

All Severn House titles are printed on acid-free paper.

Typeset by Palimpsest Book Production Ltd., Falkirk, Stirlingshire, Scotland.
Printed and bound in Great Britain by TJ Books Ltd, Padstow, Cornwall.

For Belinda

ONE

Henry Christie could see – even though he couldn't hear – that the couple were having one of those hissed, teeth-clenched and very strained disagreements as he walked towards them, stiffly sliding his arms into his hi-vis jacket.

The couple – Henry guessed they were in their mid-thirties – were standing next to the portable counter with the sign above it, located by the entrance to the car park of The Tawny Owl, the combined pub and country hotel Henry half owned in the village of Kendleton in the wilds of North-East Lancashire. The sign above the counter read, *Information, Meeting Point, Lost Children.*

Henry studded up his jacket, glad it was one of the webbed, breathable types allowing air to circulate and keep him relatively cool, and threaded his way slowly across the front terrace of the pub on which every table was full of drinkers and diners, with even more customers sitting and lounging on the low walls of the terrace, on this extremely warm Bank Holiday Monday afternoon, the third day of the Kendleton Country Fair. Probably because the annual fair had been postponed three times because of the pandemic, thousands of visitors had flooded into the village over the three-day period. Not that Henry was moaning; the influx had seen takings at Th'Owl (as the pub was known locally) rise exponentially and a lot of money had flowed into the village as life returned, more or less, to normal.

Henry had been press-ganged by the village council – the voluntary group that ran the show – to supervise the stewards and to keep an eye on the information counter, hand out leaflets, give directions and deal with any lost children that might come his way. So far, only one child had gone missing, albeit briefly, but as Henry walked down the steps towards the arguing couple, he had one of those 'moments' when that intuitive feeling of dread, honed over thirty-plus years as a cop, most of them as a detective and then latterly as a civilian investigator, shimmered through his whole being, telling him that there was more to this than met the eye.

Or maybe it was nothing at all, and he was just imagining things because he was inherently suspicious of almost everything.

The disagreement between the couple continued right up to the moment Henry stepped behind the counter, smiled at them and tapped the sewn-on badge on his jacket that declared, *Kendleton Country Fair – Here to Help.*

'Are you folks OK?' he asked.

Their strained conversation stopped, and they turned slowly to him, the lips on both their faces tight across their teeth.

'We've lost our daughter,' the woman said. She was about to say more, but the man interjected, making her snap her mouth shut irritably.

He said, 'It's nothing, I'm sure. She's just overreacting.' He rolled his eyes in the kind of knowing man-to-man gesture that Henry detested, then pointed to the village green across the road, which was teeming with people, fairground rides, craft displays, steam engines, classic cars, beer and burger tents – all the things that went to make up a typical, if very large, country fair. The man turned back to Henry. 'Look, we don't want to bother you; she'll turn up.'

Henry looked away from him and turned to the woman – he assumed wife – who was both stressed and angry, judging by the expression on her face. Henry said, 'Actually, it's no trouble,' then had to wince as the exceptionally loud public address system blared as the announcer – Mr Darbley, the local butcher – coughed and gave the ten-minute warning that the lawnmower derby was due to start on the showground on the other side of the village. Henry waited for him to finish the announcement and, once the din stopped, said, 'As you can hear, we have a very effective tannoy, plus our volunteer stewards are all over the place. We are here to help.'

The woman glanced at the man – Henry assumed husband – then to Henry said, 'She's called Charlotte Kirkham . . . I'm her mother, Melinda West, and this is . . . her, er . . . stepdad, Dave West.' She jerked her thumb at him, making him pull a sour face. 'She's thirteen, headstrong, and doesn't want to be here today, because it's not cool,' she went on, only to be interrupted by Mr West again.

'Which is exactly my point, Mel. She's almost a grown woman and you always overreact when you haven't seen her for more than five minutes.'

Melinda scowled at him, then turned back to Henry. 'I'm sorry to have bothered you, but I'm clearly an over-protective mother . . .'

'She's probably just watching the sheep-shearing competition,' Dave West said, 'with an ice cream in one hand and her bloody phone in the other – in her own little world as usual.'

'Have you actually phoned her?' Henry enquired.

'Repeatedly,' Melinda said.

'Does she usually answer you?'

'Yes . . . but there's something else.'

'What would that be?'

'Some lads . . .'

'Some lads?'

The husband tutted, rolled his eyes and gave his head an irritated shake. Once more, the wife shot him a barbed look.

Henry was about to give him the same but held back and asked, 'Which lads?'

'Some . . . er . . . three or four of them, I think – teenagers,' Melinda said. 'They'd been following us around the showground – y'know, horsing around, showing off to Charley – Charlotte – and I didn't like the look of them, though she was obviously entranced. I told them to sling their hooks, but they just sneered and laughed at me . . . And what did you do, Dave? Sod all!'

'They were just having a lark, like lads do,' he said defensively.

'OK, OK,' Henry said, patting fresh air in a gesture designed to bring peace, love and tranquillity. 'Give me a description of Charlotte, what she's wearing, her full name, and I'll let all the volunteers and stewards know, and I'll get it shouted out over the tannoy and ask her to meet you here. How about that?'

Melinda nodded with some degree of relief.

Henry added, 'You've probably nothing to worry about, but let's at least go through the motions. Nothing to lose by doing that.'

'Thank you.'

They exchanged phone numbers, and Henry said that at least one of them should remain at the counter. Melinda said she would. After she'd given him a brief description, which he jotted down on the back of one of the show's information leaflets, she also sent Henry a photograph of her daughter, taken that day. Henry looked at the picture of Charlotte, who obviously did not want to have the photo taken and was holding up her hand to partly cover her face in protest. That said, Henry could see she was a bonny girl.

'That's brilliant,' he said.

'Well, actually, I'm not happy about it,' Dave West cut in authoritatively. 'You having a photograph of our daughter. You could do anything with it. We don't know you from Adam. You could be a perv.'

'Dave!' Melinda admonished him. 'Suddenly she's *your* daughter and *you're* worried about her . . . as if.'

'I understand,' Henry said. 'It's a weird world we live in, so just so you both know, I'm Henry Christie, I own this place' – he pointed to The Tawny Owl – 'my name's over the door, and I'm also a retired police officer.' He gave them one of his winning smiles. 'A detective, even.'

'Good enough for me,' Melinda stated, giving her husband a look designed to brook no argument and at which he wilted.

'Right,' Henry said, 'I'll keep the photo on my phone, but I will pass it on to our stewards and any police officers I may come across if that's OK?'

'Yes, it is,' Melinda said before Dave could open his mouth to object.

Henry nodded and turned away to walk towards the village green, wondering just what sort of place the world had become. He walked slowly and stiffly, more of a shuffle than anything. He was still recuperating from a knife attack several months earlier, which had left him fighting for his life in intensive care for several days. The Kendleton Country Fair was his first proper outing and test of his recovery, three long days of fairly intense activity which – and here he touched his skull in lieu of wood – was going quite well so far.

The back left-hand quarter of his chest cavity still felt as though it had been packed with scrap metal from both the actual stabbing and the surgery he had undergone. As he walked, he rolled his left arm from the shoulder and tried to stretch the muscles around his shoulder blade without splitting any of the vast swathe of almost healed stitches around that area, which still had a tendency to weep occasionally.

It was getting easier every day, but it was a slow process.

He shook his head at the thought and the memory. Of standing in the doorway of St Andrew's Church in Kendleton, becoming aware of a movement behind and to one side of him, then the brutal, surprise attack – three thrusts – that had floored him instantly, and those few moments when he hadn't realized he'd been stabbed. At first, he thought he'd been punched. Hard, but punched.

The blood made him realize different. Then the agony.

Now he shook his head to rid his mind of the thoughts and the bitterness that no one had yet been identified or arrested for the assault.

'Fucker!' Henry said under his breath. He was sure he knew who his assailant had been, but, as ever, knowing and proving were two different beasts.

'Oi! Language! You could get yourself arrested for saying stuff like that!' came a voice from his left, a voice that he knew well. What was still unfamiliar, however, was the way in which Debbie Blackstone dressed, and it was taking Henry a bit of time to get his head around the change.

He'd first encountered – he preferred that word to 'met' because it seemed more appropriate – Detective Sergeant Debbie Blackstone when he had been lured back to work for Lancashire Constabulary as a civilian investigator on the Cold Case Unit, which was a department of the Force Major Investigation Team – FMIT. 'Lured' was probably not the correct word; it had been financial necessity at the time, something to keep the wolf from the door during the height of the pandemic when The Tawny Owl had been all but closed down.

Blackstone had been the DS on the CCU, and she and Henry, paired up, had blundered unwittingly into an investigation that went on to expose a decades-old criminal conspiracy; as a side issue, it firmly cemented their friendship. Initially, Blackstone had pretty much blown Henry's mind with her (to him) outrageous attitude, behaviour and dress sense, but underneath this veneer he had discovered a troubled but caring woman and also a very skilled and dedicated detective who wasn't being given the opportunity to prove herself.

Since then, and after Henry had more or less packed in his investigator's role, Blackstone had moved across to be a DS on FMIT, but that had proved to be as short-lived as her personal blue touchpaper. Henry, in recovery from the knife attack, had learned that while he was out of it, Blackstone had reacted badly to *something* and said or did *something* out of order, and a swift decision had been made to oust her from FMIT completely and turf her back into uniform.

What these somethings were, Henry had yet to discover, but he guessed Blackstone would reveal all when ready. Although curiosity was gnawing away at him, he had learned never to push her.

And the strikingly visible representation of Blackstone's new position in life was what Henry was now having to accept as the new normal.

Gone – obviously – were the speckled pink Doc Marten boots, as were the purposely torn fishnet tights, micro denim skirts and most of her facial adornments, and although her hair was still an ever-changing hue dependent on her mood (today was fire-red), she was now pretty much obliged to adapt to the constraints that a straight-laced police uniform imposed on her.

'Debs,' Henry acknowledged her. 'Just muttering to myself.'

'When men get older, they are often driven to verbalize their thoughts without even knowing it, apparently,' she warned him with a cheeky grin, never one to miss an opportunity to mock his age. In a friendly way, obviously.

'I knew I was saying it out loud,' he assured her.

'Course you did.' She shrugged.

The transfer out of FMIT into uniform had been on to Northern Division's Rural Crime and Wildlife Task Force based in Lancaster, and she was now the sergeant overseeing the force's response to the huge rise in rural crime across that swathe of the county from the coast at Morecambe right over to the boundaries with Yorkshire. It was a big area with a lot going on.

Henry gave her a critical once-over and winked. 'You look good in uniform,' he teased her.

She blinked, mock-affronted. 'I look bloody good in anything, matey,' she corrected him as she hitched up her ill-fitting trousers. She was in shirt-sleeve order because of the warm day but was also wearing a stab vest and all the other hefty accoutrements that came with being a uniformed cop: rigid handcuffs in a pouch, extendable baton, incapacitant spray, a personal radio attached to the stab vest and a police baseball cap pushed back at a jaunty angle on her head.

'Have you got everything set up?' Henry asked.

'Yep, I'm the official poster girl for the rural crime team today,' she said. She tilted her head sideways, rested her cheek on her clasped hands and flashed her eyelashes, which Henry saw were as long as spiders' legs.

Henry knew her team had a mobile display unit at the fair that day. It included three members of her staff, a PCSO and two PCs who were there in a law-and-order capacity as well as to sell the effectiveness of the team, which Henry knew was excellent at rural crime prevention as well as arresting offenders. He guessed it would be even better with Blackstone at the helm.

He knew all this because Blackstone had taken roost at The Tawny Owl and lived in the guest room in the owner's accommodation area where Henry also resided. She actually owned a nice penthouse apartment on Preston Docks but had moved temporarily into Th'Owl; initially, this was to help her cut down on the length of her commute, but when she was unexpectedly booted off FMIT – which had headquarters based near Preston – on to the rural team working out of Lancaster nick, she'd decided to sell the apartment and buy a property in Lancaster. She asked Henry, *pretty please*, if she could continue to remain in The Tawny Owl, but this time as a fully paying lodger as opposed to a freeloader.

She had used the term 'freeloader' herself, but Henry had never seen it that way. He was just happy to have her knocking about, whether she stumped up for food and board or not.

Henry and Blackstone walked across the road on to the heaving village green.

Although Henry knew Blackstone was displaying her police-related wares at the show, he hadn't seen much of her over the last few days – weeks, even – other than in passing. She was working long hours now with her new team, getting used to being back in uniform and getting her head around rural crime and all its idiosyncrasies. She tended to start early and finish late, and, on her return to her room at night, just wanted to crash, so this meeting was a chance for the two to have a quick catch-up.

'How's the apartment sale going?' he asked.

'Keen to get rid of me?' she asked.

'Quite the opposite.'

'Well, it's still happening, but you know what it's like – many a slip – so I'll believe it when it's done and dusted.'

'Any properties come up in Lancaster you fancy?'

'A couple . . . even a doer-upper in Thornwell,' she said, referring to the next village along from Kendleton, 'but that might be a step too far for me. It would have to be my forever home if I did that.'

'Intriguing. Anyway, no rush from my perspective,' Henry assured her.

'Thank you, but if I have overstayed my welcome, just say.'

'You haven't.'

'Appreciate it . . . Anyhow, what are you in such a rush for? Doing all that muttering?'

'Just taken the report of a missing girl.' He held out his phone and showed Blackstone the photo of Charlotte Kirkham. 'May have wandered off with some lads – some ne'er-do-wells.'

'*Ne'er-do-wells?*' Blackstone scoffed. 'Is that one of those Dickensian phrases you're so fond of saying that no one else understands?'

'One of those wonderful phrases that perfectly encapsulates the type of people who are villains or ruffians and which is, sadly, slowly being consigned to history,' Henry said tartly. He liked his old-school phraseology and was loath to let it go.

Blackstone glanced at the photo.

'Taken today and she's wearing that top and that jewellery,' Henry said, referring to the numerous bracelets on her right wrist. 'Pity Jake Niven's on leave this week,' he added, referring to the local beat cop who lived in Kendleton. 'This could have been a job for him . . .'

'I've seen this lass, actually,' Blackstone said. 'Earlier, with her parents, trailing behind them like a moody teenager – she looked miserable as sin. Her dad had a look around our display . . . Send me the mugshot and I'll pass it on to my lot to keep an eye out.'

Henry sent it over. 'I'm going to the PA tent to get them to ask her to make her way back to our meeting point, so if you or your crew spot her, tell her that her mum and dad will be over at The Tawny Owl.'

'Gotcha.' Blackstone made to punch his shoulder but stopped with her fist an inch away as she saw the grimace on his face. 'Not ready for roughhousing yet?'

'Roughhousing? And you slag off my ancient turn of phrase?' Henry smirked.

'Good point.'

'And no, I'm still a delicate flower,' he admitted.

'And no one's been locked up yet?' Blackstone said.

'Nope.' Henry's lips closed sharply.

'But you're still thinking you know who it was?'

He gave her a meaningful look.

'OK, won't go there . . . Laters,' she said, gave him a quick wave and veered off towards the rural crime team's gazebo.

Henry headed towards the PA tent, negotiating his way carefully around people so as not to get barged or bumped. He knew if he did crash into anyone, it would hurt him more than it would hurt them, but he also realized he could not go on living his life wrapped in cotton wool.

He nodded amicably to many folk, but then, across the opposite side of the small animal show-ring, he spotted Maude Crichton with her spoiled pooch, a Bichon Frise called Manderley, chatting to a couple of other dog owners with similar-looking animals. Maude glanced up from her conversation and, even across the expanse of the ring, caught Henry's eye. He quickly turned away, not wishing to have any interaction with her. He did see, however, that she made a quick, apologetic gesture to the people she was with and immediately set off towards him, pulling Manderley with her.

Henry groaned inwardly, knowing he was about to get doorstepped unless he upped his pace and managed to disappear into the PA tent without her seeing. He knew this was unlikely, not least because when he reached the tent, he realized it had a completely open front with nowhere for him to hide, and the two guys in charge of the system were visible for all to see, sitting behind an extended trestle table surrounded by amplifiers and lots of food.

Henry knew both men. One was Dave Darbley, the village butcher, and the other was Dr Lott, the local GP, both seemingly having a sideline as announcers and commentators. Darbley, with a chunky radio microphone in hand, had just risen from his seat and explained to Henry he was on his way to the main showground to commentate on the lawnmower derby.

Glancing over his shoulder and spotting Maude coming towards him like a heat-seeking missile, Henry explained to both men about Charlotte Kirkham and asked if they would use the tannoy to ask Charlotte to check in with her parents at The Tawny Owl meeting point.

Dr Lott said he would do so immediately and began to broadcast the request, leaning into his table mic like an old-fashioned TV presenter. Henry backed off but reversed into Maude, who had him cornered.

He attempted a nifty sidestep but got his leg caught in Manderley's extendable lead and, within seconds, had done a perfect pirouette. The lead wrapped around his calves as though he were a steer that had been lassoed by a cowboy's bolas.

'Jeez!' Realizing the situation and not wanting to do anything as stupid as fall over, Henry stopped moving. He gave Maude a stony expression and said, 'Untangle me, please.'

Biting her lip apologetically, she circled Henry slowly while also drawing in the lead until he was finally free.

'Thank you,' he said caustically.

'Sorry.'

His initial annoyance dissipated quickly as he exhaled, relaxed and said, 'Accidents happen . . .' at which point Manderley suddenly realized who Henry was and, without any foreplay, reared up and seized Henry's lower right leg and began to shag it. It was like being humped by a small sheep.

'Oh, for . . .' Henry began, trying to kick out and free his leg.

Manderley had a very bad habit of doing this to Henry, and it seemed the dog had been missing him.

'Sorry, sorry, sorry,' Maude cried and roughly grabbed her little dog's jewel-encrusted collar to yank him away from Henry's tasty leg. She then crouched down next to the beast and held him back from continuing the assault. 'Not a good start,' she admitted, close to tears.

'No, it wasn't,' Henry said curtly.

'Can we talk?'

'Not right now, eh?'

'Later?'

Henry considered the request. He sighed, not wanting to be horrible but not wanting to engage with Maude either – mainly because he suspected her son was the one who'd almost knifed him to death. It was an allegation that could not be proved, but one that Henry believed to be true and that Maude, in full protective-mother mode, was unwilling to even entertain.

'I should be at The Tawny Owl around nine this evening,' he conceded.

'OK, that would be good.' She stood up, gave Manderley's lead a tug and, with one last, lingering look at Henry, turned and headed back into the throng of fairgoers.

Henry frowned, ill at ease. It had got too complicated with Maude anyway. All he wanted was a simple existence now that he had survived the attack, and if he was honest, that meant a life without Maude, even if her son hadn't been his attacker. Her offspring – son, daughter and their partners – all suspected that Henry was after her money, and if he had kept seeing her and it got really serious, it would be a self-fulfilling prophecy as far as they were concerned. Henry didn't need any of that grief. Certainly, he didn't want a return visit from the nasty bastard to finish off the job one dark, moonless night.

He looked at his phone and began to compose a message to the stewards with details of Charlotte Kirkham, the missing, petulant teenage girl, then started a slow walk-through of the fair, here on the village green and then over to the other side of the village on the much larger showground, all the while wondering if there really was anything to worry about.

He called her mother, Melinda.

She answered, worry in her voice.

'Hi, no news as yet,' Henry said, 'but I have, as you may have heard, got the guy on the tannoy to do a shout-out. The police and the stewards have all got details. I'm doing a walk-through, and if we haven't heard anything in half an hour, I'll get a more coordinated search underway.'

'Thank you, thank you.'

'Are you and your husband still at the meeting point?'

'Yes.'

'Tell you what, one of you go into the pub and get a couple of coffees or teas from the bar, on me. I'll phone the lady in charge to let her know. She's called Ginny.'

'OK, thank you again.'

Henry hung up and called Ginny to alert her while he continued his stroll.

He went through the village and on to the vast showground beyond, which was packed with even more visitors on this glorious day. There were beer and wine tents, lots of fast-food (and class-food) tents, marquees and caravans, and multiple displays of crafts and arts, plus fairground rides including a massive space wheel that hurtled people around at what seemed a million miles per hour.

There were a few noticeable gangs of lads in evidence; some Henry recognized from the adjoining village of Thornwell and the huge new housing estates that had been built there. But most of the lads he didn't know. On the whole, they seemed good-natured, but all affected by drink and sunshine, a combination that Henry knew could change anyone's demeanour quickly.

He continued to stroll.

The atmosphere was pretty much as light-hearted as it should be, he had to admit, and although this kind of event wasn't something he liked much, it was a much-needed shot in the arm for the village, not just financially but socially. A touch of rural normality.

Henry made his way to where the lawnmower derby was about to commence in a field blocked off by hay bales. A dozen eager young lads and girls with ruddy, chubby faces perched precariously on their homemade machines which revved ear-splittingly on the start line.

Henry grinned. Good fun.

This was also close to the location where the sheep-shearing competition had taken place, as referred to by Charlotte's stepdad earlier. A small herd of sheared sheep had been corralled into a fenced area behind a livestock lorry, with a stack of newly shorn fleeces next to the fencing.

Henry leaned on a post and watched the naked sheep for a while as they moved in and out and around each other, bleating continually. He wondered if they were as dim as they were stereotyped to be. He doubted it.

Something caught his eye on the grass being trampled flat by the sheep. A small, black, slim, rectangular object.

A mobile phone.

Henry clambered clumsily over the fence and pushed his way between the sheep until he reached the phone, dropped slowly on to his haunches and picked it up, a feeling of trepidation zigzagging through him.

He stood up and looked at his find.

It had a cracked screen, maybe caused by the sheep treading on it.

Even so, as he swept the tip of his forefinger across the cracks, it came to life and the screensaver photo on it made him gulp: a family group – mum, dad, daughter – clustered together for the selfie. Melinda, Dave and Charlotte, all smiling.

Even as he looked at it, the phone started to vibrate as a phone call came in, identified as *Mum*.

TWO

Henry had a terrible sense of foreboding – like a clenched fist or half a house brick – in the pit of his stomach as he leaned on the wall at the back of the function room at The Tawny Owl and watched a line of Support Unit constables, led by their sergeant, troop in, chattering among themselves, then sit on the row of plastic chairs Henry had arranged for them at the front, opposite the low stage.

Debbie Blackstone watched them also, resting her elbow on a lectern, as they finally sorted themselves out and settled down for a briefing.

The Support Unit had been on some sort of public order deployment in Morecambe, and half their number – this lot, eight including the sergeant – had been pulled off that job and hustled over to Kendleton in their personnel carrier.

'OK, people,' Blackstone said finally when she was certain all eyes and attention were on her. She checked her watch, and Henry glanced instinctively at the wall clock behind her, which showed that almost ninety minutes had passed – very quickly, it seemed – since Henry had found Charlotte Kirkham's damaged mobile phone in the sheep pen. That meant, in theory, that the 'Golden Hour' had passed. Henry knew this phrase was usually misquoted as being limited to an actual hour following the commission of an offence or the discovery of suspicious circumstances. In reality, it was *not* limited to one hour and, in a serious investigation, it could encompass several hours or even days. It referred to the moments that should be used to full advantage to maximize opportunities to get to the truth of what had happened and make progress in an investigation.

That said, even though it had taken well over an hour to get some meaningful numbers of police on the scene in Kendleton that day, the intervening time had not been wasted by hanging around.

Henry had been quick to ensure several things happened after finding the phone and answering the incoming call from Charlotte's mother.

After a couple of minutes trying to explain to the almost hysterical woman who he was – because a man's voice had triggered her right off the scale – and why he was in possession of the phone, and trying to calm her as to the possible implications, he'd upped his speed and scuttled through the showground to find Blackstone at the rural police display to report his discovery to her. Her face had clouded over instantly.

'I'll get things moving,' she said and told Henry she knew the Support Unit was over in Morecambe, which was not too far away.

He nodded and started to make his way back to The Tawny Owl while transmitting over the dedicated radio system to call all the stewards to muster at the meeting point outside the pub as soon as possible.

They'd all managed to get there in ten minutes – which was good going for some of them who were in their seventies. He gave them a short briefing, sent Charlotte's photograph to their phones again and dispatched them to start to search the village green and the showground, ensuring the task was carried out with some logic and not too much overlap. He wanted them to look everywhere – behind stands, inside tents, underneath vehicles – and to ask all stallholders and exhibitors if they'd seen Charlotte, and also to record everything they did and where they'd been. They weren't trained to search or to ask questions of possible witnesses, but at least something was being done, and there was the possibility of striking lucky, in which case this incident would quickly be closed down as a nothing job or quickly escalate into something possibly terrible.

Whatever, Henry knew it had to be approached as the latter; if it turned out to be the former, at least there would be no egg splattered on anyone's face.

Blackstone took no convincing whatsoever to take it seriously, even though initial police resources, despite getting eight experienced uniforms on the scene quickly, were pretty limited at the moment.

One thing Henry knew for certain was that Blackstone would not get caught, metaphorically speaking, with her knickers around her ankles.

Yet, even as Henry watched her start to speak to the newly arrived cops, he had a horrible feeling about this.

Behind him, the door to the function room opened and Ginny entered, pushing a trolley on which were a dozen mugs and large coffee and tea urns, plus biscuits, for the Support Unit. Henry had ordered the refreshments based on his previous experience – thirty-odd years as a cop. It was basic stuff, but he knew a brew and a chocolate biscuit went a long way to making a bobby happy.

He gave Ginny the nod to leave the trolley.

'How are the parents?' he whispered to her. She had been looking after Melinda and Dave West in the owner's accommodation.

'On pins.'

'I can imagine.'

Ginny hesitated.

Henry said, 'You OK?' He sensed something amiss.

'Er, yeah. Um, I need to have a chat with you later, if possible, when you're free, yeah?'

'Yeah, of course.'

She nodded and left Henry wondering what she meant as he turned back to earwig Blackstone's briefing, but before he could listen in, one of the stewards called him up on the radio.

'Bob to Henry, Bob to Henry, come in.'

They didn't have call signs – they weren't so sophisticated – so they stuck to forenames, although 'Bill One' and 'Bill Two' did cause some confusion. 'Bob' was a local builder.

'Henry to Bob, go ahead, mate,' Henry answered and twisted out of the function room so as not to interrupt the briefing.

'Yeah, Bob here, Henry,' Bob said.

Henry rolled his eyes. 'I know, you're calling me, Bob.'

'Oh, yeah, right, good . . . Henry, I'm with the guy who has the falconry display – you know him?'

'Affirmative.' Henry knew who he was but did not know him personally. He also knew the bird-of-prey display was somewhere behind the sheep pen where he had found Charlotte's phone. 'Yes, go on, Bob,' Henry urged him.

'I think you need to get over here, Henry. This guy thinks he saw our missing kid, Charlotte, with some lads.'

'I'm pretty sure it was her,' the man said, taking another look at the image on Henry's phone. He, ironically, called himself Tony Owl, which was his business name; his real name was a rather less impressive Jim Taylor. That said, Henry thought he ran a very professional and popular business.

On his forearm, a large Russian steppe eagle gripped the leather gauntlet and looked balefully at Henry, who felt a tad uncomfortable under the watchful eyes of a bird that seemed to be checking him out as its next meal.

Tony Owl grinned slightly as Henry took a step backwards. 'Don't worry, she's a softie,' Tony assured him, but Henry didn't think that was the case.

The falconer looked down at the photograph again, pursed his lips, then nodded. 'Yep, I'd say so.'

'What were the circumstances?' Debbie Blackstone asked. She'd curtailed the Support Unit briefing, got the officers turned out and accompanied Henry to the falconry display.

'I'll be honest, I didn't really take too much notice,' Tony said. 'Y'know, just another group of kids messing around . . .' The birdman stopped speaking and looked up quizzically and frowned as he tried to recall the sighting in more detail.

'You remember something else?'

'Er, maybe . . . now I think about it, they were acting a bit odd.'

'In what way?' Blackstone asked.

'Oh, it's probably nothing.'

'Never make that assumption,' Henry said. 'What was strange?'

'How they – the lads – seemed to be surrounding the girl, throwing something and she was trying to catch it.'

'Throwing what?'

'Um . . . mobile phone, maybe. I think she looked pissed off and also, *also*, they seemed like they were herding her, pushing her along.'

'Did she seem uncomfortable with that?' Blackstone asked.

Tony shrugged. 'Wouldn't like to say. Let me see her photo again,' he said to Henry, who showed him Charlotte's photograph once more. The man nodded now. 'Yep, it was definitely her, and now that I think about it, it didn't seem quite right, I suppose.'

'OK, thanks for that,' Blackstone said. 'I take it you're here for a few more hours?'

'I've got one more display of the birds which takes three-quarters of an hour or so, down by the stream. Then I'll start packing.'

'Can I ask you not to go before we come and see you again?' Blackstone added. 'Just in case we need a statement.'

'You think something might have happened to her?'

'We're keeping an open mind for the moment,' Blackstone said. 'But, whatever, please don't leave the site before we speak to you again.'

'OK, no worries.'

Henry and Blackstone were about to turn away when Tony said, 'I've just remembered something else!'

They stopped abruptly and looked at him.

'One of the lads. I'd seen him earlier.'

This was the second pair of eyes within minutes that was looking balefully at Henry, except this time it wasn't an eagle looking at him; it was a man, but the look in the eyes was exactly the same: boredom tinged with danger.

Henry felt the skin crawl and tighten at the back of his neck, but he also got the twitch of excitement that he always got in his arsehole when he knew he was on to something or someone, even if he wasn't yet sure what it was.

Following the snippet of information given to them by Tony Owl, Henry and Blackstone had, as quickly as his body would allow, trudged across the showground to a row of food stands, stalls and vans, several of which were serving burgers and suchlike, and the pair were now standing at the back of a long-wheelbase burger van, looking up at the owner who was leaning over the half-door at the top of a short flight of metal steps. He was wearing a full-body apron, splattered with grease and speckled with blood, which was partly explained by the fact he was in the process of preparing a beef burger, currently slapping it from palm to palm as he shaped it, making a disgusting slurping noise that caused Henry to feel slightly queasy.

'What?' said the man. 'I'm busy . . . been a good day for business.' He was clearly impatient about being interrupted. 'Got loads more of these beauties to make and sell,' he added with a half grin while looking at Blackstone and bouncing the burger on his hand. It was ready to cook.

'This is your burger van?' Henry asked. He had a list of everyone at the show involved in selling or displaying goods. It was a tightly typed list, tiny letters, single-spaced, on two sheets of A4 paper. 'You are Mr Lennox?'

His name was Leonard Lennox according to the list, but he didn't acknowledge that it was, just waited for the follow-up question as Henry raised his head from the list and looked at the burger guy – which was the name of the business painted on the front of the van, on the awning and underneath the serving hatch.

Lennox was fifty-ish, slightly chubby but with a pointed face and a crooked nose that looked as though it had once been broken, a thin, almost invisible scar down the right side of his face, and suspicious eyes. He said to Henry, 'You got some sort of a problem?'

'Missing girl. A teenager,' Blackstone cut in. She turned her phone so Lennox could see the screen photograph of Charlotte.

Lennox shrugged. 'And?'

'You've not seen her?' Henry asked for clarification.

'Nope.' The burger continued to flop from one hand to the other with a slapping noise.

'Have you come with your son today?' Henry asked.

Henry saw the almost imperceptible twitch in the eyes of the man – just a micro-flash – and he knew the next words coming out of this man's mouth would be lies.

'What son?' he lied.

Henry blinked, aware that Lennox had picked up on the fact Henry knew it was a lie.

Henry cocked his head and said, 'We'd like to speak to him.'

'Urgently,' Blackstone added, also having picked up on the fib.

Lennox shrugged as if he didn't give a shit. 'He isn't here.'

'But he's at the fair?' Blackstone pressed.

'I have literally no idea where he is,' Lennox said and eyed the policewoman up and down in a way that made Blackstone want to retch.

'OK,' Henry said, 'has he got a phone? We'd like to call him.'

'He doesn't have a phone.'

'I find that hard to believe,' Henry said, looking at him challengingly, 'just like I find it hard to believe you don't know where he is. Is he with his mates?'

'I've got to get back to work,' Lennox declared and tossed the burger high in the air and caught it expertly. 'Best burgers in town,' he said.

Henry peered up and beyond Lennox into the space behind the counter of the van where a youngish girl was serving customers. Then he glanced behind the van and saw a long-wheelbase Ford Transit van which had obviously been used to tow the burger van to the fair. He quickly exchanged a look with Blackstone and jerked his head towards the Transit.

Blackstone picked up on the intent and to Lennox said, 'Do you have any objection to us looking in your van?'

The burger guy looked at them with growing impatience as if he was about to demand a search warrant, but then relented and said, 'Knock yourself out.' He turned and slapped his burger down on the griddle where it began to sizzle.

Henry and Blackstone walked the few steps to the Transit, which had a sliding side door and double doors on the rear. Blackstone opened the side door and the pair of them peered in. The space was essentially empty, in as much as there was no trace of Charlotte, just a jumble of junk, car parts and other accumulated bits of rubbish.

'Not here,' Blackstone said. She slammed the door shut.

'We need to speak to his son PDQ,' Henry said. 'I know when I'm being lied to.'

'Me, too,' Blackstone said. 'He's probably gone into default protective mode. Anyway, I'll get the lad's details from him even if I have to wring his neck.' She went back to the side of the burger van, leaving Henry at the Transit, which he slowly stalked around, wondering, in his usual ultra-suspicious way, if there might be a hidden compartment large enough to hide a kidnap victim. He looked in through the back doors, weighing up the dimensions by sight, but concluded that the van didn't have anything so horrific hidden within its construction. In his time, Henry had come across many vehicles that had been adapted by criminals for all sorts of purposes – to hide bodies or stolen goods or drug shipments – and some had been so cleverly constructed, almost like an optical illusion, that it had been impossible to find the spaces without actually taking the vehicles to bits. But, after getting down on his hands and knees and looking at the Transit's chassis, he didn't think there were any hidden compartments in this vehicle.

Blackstone returned.

At that moment, Henry was slowly getting back to his feet. She gave him a hand and hoisted him up, for which he was both grateful to her and annoyed by his own lack of mobility. He expected her to quip something derogatory, but she kept quiet and read out from her pocketbook: 'Ernest Lennox, nineteen years old, born in Morecambe.' She read out the lad's date of birth and added, 'Details reluctantly provided by Dad, who still insists he doesn't know where his son is.'

'Do we know him – the son?' Henry asked, the 'we' meaning the police.

'I'll PNC check him in a moment.'

'How about we get his name broadcast over the PA system?' Henry suggested. 'Tell him to make his way to the meeting point.'

'Like he would?' Blackstone scoffed.

'Even if he doesn't, he'll know we're interested in him. If he hasn't any connection to Charlotte, he might pay us a visit, and if he has, it might panic him into doing something stupid. Did you ask about his mates' names?'

'Mr Grease said he had no idea what I was talking about. It was like getting blood from a stone just to get him to tell me his son's name, and, of course, he has no idea where he is. Shifty twat,' she spat.

'But you insisted?'

'I insisted,' she confirmed. 'And I don't like the feeling I'm getting, Henry.'

Henry was scowling thoughtfully.

'What?' Blackstone asked.

'There is something vaguely familiar about him,' Henry mused.

'From your past life?' Blackstone asked. 'When you were a proper cop?'

'Damn!' Henry said, irritated at being unable to pinpoint the memory.

'Why don't we go and ask him?' Blackstone suggested.

'I think we should. He unsettles me somewhat.'

Armed with this intention, he and Blackstone went back to the side door of the burger van and stood there like two puppies, although in reality they were like dogs with a bone. The level of the van was higher than the two of them, and Henry didn't particularly like looking up at people, especially ones who were not pleased to see him. He liked a level playing field or, better still, liked to be the one looking down on others. It was all psychological games.

Lennox saw them. 'Really? You're back! *Really?*'

Henry and Blackstone gave him a pair of winning smiles.

Lennox was busy flipping burgers with a spatula, but even so, Henry beckoned him with a crooked finger. 'Down here, please.'

Shaking his head and beginning to get angry, Lennox moved away from the counter and came towards them, wiping his hands on his soiled apron. He came down the steps.

'Just one more question,' Henry said.

'What would that be?'

'Do I know you?' Henry asked deliberately slowly, tilting his head as he looked closely at Lennox.

The look of a trapped animal instantly told Henry everything as Lennox's expression changed from one of annoyance to guardedness, and back again.

'Why would you know me?'

'Have you been doing this long?' Henry gestured at the van.

'A fair while . . . and again, why would you know me?'

Henry was proud of his memory for faces and names. That, he thought, was one of the elements that had made him a decent cop – that plus an eye for detail and other traits that went into being a detective. He knew his mind wasn't what it used to be, but it wasn't too bad. Somewhere in the mists of his grey matter, he recognized Lennox but was struggling to exhume the recollection fully.

'I used to be a cop in Blackpool,' Henry frowned. 'And if I'm not mistaken, you once had a burger stall on the front, didn't you?'

The mist was clearing slightly, but the recall still wasn't fully emerging.

Lennox swallowed. 'Long time ago, that.'

'Maybe so, but that's how I know you, isn't it?'

'Maybe you do, maybe you don't.' Lennox shrugged. 'Whatever, I don't see how that has anything to do with anything.'

'Perhaps you're right,' Henry conceded. 'Whatever, we need to speak to your son Ernest as soon as possible, and I'm pretty sure you're lying to us about knowing where he is, but so be it. We have something to discuss with him, and I don't for one moment believe he hasn't got a mobile phone, so I suggest you call him and tell him to get his backside to the meeting point at The Tawny Owl or tell him to his face if he turns up here, OK?'

Lennox held Henry's gaze for a few seconds, then nodded.

'See how simple that was,' Blackstone said to him. She jerked her head at Henry. 'C'mon, let's go for a look around.' To Lennox, she added, 'Back soon if we don't hear from you.'

They turned and walked away, only to hear Lennox call, 'Fucking police harassment!'

Henry stopped abruptly, jarring himself painfully in the process, then spun back to Lennox who had his foot on the first rung of the steps up into the van. Henry stalked up to him and growled furiously, 'We've not even started, mate. Get your fucking son to make contact with us and then we might – *might* – back off.'

'You're not even a cop. You can't threaten me,' Lennox sneered, looking derisively at Henry's hi-vis jacket.

'It's exactly because I'm not a cop that I can threaten you, Mr Lennox. I do not need to play by the rules.' Henry studied the guy's face, gave him a wink and turned back to Blackstone, who had witnessed the brittle exchange with a smirk.

As they walked towards the PA tent, Henry said, 'You know when you get a bad feeling about somebody even though there's technically no real reason for a bad feeling? No evidence, nothing . . . just a feeling?'

'It's what keeps cops going and digging,' Blackstone agreed, knowing exactly what Henry was talking about. 'Not that we're a suspicious bunch.' She smirked again. 'Does your anus twitch "half-crown, thruppence" when you get that feeling? Mine bloody does and it's going like the clappers at the moment, even though I've had it bleached.'

'Too much information . . . but yes, and right now.'

'Thing is . . .' Blackstone began.

'What?'

'Do I want to look stupid or what?'

Henry stopped suddenly again, as did Blackstone. He was no mind reader, but he knew they were very much on the same wavelength at that moment. 'Honest opinion from an old lag?'

'Do I have an option?'

'No . . . I now quote, or paraphrase, from the Murder Investigation Manual: "Every missing-person report has the potential to become a murder investigation". And, without being too dramatic, "Think murder and investigate it until the evidence proves otherwise". Old lag, over and out.'

She blinked, impressed. 'You really remember all that shit?'

'I wrote most of it – well, odd bits – and it'll be ingrained in me until I turn my toes up, as will most of my police training, just like the stuff I had drilled into me on my police driving courses by cruel and unusual instructors.'

'You remember that stuff, too?' Blackstone asked incredulously.

'Word for word, but I don't think they do it to that nerdy degree any more. However, we digress. We were discussing egg on face.'

'And I was waiting for an old lag's opinion.'

'You've got the ball rolling with the Support Unit. Now get the whole machine cranked up. Get on to your former boss, Ricky Boy Dean and run it past him. He'll go for it, especially if I'm perched on your shoulder. If, in the meantime, Charlotte turns up unhurt, then we'll do a dance of joy, but at least you'll know you did the right thing.'

'What if I'm accused of overreacting?'

'Better that than do nowt and find her dead in a ditch . . . which,' Henry said sombrely, 'is entirely possible and why our arses are twitching in unison.'

Lennox paused on the top step of the entrance to the burger van and, through narrow, scheming eyes, watched Henry and Blackstone walk away into the crowd, talking to each other, obviously about him.

When the pair had finally been engulfed by the milling throng and Lennox was as sure as he could be they were not going to return and ask more pesky questions he couldn't or didn't want to answer, he removed his apron, lobbed it into the van and shouted to the girl working the griddle, 'Back soon, Ella.'

He slithered down the steps and walked quickly in the opposite direction to his questioners, weaving between parked vehicles, towing caravans and mobile homes all located in an area set aside for exhibitors; many were there for the whole weekend and had arrived on Friday with their mobile living accommodation, establishing a little community where most knew each other. Although Lennox knew quite a few of them, he didn't like them, and none seemed to take to him either.

As he walked along, he felt anger start to grow and surge inside him because he didn't want anything to jeopardize this weekend; money had been tight because of the pandemic, and he needed everything to go to plan in order to set himself up for the next few months. Being linked to the investigation of a missing girl was the last thing he needed right now because it would mean a sudden, huge influx of cops which would probably shut the fair down while they carried out searches of likely places, including vehicles and caravans, intrusions that had the potential to screw up everything for Lennox.

He felt himself growling as he walked.

And even then – paradoxically – although he did not know for certain whether his son really was involved in a girl going missing, Lennox knew in his soul that he was involved.

As soon as the cops (and try as he might to do otherwise, he included Henry Christie in that category – he might be retired but he was still a cop to all intents and purposes) had painted the scenario

Nick Oldham

and mentioned his son, though not by name to begin with, Lennox knew the stupid little twat had done something ridiculous, despite the warnings.

The lad was someone who just couldn't keep it bottled up and under control.

He went through phases – 'like father, like son,' Lennox thought crossly – when a barren period became something else, something scary and uncontrollable, like a geyser bursting out of the earth's crust.

So far, the lad had been lucky, but that wouldn't last. That was something Lennox knew about all too well because many years before, from his late teens into his early twenties, he had also been that boy, consumed by uncontrollable lusts that had to be satisfied at all costs . . . something that had once resulted in a terrible showdown.

He was only surprised that Henry Christie hadn't yet recognized him. He'd seen the look cross the guy's face – that 'I know you, but I can't put my finger on it' look.

Without a doubt, the penny would drop even though the years had passed.

Lennox ran his thumb and forefinger down from the bridge of his crooked nose to its tip, then the tip of his finger down the very faint scar that ran from the corner of his left eye to the corner of his mouth.

Now Lennox was different, though. Older, wiser, more able to put a lid on things, much more careful . . . but his son, who had his blood flowing through his veins, was going through something similar to what he himself had gone through way back. Because Henry Christie had been correct: they had indeed met before and not in very convivial circumstances.

'You've gone extremely quiet,' Blackstone remarked.

'I'm thinking,' Henry said.

'What about?'

'Mr Lennox, the burger guy.'

'You really do know him, don't you?'

In that exact instant, it slotted into place for him as clarity returned to his brain and the fog lifted.

To Blackstone, he said, 'Bingo!' But it wasn't said in a happy way as though he'd won a jackpot; it was more that he'd pulled up

a manhole cover, peered down into the sewer and discovered something particularly nasty slithering about in the shit-filled water down
below. He added, 'It's not good.'

THREE

'Tell me!' Blackstone grabbed Henry's shoulder, not for the
first time, but this time a little too roughly.
'Ow-uh!' he said, stopping and swiping her hand away.
They faced each other, surrounded by a swirl of people, blaring
music, the sweet smell of candyfloss, electricity generators running
with deep throbs, kids' laughter. And it was this miasma of assaults
on Henry's sight, smell and hearing that had triggered it for him, and
suddenly he saw himself back in the very early 1990s when he was
a Detective Constable on Blackpool CID.

He could visualize himself weaving through the crowds of people
on the Pleasure Beach amusement park in Blackpool South, shouldering or pushing folk aside on a hot Sunday afternoon of a bank
holiday weekend in pursuit of a suspect who had fled from him
across the promenade. The guy had slithered spectacularly across
the bonnets of two cars, then zigzagged his way through queues of
people waiting to enter the Pleasure Beach, vaulted a turnstile in
the hope of vanishing among the crowds inside the vast park, which
provided many hiding places and routes for escape.

Henry's fingers had only just missed him, but he had been close
behind and wasn't about to give up the chase (never had, never
would) and he'd hared after the guy across the prom, avoiding being
mown down because the road was heaving with traffic. Henry had
leaped across the same turnstile but had stumbled inelegantly on
landing – to some cheers from onlookers – not badly but just enough
to hold him back a touch, thereby allowing the young feral lad he
was chasing a few extra, precious yards.

Yes, there was no way on earth that Henry would give up on this
one because that young, scrawny guy he was chasing had abducted
a young girl – young meaning eight years old – almost from under
her parents' noses, then had bound and gagged the little lass and
stashed her alive but otherwise untouched for the moment in a

disgusting bedsit on a road close to the Pleasure Beach. He intended to return later, and Henry could only imagine what horrors were in store for the girl.

Henry had been very much on the case from the start, more by luck than judgement.

At that time in his career, he had been mostly on the reactive side of the CID working from Blackpool Central nick. That basically meant he turned out to any crime-related incidents where a detective was required. And it had been one of those days in Blackpool that would stick in his mind forever, one of those days when, as a cop, you realized that all human life, good and bad, could be found in the resort of Blackpool, that place that lured in millions of visitors every year, and veered from the sublime to the ridiculous, from the trivial to the most serious life-threatening, life-changing scenarios ever.

Straightaway, when he had come on duty at eight that morning, his DS had tossed an overnight file over to him with a gruff 'Deal with that.' The cells on the lower ground floor of the station were packed – the usual for a Saturday night/Sunday morning – and Henry had been given the task of interviewing a teenager who'd driven a screwdriver into another lad's guts in a brawl outside a nightclub in the early hours.

That had been a fairly easy, run-of-the-mill job: an interview during which the offender admitted the stabbing, a quick visit to the hospital to speak to the very much alive and very angry victim, then back to the cop shop to complete the processing of the prisoner. He wouldn't be going anywhere other than to stand in front of the magistrate the next morning on a charge of wounding with intent.

When Henry sauntered back to the CID office, his DS said, 'Four burglaries, same street, South Shore.' He dropped a slim file containing four printed crime forms in front of Henry.

Half an hour later, after a swift visit to the top-floor canteen, he was at the first house – those were the days when detectives actually turned out to break-ins and reassured victims, even though the writing was on the wall for that, even then – and taking down details from a distressed old couple (the burglary had taken place overnight when they had both been in bed). He was just about to go to the next one, next door, when the day kicked off big style, and because he was out and about, as keen as anything, and uniform resources were stretched, he could not keep himself from calling up for some of the jobs that were coming in thick and fast.

The first one was to show his face at the sudden death of an old lady who'd been found after not being seen for a few days by neighbours. Henry helped force entry to her flat, then after ensuring it wasn't a job for CID – no suspicious circumstances – he waited for the undertaker to turn up, watched the body get bagged up and taken away, then left the job for the constable who had attended. Bread-and-butter stuff for most cops.

Almost before he could draw a stuttering breath, the next job came in: a young boy had been hit by a bus on Talbot Square and was trapped underneath the wheels. He was badly injured but still alive, and although this was not really a job for CID, Henry went, driven as always by his inborn desire to help people. All he could do in the circumstances was to hover about in the background while the bus company and the fire brigade rushed lifting gear to the scene and managed to raise the immensely heavy bus just the few inches needed to drag the lad free.

Next up was a huge lunchtime brawl in the resort centre that became a running battle. It had started as a shouting match between local youths and a coach full of day trippers from Glasgow and ended up like a scene from a saloon in Dodge City in the Wild West. Pretty much usual at any time of day for Blackpool.

The uniform branch plus dog handlers were soon on top of it, breaking it up, making eight arrests for public order offences and drunkenness.

After that, Henry decided to make his way back to South Shore to visit the remaining houses that had been burgled, but on the way a call came over the radio that a man had been beaten and robbed close to the Pleasure Beach. Uniform were in attendance, and Henry shouted up that he was on his way also.

The victim was a drunk who had been battered and rolled by three well-drilled lads who fitted the description of a trio who'd been working the resort for a few weeks, specializing in clinically assaulting and overpowering drunks and stealing cash from them. That day's victim had been punched down and kicked, and had lost somewhere in the region of £200; he was an out-of-towner, here on a work's outing, and had become separated from his colleagues. He was also very, very drunk.

By the time Henry got to the scene – traffic was agonizingly

slow and he was driving an unmarked CID Mini Metro with no
blues and twos, so he had to content himself with going with
the flow – the victim was being loaded into the back of an
ambulance.

Henry decided he would catch up with him at the hospital, so
spun his car around, intending to go to the remaining burglary
addresses, which was when the report of the missing girl came in.

He responded to that immediately.

Even though he knew the odds were in favour of her turning up
within minutes – as most did in spite of lurid, scaremongering
newspaper headlines – Henry preferred to work on the assumption
that she might not. He made his way to where two uniformed
constables were in deep conversation with two terrified parents,
obtaining details to circulate.

Henry flashed his warrant card, listened in.

There was a children's play area on the opposite side of the
promenade from the Pleasure Beach where the eight-year-old had
been playing on the swings, slide and roundabout. Her mum and
dad had been watching like hawks because the whole area was
teeming with people, up to the point where her dad had gone to
buy ice creams from a van parked close by. The serving hatch was
on the opposite side, facing away from the play area, and he joined
a short queue only to discover he did not have enough change when
he reached the hatch, so he bobbed his head around the side of the
van and mee-mawed to his wife who, keeping an eye on her daughter,
jogged over to her husband, rooting in her handbag for her purse,
taking it out and giving him a handful of loose change.

The time spent distracted doing this was minimal. Seconds. A
minute, tops.

But long enough.

When the mother began to walk back to the play area, she could
not see her daughter.

Panic engulfed her like a shroud.

A quick search of the area with her husband revealed no trace
of the girl; either she had simply wandered off, as kids that age are
wont to do, or something more sinister had happened.

Henry heard the wife saying to the uniformed cops, 'She wouldn't
wander off, she just wouldn't. She's a good girl.'

'Well, y'know, it happens,' one of the officers said a bit
unsympathetically, and Henry winced.

'And she certainly wouldn't have gone off with a stranger,' the dad interjected. 'We drill that into her.'

'Oh, God.' The wife gasped at that prospect. Henry could see the terrible fear and pain on her face. By that time in his life, Henry had two young daughters, the lights of his life, and he couldn't even begin to envisage how he would feel or react in similar circumstances, other than that he knew he would be terrified and demand a serious, immediate response from the police.

The woman's mouth popped open and she looked horror-struck at the PC who had made the blasé remark. He in turn went pale, knowing he'd put his foot in it.

Henry stepped in. 'DC Christie,' he reiterated, knowing that flashing his warrant card had probably meant little to the parents. He knew they were only feet away from where the girl had gone missing; even so, he said, 'Take me through it once more, please,' and gently steered husband and wife towards the play area. 'Quickly,' he urged them.

'I hope you're going to take this seriously,' the mother said.

'Very,' he assured her.

She seemed to believe him and once more quickly ran through the scenario, after which he checked his watch and said, 'This was all how long ago?'

'Fifteen minutes, I'd say.'

Henry's heart sank just a little. You could go a long way on foot in that time; in a car, you could be more than halfway to Preston. He could feel the nerves in his face twitch as he wondered if the girl had simply walked away – hopefully – or been taken.

Sometimes, though, even in cases like this, cops can get a break quickly.

And in this one, they did almost immediately. Henry was just piecing the story together in his mind, deciding what best to do, how to get the ball rolling as soon as possible. Obviously, it would entail a coordinated response from the uniform branch, and he knew that because this was a bank holiday weekend, the numbers of such officers had been bolstered by the arrival of two serials from the Support Unit which had arrived for the day, numbering almost twenty-two extra cops. Henry knew the resort was heaving and very busy police-wise, but he was pretty sure supervision would allow him to organize a street search plus door-to-door operation.

Just as he was about to call the patrol sergeant, he glanced at the two constables who had been on the scene to take the original report of the missing girl. They were being spoken to by an elderly woman who was gesticulating as she explained something to them urgently.

For a moment, Henry thought nothing of this until one of the officers beckoned him over.

He told the girl's parents to wait a moment while he went across. 'What is it?'

'This lady,' one said, 'has seen something of interest in Balmoral Road.' He pointed towards the road that ran down the northern perimeter of the Pleasure Beach, one of those streets typical of that area with large, terraced houses, many of which had been converted into houses of multiple occupancy, divided into numerous pokey flats, providing accommodation for people on social benefits, often run by sleazy landlords for guaranteed, easy incomes.

Henry had spent quite a lot of his police service knocking on doors, or kicking them in, in such houses.

'Hi, I'm DC Christie. What did you see, Mrs . . .?'

'Grace,' she told him, 'Edna Grace. I,' she continued proudly, 'am one of the few people who still have a real home on Balmoral Road.'

'OK.'

'Mostly they are now owned and inhabited by fly-by-nights and rats – real rats. I still run a respectable B and B.'

'OK,' Henry said again, counting more seconds wasted in a search for a vulnerable kid. 'What have you seen, exactly?'

She turned, and Henry followed the gnarled, arthritic finger that pointed towards a small caravan close to the entrance of South Pier, which had been converted into a burger van, but which currently had the shutters down and was closed for business.

'Right?' Henry said.

'The man who owns that cesspit of germs and vomiting,' Mrs Grace almost spat, 'lives on Balmoral Road, and I live opposite the little turd.'

Henry tried to hide his surprise at the old lady's turn of phrase. She seemed so nice and kindly, but clearly she had a harsh tongue on her.

'Always suspected him of wrongdoing,' she went on. 'Young kids always coming and going all the time into his flat . . . He's a perv, is my guess.' She paused, refitted her top set of teeth and went on, 'I saw him actually carrying – yes, carrying – a young lass in through the front door. He was moving really quick. He had her in a sort of bear hug, but I couldn't tell if she was struggling or what. But it didn't look right.'

'Could you remember what she was wearing?' Henry asked quickly.

Mrs Grace struggled and frowned deeply as she thought. 'Red top, a cardie, I think.'

Which matched the description the girl's parents had given Henry of their daughter's clothing.

'What number, what flat and what is this man's name?' Henry asked.

'Lives in number ten, directly opposite me – I'm at number seven, Grace's Bed and Breakfast. He goes in through the front door but his flat's the basement one, and he's called Leonard Lennox and he also has *that* burger van.' She pointed to it again.

'Thank you.' Henry gestured to the two constables and said, 'With me, guys.' He dashed back to the parents and said, 'Please stay right here, will you? We may have something and we're going to check it out, OK?'

Their expressions were confused but hopeful, and they nodded. Henry turned and began to run, crossing the promenade so he was back on the Pleasure Beach side, then ran north with the front elevation of the amusement park on his right. He turned right into Balmoral Road, taking the steps up to the front door of number ten three at a time.

This was one of the few houses Henry had not visited previously, but he knew they were all pretty much the same template: in at the front door, through a short vestibule and into the ground-floor hallway; there would be a few doors on either side to the flats and a set of stairs up to the first-floor landing; there would also, usually, be a door on the ground floor that would lead to the basement flat.

Number ten's front door was locked as Henry barged into it.

He stood back, braced himself, choosing the perfect spot – just below the Yale lock – and then, in a well-practised, powerful move, he flat-footed the door.

First time, nothing gave.

He set himself again and counted down from three. Then booted it again. With a splitting of cheap wood, the door clattered back with a bang and the police were inside the property with no need for a warrant as he had reasonable belief that a person's life was in danger. English law is good like that.

They went in through the vestibule, into the hallway. The first door on the left was open and was the one, Henry guessed, that led to the basement. Henry stepped through. He was correct. Narrow, steep steps led down, so he shot down and found a door at the bottom which was secure and sturdy and made of thick wood edged with steel plate.

Henry tapped on it.

No response.

Then he knocked more loudly, but still nothing.

The two PCs were behind him on the steps with not much room to manoeuvre.

Henry tried the doorknob and pushed, but it was locked, no give in it, so he knocked again and this time shouted, 'Police – open the door!' All the while, he rattled the knob and kicked the bottom edge of the door with the toecap of his nice brogues. 'Open up, please.'

Again, nothing.

Henry eyed the two uniformed lads. 'We need to get in here; you think you can do this?'

Their expressions said, *Piece of piss.* Henry stood aside and squeezed back up a couple of steps to give the two big guys as much room as possible in the confined space. They managed to align themselves side by side and raised their legs, leaned back slightly, counted down and simply attacked the door with the soles of their size elevens, two feet in unison. Their synchronized door bashing would have got a gold medal in the Olympics had it been a sport.

It took four solid blows. Each time, the door visibly weakened slightly in its frame until it finally splintered open and they entered ahead of Henry into a very grotty basement flat that stank of damp and weed. Sitting, slumped on a rickety cane chair in the middle of that single, horrible room, was the missing girl. There was no one else present.

At first, Henry thought she was dead, gaffer-taped to the chair, her head lolling forwards, but as he stepped between the two constables, he saw her move. She raised her face, and Henry saw there was a strip of tape across her mouth. He swooped down beside her on one knee.

'You're safe now; we're the police. No one will hurt you, and you'll be back with your mum and dad in a few minutes, OK, sweetheart?' As he spoke these words, he gently eased the tape from her mouth.

Henry almost couldn't breathe. The whole thing – over within minutes – had filled him with rage and worry and now blessed relief at finding the girl unharmed, hopefully. He now felt an all-consuming desire to lay his hands on the offender and yank him screaming and kicking to Blackpool nick and hurl him bodily into a cell. For starters.

He began to unwind the tape from her wrists and ankles in order to release her, and although he did it as quickly as he could, he also did it carefully as there was every chance there would be fingerprint evidence on it that could link the offender to the crime.

As he did this, he said, 'Did he hurt you at all?' quietly.

'No, no,' she gasped. She was traumatized, confused and afraid. 'I don't think so . . . but I scratched him, I scratched his face. Did I do wrong? He called me a naughty word.'

'No, you did exactly right,' Henry said as he unwound the last bit of the tape, already thinking one step ahead about evidence and what could be underneath the little girl's fingernails.

The little girl added, 'He smelled of beef burgers.'

Her name was Elizabeth – Lizzie – and she was back with her parents sitting in a police van just minutes later.

Henry and the constables had done a very quick, intentionally superficial search of the basement bedsit, just to check there wasn't anyone hiding there – there wasn't – and with a view to getting Scenes of Crime to do a proper search later.

Henry then walked nonchalantly back down to the promenade, keeping to the inland side. He looked across at the burger van Mrs Grace had pointed out to him and saw the front canopy had been raised open with a young man serving. Somehow that man had managed to abduct Lizzie, carry her to what Henry, in his head, was already calling a lair, where the guy had then dumped her, tied her up, no doubt intending to return later; then, Henry thought, the cheeky bastard had gone back to serving burgers swathed in slavering, dripping fat.

He had gone back to work, which told Henry he was one hundred per cent confident he was home-free: kid abducted, stashed, be back later.

Henry had no adequate words for this guy other than the obvious 'scum', and he could not wait to arrest him and hope the guy tried to squirm away from him and resist arrest, which, although Henry would never admit it to anyone, would provide a bloody good excuse to give him a few well-placed digs, circumstances and (lack of) witnesses permitting.

He stepped into a recess in the wall surrounding the Pleasure Beach, which might have been a shop doorway once upon a time and from which he was able to see the burger van diagonally across the road on the wide promenade area in front of South Pier.

A couple of customers formed the queue, but because the awning cast a shadow across the serving hatch, Henry could only really make out the form of a young man, a bit scrawny, in a tatty T-shirt and apron, serving the food.

Henry backed fully into the recess and brought his PR up to his mouth and said, 'DC Christie to PCs Wallace and Ollerton. Are you guys in position?'

The plan was a military-style pincer movement. The two constables who had been with him from the start of this, Wallace and Ollerton, would edge around in a big loop, keeping out of sight so as not to spook the burger guy, and get themselves into a position behind the van ready for when Henry gave the word. He intended to join the customer queue for a burger. When he got to the front, he would check the lad out, and if he thought he was on to a winner, which he was certain he would be, he would give the burger guy the good news concerning his arrest. As soon as he had done that, the two uniforms would materialize at the side door of the van and the burger guy would be trapped.

Of course, the old adage was true: plans always go to rat shit once they are implemented.

Henry slotted his PR into his inside jacket pocket, crossed the road swiftly and joined the queue, which consisted now of four people, two of whom were at the counter being served.

Henry got a better look at the lad serving.

Scrawny. Hair cut almost to the bone. Some tattoos on each arm as if they'd been home inflicted, more blue blurs and misspelling than anything, but he did have the obligatory swastika on his forearm.

He also had a fresh scratch on his left cheek from the inner corner of his eye in an almost perfect straight line to the corner of his thin lips – the one inflicted by Lizzie.

Henry's scrutiny must have lasted a tad too long because as the lad raised his eyes ever so slightly, even though he was serving a burger to someone else, they locked with Henry's, and in that microsecond, Henry knew the guy realized he had been rumbled.

Henry also realized that what he was wearing probably screamed *Cop!* His suit certainly wasn't saying he was a day tripper, and the guy processed this quickly.

Without hesitation, he flung the burger at Henry. It spun through the air like a discus, but came apart as it did, the bread going one way, the heavier burger going straight towards Henry's upper chest. As the burger was in mid-air, the guy ripped off his apron and, in one flowing motion, twisted sideways and jumped towards the van door.

If Henry hadn't instinctively ducked so that the constituents of the burger – including lettuce, a slice of tomato, fried onions and some sort of relish – didn't slop on to his natty suit (detectives were a bit anal like that), he would have managed to catch the burger guy jumping out of the van door, but his split-second decision to avoid the flying food meant he was also a split second too late in reaching out for him, his fingertips just missing. The next thing he knew, the guy was haring across the road and moments later was inside the Pleasure Beach complex, where he went to ground almost as soon as Henry had managed to negotiate the turnstile after him.

This was one of the busiest days of the year, and if there was anywhere better to hide from a cop, Henry couldn't think of it.

Hundreds, thousands of people, all shapes and sizes: singletons, pairs, family groups; fat, thin and, from behind, lots of similar-looking youths. Henry started to thread his way steadily, checking all the gaps between the stalls, at the same time calling the job in on the radio and getting as many cops as could be spared to make to the Pleasure Beach, so that all exits could be covered and a methodical search could begin.

However, Henry knew that if the lad wanted to stay out of the grasp of the police, then he would have a good chance in this environment which, while enclosed, offered hundreds of hiding places.

And if he wanted to get away, which he no doubt did, if he had run immediately to one of the other exits, he could have already left the park, and finding him would be a whole lot harder.

Henry hoped he was still inside.

He became angrier as he made his way through the throng of

holidaymakers, thinking about what this young guy had done and what he might have done if the police hadn't got lucky.

All the while, he was relaying information and requests back and forth between himself and the comms room at Blackpool nick, patrol supervision and his own detective sergeant who was rushing to the scene. It wasn't long before all the park exits were covered and there were bodies ready to enter the park to begin a proper search, rather than just Henry doing his best, as useful as that was.

He was beginning to think of taking a back seat and allowing the uniform branch to do what they were good at. With that thought in mind, he radioed the patrol sergeant and set up a meeting point with her just inside the entrance he had come in at in order to give her a good description of the guy who, if spotted, should be fairly easy to identify because of the scratch down his face.

'You a cop?' a voice interrupted as Henry spoke over the radio.

It belonged to one of two young girls around the eleven-year-old mark, both licking ice creams.

He nodded. They had obviously put two and two together if they had seen him walking around, speaking into his PR. 'I'm Detective Constable Christie from Blackpool CID,' he confirmed.

'Are you looking for someone?' the second girl asked.

'I am.'

'Lad with a scratch on his face?'

'Yep.' Cautious.

'Told you!' one girl said smugly to the other. 'What's he done?' she asked Henry.

'You don't want to know,' he said and added, 'Honestly, you don't.'

'Perv, then,' the same one said to the other. 'Told ya!'

'And?' Henry said impatiently.

'We saw him duck out of the way when he saw you,' she said. 'We was sitting on that wall.' She pointed to a low wall close to a cafeteria.

It had only been a short conversation, but Henry was already irritated by it.

'Where has he gone?'

'Men's bogs – there!' one of them said and pointed to a brick-built, single-storey toilet block of the most unprepossessing variety. Split in half, one entry for the women, the opposite end for the men.

'Is he still in there?' Henry asked.

'Unless he climbed out of a bog window.'

'Thank you,' he said and crossed the walkway towards the block, radioing in to report the possible sighting. Moments later, he was standing on the threshold, inhaling the heady reek of urine from within.

He stepped inside.

There was a long, tiled urinal on the right-hand wall, a few metal sinks on the back wall and six stalls on the left, made of veneered wood panelling with gaps at the bottom and the top and not designed for privacy or comfort. On the plus side, if you were a cop chasing a villain, they provided no real hiding place. Which was good.

No one was having a pee at the urinals or washing their hands at the sinks.

There were high windows above the urinals made of thick, toughened, frosted glass, none open or broken, which meant that if the suspect was in here, he had to be in one of the stalls.

Henry smiled grimly and with satisfaction, then bent over and peered along the full length of the half dozen stalls and saw no feet.

Henry kept smiling and said firmly, 'I'm DC Christie from Blackpool CID, matey. You need to come out.'

As expected, there was no response, so Henry stood upright and went to the first stall door and pushed it open.

No one inside.

The odds were shortening in Henry's favour. Up until the moment the lad had decided to duck into the toilets, the odds had been pretty evenly balanced. He'd had all the space in the world to disappear but, having made a poor judgement call and having a particularly determined cop on his tail, now he was backed into a corner.

Henry moved to the next cubicle.

'Not long now,' he called out, listening for a sound or a response.

None came. Henry guessed he was balancing on a toilet, holding himself in place with a hand on each wall.

Henry booted the next door open just for a bit more drama: another empty one.

And the next one along got booted too: empty. Two remaining.

Henry's patience had worn thin by that point, so he kicked open the fifth door – no one inside – quickly followed by the sixth. As it clattered open, he saw the lad slithering like a fast-moving rodent

underneath the partition wall, confirming he really was built like a
rat.

Back then, Henry was fit and fast. He played five-a-side football
once a week, squash twice, proper football and rugby for the division, and jogged four miles most days with a bit of weight training
chucked into the mix, so he sidestepped as the young guy rolled
into the cubicle next door and he had him. He hauled him bodily
out and the guy fought back like a cornered wildcat – fists, feet,
scratching, screaming – all of which gave Henry the opportunity,
legitimately, he'd been hoping for.

Henry wasn't a puncher by preference.

He usually grappled violent suspects into submission if it was
necessary, which he found to be the safest course of action and
prevented the Police Complaints Authority (as it was then) from
getting involved and making life uncomfortable.

But he knew he wanted to hit this guy for what he had done.

So he did: twice.

One a good, deep punch to the lower gut with the immediate
effect of winding him, sending all the breath out of him like a steam
engine and doubling him up. This opened him up to a straight, hard
blow to his nose, which sent him staggering backwards into the
stall where he plonked down heavily on the toilet. His head lolled
and blood gushed from a nose that Henry knew he had broken.

He'd felt it crunch.

By the time back-up arrived, Henry was pinning the guy face
down in the urinal channel, into which the blood from his
face flowed.

FOUR

On the day of the Kendleton Country Fair, Henry hadn't
recognized Lennox. A lot of years had passed, a lot of
villains much more memorable than him had been dealt
with, a lot of faces had become blurred and were half forgotten in
the mists of time, but the face and name finally jogged Henry's
memory as he and Blackstone walked through the crowds.

Obviously, the guy was older and his face was puffed out, but the scratch the little girl had given him had been deep enough to have turned into a thin, very slightly raised scar down his mean face, almost impossible to see clearly. She had given him something that would last a lifetime. Good for her.

And so had Henry – a crooked nose.

They had stopped at Blackstone's insistence, and Henry had briefly regaled her with an account of the time he'd come across Lennox who, following his arrest on Blackpool Pleasure Beach, had been jailed for twelve years for the abduction and released after ten.

'Hell!' Blackstone exclaimed, aghast. 'And he's still serving burgers to kids.'

'I guess you don't need a DBS check for that,' Henry said wryly, referring to criminal record checks. 'But it turns out that is what he was doing way back – burger vans, burger stalls, all ideal ways of getting to know kids, especially vulnerable ones or runaways, which Blackpool has oodles of. The little girl on the prom was just opportunistic, and who knows how that would have panned out? Even now, when I think about it, I get that queasy sensation in my legs, which is why he got such a long jail sentence, because when I got to court, I trowelled it on thick – the anguish the parents had felt and the terror the daughter had experienced. I was pretty good in those days.'

'You're not such a slouch now,' Blackstone complimented him.

'Let's get this lad's name over the tannoy,' Henry said and set off with purpose in his stride to the PA tent.

Two of the lads were sitting on knackered plastic chairs by the side of the old mobile home in the main car park, an ancient Hymer that looked as if one half-decent collision would make it crumble to pieces. They were sipping beer from bottles, and when Lennox first saw them, they were also messing about with their mobile phones, but as he closed in, they spotted him and sat upright.

By this time – in the distance from the burger van to the mobile home – Lennox had become furious but held his rage in check for these two lads: Benny and Jimbo were skilled at what they did for Lennox – good thieves – but they were essentially followers and had to be told what to do.

Although Lennox senior was the boss of this little crime outfit, it was very obvious where the real influence on these two (Lennox would say 'slightly simple' lads who'd spent too much time in bad care homes) lay.

That was with Ernest Lennox, his son.

Cocksure, smug, arrogant, violent – all these traits ran through Ernest's core. All those, plus an inability to control any of his urges.

'All right, lads?' Lennox greeted the two beer drinkers, trying to remain affable but unable to stop his teeth grinding and hearing the noise reverberate around his cranium. 'How's it going?'

Neither could hide their guilty look.

'Good, boss.' Benny coughed nervously, his mop of unkempt red hair flopping untidily around his ears.

'How have you gone on?' Lennox asked.

'Brill, brill,' Jimbo cut in because Lennox had caught his eye.

'How many?'

'Twelve,' Benny replied.

'No, no,' Jimbo disagreed, 'I'd say a dozen, easy.'

And that, Lennox thought, was the level at which these two dimwits operated. He also knew for a fact that neither of them could tell the time with an analogue watch or clock. 'Fuckwits,' he grumbled under his breath, then said, 'So, twelve catalytic convertors, give or take, yeah?'

They nodded as Lennox did the calculations in his head. Thing was, as much as he looked on these lads as Lancashire hillbillies, they did a brilliant job for him; they had become adept at wriggling under targeted vehicles without having to use a jack and efficiently removing the catalytic converters from the exhaust systems. The lads were built like long-distance runners, thin, agile, lightweight, rolling under SUVs, which were slightly higher off the ground than normal cars, and doing the business, usually in less than sixty seconds.

Twelve that day meant a good cash return for little effort on Lennox's part. Money in pocket, cash in hand, just the way he liked to operate . . . but that haul was by no means everything planned for that day. It was, in fact, just the beginning.

'Nobody saw you?' Lennox asked the two lads.

'Nope,' Benny replied confidently. 'We worked the back end of the field. No one saw us.'

'Good.' Lennox nodded. These lads were like ghosts.

He looked up at the side door of the Hymer as Ernest stepped out, not having noticed his father's appearance, but then he did see him and, in a croaky voice, said, 'Hi, Dad,' and rearranged his face into a smile.

'Ernie.' Lennox nodded curtly at his son, who, like the other two lads, was thin and equally adept at the speedy removal of catalytic convertors and, like the other two, stealing most other things.

These three were a pretty good, well-drilled crime-committing team, if all slightly dim. Over the course of the pandemic, they'd stolen hundreds of converters for the precious metals – rhodium and platinum – contained within them which were used to filter much of the toxicity out of engine transmissions down to acceptable levels when they came out of the exhaust.

It was an irony not lost on Lennox that these lads almost mirrored the poor kids in the countries that produced those precious metals, who were used as slave labour. The big difference was that, apart from the colour of their skin, Lennox used these youngsters to steal the finished products and then put them back into the system again, whereas the kids in the other countries mined the raw materials. Lennox also gave these guys a good, if sleazy lifestyle. If you wanted to live like a thief, that was.

Another money-making scheme that they'd entered into during the pandemic was the acquisition and export of dogs.

These lads loved that, too: usually targeting lone females out walking their treasured, thousand-pound-plus pooches, scaring the crap out of them and stealing their beloved pets.

Sixty dogs down the line proved a very lucrative business because people paid stupid money for them.

But that – dognapping – had been a needs-must scenario to tide Lennox over the lean period of the pandemic until things got back to normal.

And the weekend of the Kendleton Country Fair would be the first time of being back to that normal, a return to what had mostly funded his lifestyle over the last two decades or so.

And he could do without it being jeopardized by the reckless actions of Ernie.

Lennox growled, 'What've you been up to, lad?'

Ernest did not reply, but in that one glance, one lowering of his gaze, that brief inability to look his father in the eye, Lennox knew everything.

Lennox walked up the steps into the motor home, making Ernest shuffle backwards.

'Where is she?'

Ernest half shrugged, trying to be cool, half shook his head and said innocently, 'Where is who?'

'The girl . . .'

Before Lennox could say anything further, the public address system blared out, 'This is an appeal for Ernest Lennox, that is Ernest Lennox, to please make his way to the meeting point in front of The Tawny Owl, please . . . that is Ernest Lennox . . .' The voice began to repeat the message, and throughout the course of it, Lennox senior kept his eyes rigidly on his son's eyes, watching them dart left and right, left and right, as though looking for an escape route.

Lennox waited for the announcement to finish, then said, 'The police want to talk to you.'

'Why, Dad, why? I ain't done n—'

He was about to say the word 'nowt', but before it left his lips, his father had slapped him hard across the face, snapping the lad's head sideways and knocking him back against one of the cupboards inside the motorhome.

'Aww, what was that for?' Ernest clasped the palm of his hand over his already reddening face, eyes watering, and glared at his father. 'What was it for?' he demanded.

'I'll tell you what it was for.' Lennox's voice was deep and threatening. His arm shot out as fast as a rattler's strike, and he grabbed Ernest's face in his hand between his finger and thumb and squeezed the lad's features out of shape, then went nose-to-nose with him. 'You were seen; there's a girl missing, so where is she?'

Ernest screwed his face out of his father's grip. His lips were twitching, and his cheek was starting to swell as a result of the slap. He scowled and turned into the motorhome and walked through it, dragging his feet, his shoulders hunched miserably like a scolded child, to a door in the back third of the vehicle which he opened. This was the built-in shower unit, a tight, uncomfortable space.

He stepped aside to allow his father to see in.

Lennox drew his hand down his features, stretching them, and swore unpleasantly, but yet a strange shimmer of excitement and breathlessness skittered through him as he looked at the bound and gagged form of Charlotte Kirkham, trussed up into a tight foetal position in the shower tray. Her shorts exposed her thin white legs and her ragged short-crop T-shirt showed her back from her waist to her shoulder blades. She twisted her head and her wide eyes, above the duct tape gag, were pleading and terrified.

'You fucking idiot,' Lennox said, overriding his own inner feelings that had suddenly ignited at the sight of Charlotte. He closed the shower-room door and looked menacingly at Ernest who cowered away, expecting a fully fledged assault this time. 'Did you honestly think you could get away with this?'

'Dad, she were there for the taking. You know how it is,' his trembling voice tried to say reasonably. 'It were like a spider's web.' He had a perverse gleam in his eyes.

'You know we have stuff to do here, don't you? This day isn't over by a long shot and this' – Lennox flicked his fingers towards the shower – 'this just complicates things, brings attention on us we don't need.'

'I know, I know,' Ernest said contritely.

'What are you aiming to do with her?' Lennox demanded.

Ernest didn't say it loud, but loud enough for his voice to travel through the shower door and to Charlotte's ears, making her emit a terrified whimper.

Ernest's eyes sparkled. And the words were: 'Keep her.'

Henry and Blackstone stood by Mr Darbley as he spoke over the PA system and asked for Ernest Lennox to make his way to the meeting point at The Tawny Owl.

Neither he nor Blackstone was convinced this was the best course of action and knew it might ultimately be one of those things that could be scrutinized later under a microscope by some supposedly impartial investigative authority after the fact, but for the moment it was what it was: one of those rock-and-a-hard-place decisions made on the hoof, but with the best intentions.

All they knew at that stage was that Charlotte was missing, her mobile phone had been found, and she might or might not be with Ernest Lennox, the son of a guy Henry had once arrested for abducting a young girl, way back when.

If Ernest was with her innocently and he heard the announcement over the PA, he might turn up at The Tawny Owl. If he wasn't with her and had nothing to do with her, then he might deign to put in an appearance – or not.

If he was with her with the intention of causing her harm, then he would either ignore the announcement and go to ground or he would turn up and try to brazen it out.

Pick a card, any card, Henry thought despondently. There was no perfect answer, except that not doing anything was out of the question because there were very few police officers out there and their options were limited. At least, Henry thought, as he and Blackstone walked away from the PA tent, they had run through these scenarios in a kind of fluid risk assessment and decided on a course of action. What Henry did realize was that he wouldn't be the one in the firing line if this turned out to be more than just a missing-person enquiry. Blackstone would be the one facing the questions, having to justify her actions, not him because he wasn't a cop any more.

That was also one of the reasons why he was keen for her to delegate it upwards, which would at least absolve her of some of the responsibility.

She had kicked off the initial investigation, done her best based on what she knew or surmised, and, in Henry's opinion, for what it was worth, she now needed to pass the buck upwards – which Henry also knew might be easier said than done.

'Well?' she said, looking at him.

He gave her his thoughts on the matter, but he was certain that she knew what she was doing and what she needed to do. She was no rookie cop; she was experienced in this field and all he could tell her was what she was thinking already just to reassure her.

Then he added, 'I'm going to go back and speak to Lennox again, hopefully surprise him. It might be that his son has another vehicle on site. You never know.'

'I'll come with you.'

As they made their way back, Blackstone was on her PR to comms, requesting that the patrol inspector at Lancaster should attend as soon as possible and that she wanted someone higher up the chain of command to OK more uniforms for deployment to Kendleton. She gave Henry a sideways glance as she asked for this and raised one of her finely tattooed eyebrows at him.

'Over to you,' she said. 'Smooth the passage, as it were.'

Henry fished out his mobile phone and looked through the contacts list for Detective Superintendent Rik Dean, the head of FMIT. Until fairly recently, Rik had been Blackstone's ultimate boss on the team. He also had the dubious honour of being Henry's brother-in-law, being married to Henry's sister, Lisa. He was also a good friend and colleague going back over many years, when Henry, as a detective sergeant on Blackpool CID, had spotted Rik's thief-taking potential and manoeuvred him off section patrol on to CID. Rik's subsequent rise through the ranks had been all his own doing as he was a rare combination of a good manager and a good detective. However, when Rik stepped a bit too quickly into his boss's shoes on Henry's retirement, it did leave a sour taste in his mouth, which Henry was only just getting used to.

However, because of all this baggage and also because Rik had asked Henry to help out as a civilian investigator a few times, crossing Henry's palm with much-needed silver, Henry did have a fast track to Rik's earhole, and Henry had put it to Blackstone that it might be worthwhile going straight to Dean about the missing girl, just so he knew and could react swiftly if it became a job for FMIT down the line. Henry knew it would be quicker than Blackstone having to clamber up through the police hierarchy stage by painful stage, even if it put a few noses out of joint on the way.

'Rik Dean, you mean?' Henry asked, just to confirm what she was thinking.

'The one and only,' she said, without much enthusiasm even though she knew it was a good call.

Henry phoned him, and Rik answered.

By the time he'd briefed Dean and Blackstone had also spoken to him on Henry's phone – in a very stilted, subservient manner, which wasn't really like her – and given Henry back the phone, they were not far from Lennox's burger van.

The girl was serving alone, and they spotted Lennox appear from behind the van and scuttle up the steps to join her.

'Interesting,' Blackstone said. 'Wonder where he's been?'

'Good question. Let's ask.'

Ernest Lennox knew he'd been lucky not to get a proper battering from his father, something he'd endured repeatedly over the years, because he knew he had dangerously overstepped the mark by snatching the girl, but it was just an opportunity not to be missed.

He and the other two, Benny and Jimbo, had been rolling around the fair after having spent a couple of hours on the car park, sneaking about and doing what they were good at – getting under SUVs and four-by-fours and relieving them of their catalytic converters. It would be good money for his dad, maybe a hundred quid for each box. After stashing the convertors in the old Hymer, the lads wandered down on to the village green and showground, mingling with the crowds and doing the other thing they also did well – stealing from people, in particular mobile phones. Although they preferred high-end smartphones, they were happy to have anything that came their way – and a lot did as so many people in summer attire were happy to slide their phones into their back pockets or shorts pockets, both of which the lads were skilled in snaffling from without the owner realizing until it was too late.

They were a well-drilled team of crims, didn't particularly stand out, were at their best in very crowded situations but also very happy to try their hands at anything, and if it involved violence, they wouldn't shy away from that either and were eagerly anticipating the events Lennox planned for later that day. Ernest's foray into abduction could have scuppered or at least jeopardized those plans, but his father's quick thinking might have saved the day.

Ernest had watched his dad ruminating after he'd seen the girl trussed up in the shower.

'I did ten years for doing that and I never even touched the girl,' Lennox had said, mulling things through. Ernest knew this, and he also knew that he and his dad shared so many similarities and obsessions. 'You've got two major problems now,' Lennox senior said. 'You want to keep her and she's seen your face – and mine, now – and the lads' faces, and that means we can be identified. If that happens, you're ten years in clink for doing next to nothing and I won't be far behind. So, keeping her means getting her off-site now somehow, dead or alive . . . presumably alive for the time being.' He sighed and screwed up his face. 'And we still have a lot to do here, stuff I'm reluctant to let go.'

'Let me get her off-site then,' Ernest said.

Lennox blinked as he thought this through, but he was also inwardly cogitating about running into Henry Christie again, the man who had ruined his life. The guy was a terrier, didn't let go of anything, and the fact he wasn't a cop any more, not bound by cop rules of fair play and legality, made Lennox extra nervous.

He said to Ernest, 'You need to get moving.'

Now Ernest could really see his dad's mind racing.

Ernest said helpfully, 'They've got nothing on me.'

'Yet.'

'I even ditched her phone, just in case, and it were a good one.'

'Mm, at least that were a good move,' Lennox agreed and looked his son in the eye, feeling a parent's innate desire to protect their offspring no matter how bad or stupid they were, what they'd done or what they planned to do.

'Right,' Lennox said, reaching a strategic decision. 'Get her off-site. Bung her up in the over-cab bed so she's out of sight, and do anything to keep her still and silent, then get going, yeah?'

Ernest nodded eagerly.

'Well, what are you waiting for?' Lennox demanded when Ernest hadn't moved immediately. 'You need to get going now, because if I know anything about cops, they'll become very interested in every car in this car park and will want to look inside 'em all. So *move!*'

'Gotcha, Dad.'

Lennox gave his son another once-over, disappointed that he had evolved into his father.

He turned and exited the motorhome, waving at the other two lads and saying, 'Speak to Ernie now,' then he was gone, jogging back to the burger van and catching sight of Christie and the female cop as he came from behind the van and went up the steps into the serving area.

He cursed.

Henry and Blackstone reached the bottom of the steps just as Lennox was fastening his apron. Henry thought he looked nervous, trapped.

'Where have you been, Mr Lennox?' Henry asked.

Lennox looked up and tried to feign surprise. 'Eh? Oh, you two again? Like bad smells. Don't know what you mean – not been anywhere.'

'We just saw you come back from somewhere. Where, exactly?' Blackstone asked. 'Been to warn your son?'

Lennox shrugged. 'Don't know what you mean. Been round the back for a slash. Now, if you don't mind' – he gestured to the serving hatch – 'there's a queue of hungry people waiting to be served.'

'I mind,' Henry said firmly.

'You can mind all you want. I'm busy.'

'Where is your son?' Blackstone asked.

'I have absolutely no idea.'

'Liar!' she said.

Lennox regarded her stonily. 'There endeth the conversation,' he said.

'I've remembered where we met, by the way,' Henry interjected. 'The circumstances, everything. How you got your crooked nose, how you got that scratch down your face.'

This revelation seemed to stop Lennox abruptly. 'Well, I don't recall,' he said brazenly and irritably. 'I assume you're going to refresh my memory?'

'You abducted an eight-year-old girl from a play area on Blackpool promenade, 1991-ish, and I arrested you before you managed to do anything to her.' Henry spoke in a purposely loud voice. 'You went down for a decade.'

Lennox seemed to consider the validity of this accusation, then said, 'Nope, wrong guy, mate.'

'The little girl scratched your face,' Henry said. 'You've still got the mark. Faint, but it's still there.'

Instinctively, Lennox touched the scar and his nose.

Henry smirked. 'So, what is it?' he asked. 'You and your lad? You in business together?'

Lennox glared at Henry, who could see rage simmering, replacing the nervousness, just under the veneer of his skin, his jaw tensing and relaxing, nostrils flaring. If Henry was honest with himself, he felt the urge to drag Lennox out of the burger van and smash his face again, just for old times' sake, even though he knew he didn't have the physicality to put that desire into action. One thing he had realized as he recuperated from being stabbed was that it seemed his days of combat in any form were well and truly over.

'Whatever,' Lennox said eventually after presumably weighing up a series of responses and deciding not to mix it with Henry. 'I did my time and my lad's nowt like I was, OK?'

Henry sniggered and said, 'Although I haven't yet met him, I seriously doubt that, Lenny. A chip off the old block would be my guess.'

Blackstone cut in at that point, possibly fearing this exchange was going to degenerate into a slanging match. She said, 'Do you, or your son, have another vehicle on site – other than the Ford Transit?'

'No.'

'So you, your son and his mates, and this girl' – Henry pointed to the lass who was serving – 'all arrived in the Tranny van?'

'Ha! Good try,' Lennox stonewalled them.

There was a momentary stand-off then as Henry realized he and Blackstone were not going to get anywhere with Lennox, whose guard was well and truly up now. Blackstone seemed to realize this too and said, 'When he gets back from wherever he is, tell him to contact us, OK?'

That elicited another 'Whatever' from Lennox.

At that moment, Blackstone's PR piped up: comms were calling her.

She turned away to answer, but before Henry turned, just to wind Lennox up, he gave him the two-finger eyeball-to-eyeball 'I'm watching you' gesture.

Lennox sneered contemptuously and mouthed something obscene that Henry didn't quite catch. He let it ride.

'Go ahead,' Blackstone said into her radio.

'For your information, Sergeant Blackstone,' the comms room operator said, 'the remainder of the Support Unit serial is now attending from Morecambe for deployment in Kendleton. Also, Detective Superintendent Dean from FMIT has contacted us and asked to be kept updated, and finally the patrol inspector from Lancaster is en route with a couple of officers, plus a dog patrol is also on the way but from a job in Fleetwood so may be some time.'

'Roger that, and thanks. Please inform the Support Unit to make to The Tawny Owl pub where I'll brief them.'

'Roger, will do.'

'Things are moving apace,' Henry commented as Blackstone finished her transmission.

'Yet, as much as I do think something untoward might have happened to Charlotte, there is also the possibility she's gone off for a quick fumble in the bushes.'

'The nature of missing persons,' Henry said. Then, 'You're doing the right thing, lass.'

'*Lass?*'

'Turn of phrase,' Henry said quickly, realizing his faux pas.

They continued to walk through the crowd towards the police rural crime display. One of Blackstone's officers, a young PC, stood up with an expression of relief from behind the table he was looking after.

'Everything OK, John?' Blackstone asked, noticing the officer's stressed demeanour.

'Sarge, in the last thirty minutes I've taken the reports of half a dozen thefts from the person – wallets taken from back pockets, that is – and another five reporting the theft or loss of mobile phones, and a couple of decent cameras gone, too. We've got a team of Artful Dodgers working the show, I think.'

'That's all we need,' Blackstone said. She turned to Henry, 'I thought these rural fairs were supposed to be all nicey-nicey with ruddy-faced country folk talking about tractors.' To the PC, she said, 'What are the MOs?' meaning modus operandi.

'All either back pocket or shorts pocket jobs. Not one of the victims knew they'd been rolled until it was too late. The cameras stolen while the owners were looking the other way.'

'OK. Have you got enough details to submit crime forms?'

The officer nodded. Henry could see he didn't fancy the prospect of all that paperwork.

'Do it, then,' Blackstone told him.

Henry knew it was all done straight online so there would not be any delay in getting the crimes recorded and circulated.

Blackstone turned to Henry again. 'I need to get someone up to the car park exit to start speaking to drivers on their way out and searching vehicles, and that new Support Unit lot shouldn't be too far away now. How d'you reckon I should deploy them?'

Henry considered the question. Kendleton had a stream running through the village, which was also surrounded by a lot of trees and woodland. Henry suggested a quick sweep of the banks of the stream and delving into the clusters of trees nearby might be a good move. Blackstone thought this was a good idea, and after sending her other PC up to the car park to meet up with one of the stewards Henry had deployed there to check cars that were leaving, she veered back to The Tawny Owl where the extra Support Unit bods were due to land.

As much as Henry would have liked to put everything on hold for Charlotte's sake, he still had other responsibilities at the fair, and he got a sharp reminder of this when his own radio blared out loudly and a strident voice said, 'Ronnie to Henry, Ronnie to Henry, come in.'

This was the voice of Veronica Gough, the wheelchair-using almost nonagenarian, a true force of nature who had a huge say in many local activities and was the driving force behind the re-emergence of the Kendleton Country Fair. She had been almost solely responsible for kicking everyone into action to get an event underway again that could so easily have remained dormant forever, because that was the easy option.

She was also the person who had undoubtedly saved Henry's life on that church doorstep all those months ago as he lay there, bleeding profusely with the life ebbing out of him. When Henry thought about that statement now, it seemed overdramatic, but the truth was he had been dying, and Veronica's quick thinking did save his life, and now, even though it all still 'fucking hurt him like a bastard' (his words), he was on the road to recovery all because of her.

'Henry to Veronica,' he responded.

'You haven't forgotten, have you?' she asked him.

He was about to tease her by saying, 'Forgotten what?' But she saved him from that by quickly adding, 'You know? The dosh.'

'No, I haven't,' he said, checking the time. 'I'll be with you in a tick. Something came up, that's all.'

'Roger Dodger and out,' she said.

Henry smirked, amused by Veronica's transmission, but then had a slight pause for thought when he realized that the word or name 'Dodger' had been used twice in the last few minutes, not in any connected context, but it did make him wonder. Phones stolen, wallets going missing, cameras disappearing . . . perhaps that young PC's theory that there was a team working the fair wasn't so far off the mark. Up to that moment, there had not been one single crime reported in the previous two days. There had been some genuine property losses, but no phones or wallets; that in itself was an obvious pointer that a gang had targeted the fair today and was maybe still at large. Even though the event was beginning to wind down, Henry thought it would be remiss of him not to share that knowledge and pass on a warning to the fairgoers.

He called Blackstone on his mobile phone and ran the idea past her. She agreed, so Henry deviated from his course towards Veronica, made his way to the PA tent and asked Dave Darbley to announce the possibility that a gang of thieves was at work and for everyone to be vigilant and take extra care of their valuables.

Once he'd done that, he carried on towards the tent from which Veronica Gough ruled the roost. As she was a huge fan of the 1970s American TV comedy show *M*A*S*H*, a sign hung over the door which said *The Swamp*, which was the name of the tent the main characters lived in.

*   *   *

Despite being close to ninety years old and challenged mobility-wise, Veronica Gough still had the energy and mental capacity of someone thirty years her junior. She lived every day to the max, and although many people rolled their eyes whenever this interfering busybody's name was mentioned, few meant the slur. People like her were the heart and soul of the Kendleton community, which was all the richer for her.

Actually, though, when he'd been a cop, Henry thought he'd had his fill of the term 'community'. Everything the police did seemed to revolve around the word, but he never seemed to see real pay-off for all the hard work of so many officers. The communities Henry had served were often fractured through no fault of the police, and there was little cops could do to repair them; they seemed intent on pulling themselves apart, and the police could only achieve very short-term wins in spite of great efforts.

But since he had moved to Kendleton just before his retirement, he had truly seen what a community could achieve, but only if it was willing and had folk like Veronica Gough to chivvy it along.

Entering *The Swamp* was more like ducking into the tent of a crystal ball reader, lifting the flap to see Veronica seated behind a trestle table, but instead of wearing a flowing gown and turban and stroking the said ball, Veronica was busily counting cash. Lots of it.

It was a sight that made Henry close his eyes for a moment and shake his head at the vulnerability of it all: counting cash in the middle of a fairground was, to him, asking for trouble. But it got worse than that, at least in Henry's eyes.

Being the joint owner of the only local pub in the area, he had been co-opted on to the committee of the Kendleton Country Fair – harassed to join if he was honest – by Veronica whose trump card was that he owed her for saving his life. The truth was even-stevens because Henry had managed to help Veronica through something that had been a dark cloud over her for most of her life: she had been raped at the age of thirteen on VE Day in 1945 and the offender had never been brought to justice. Henry had righted that terrible wrong, even though the rapist was now a one-hundred-year-old man. Henry had also managed to return something priceless to her at the same time, a treasured memory of her father who had died in the war and which the rapist had stolen from her as a souvenir after violating her. So yeah, Henry could argue that he and Veronica were pretty much evenly matched.

Anyway, he found himself on the committee and, while recovering from his stab wounds, attended all the planning meetings which took place in The Tawny Owl, ended up with a list of responsibilities but mainly kept quiet and watched and listened with interest.

He learned the fair was run totally for charitable purposes and all monies raised through selling concessions, gate and car-parking receipts went to good causes. In addition, special collections were being carried out this year to provide funds for a couple of Ukraine charities because of the war.

One of the briefing spreadsheets Henry was given as a committee member was the audited accounts of the fair, detailing just how much money the previous three fairs before the pandemic had raised: an astronomical amount. Eye-watering, in fact, and all of it, minus legitimate expenses, donated to local causes mainly aimed at helping kids and with several community projects in the mix.

Henry was truly impressed.

Except for one thing. The money collected at the fair was all handed to Veronica, then counted on site, and after the fair was over, she kept the money in her house overnight and the day after she deposited it in a bank in Lancaster.

Henry scratched his head over that one.

Thousands of pounds were raised each day, and when he started doing the maths, it almost blew his mind.

And this year, as the phoenix rose from the ashes of the pandemic, more people than ever were expected to attend – more than two thousand each day – and if only half of those paid the adult entry price of £12, Veronica would be handling in excess of £12,000 each day in her tent, plus money from other sources including the charity boxes. All Henry could think was, *A little old lady counting all that cash, no matter how feisty she was, had to be a target.*

Surely.

Especially as the pandemic had put a lid on quite a few criminal enterprises, and bad guys would be on the lookout for easy ways to reline their pockets, if Henry knew anything about bad guys.

And Henry knew a lot about bad guys.

He broached the subject with Veronica after one of the committee meetings in The Tawny Owl. He had a printout in his hand and waved it as he talked to her.

'Makes a lot of money, this,' he said.

'It certainly does.' She was in her electric wheelchair and began to glide across the floor of the function room in it like some sort of Bond villain. Henry had to step aside, then walk with her towards the door which led out into the foyer of the pub. From there, Henry knew that a few diehard committee members would reconvene in the bar, including Veronica who was not averse to a snifter of good whisky and water.

'What happens to the money each day of the fair?' Henry asked innocently.

'What do you mean?'

'I mean, what happens to it?'

'Erm, it's collected by the entrance stewards and delivered to me in dribs and drabs. Then I count it, eventually.'

'Where do you count it?'

'In my tent.'

'Your tent?' Henry scowled.

'Yes, my tent, *The Swamp*. I've used the same one for the last twenty-five years, so it's still quite new by my standards. Now, do you mind?'

They had reached the door. Henry stepped forward to open it, then followed her through and said again, 'Your tent?'

She slammed the brakes on, and Henry crashed into her. 'Yes, my tent! Do your ears need syringing?'

'Hang on, Ronnie. So all the gate receipts and all the other money that comes in on the days the fair is running are delivered to you? In a tent? Which is where, exactly?'

'Village green, near the war memorial.'

'So, upwards of ten grand – ballpark figure – gets handed to you and you count it?'

'I do. Is this so hard to get your head around, young man?'

'And you've never been robbed?' Henry blurted.

'Why would anyone do that? This is for charity.'

'For an old bird, you're very naive,' Henry teased her. They had become good friends over the last months, and he knew she wouldn't be offended by his jibe, although he didn't push it. 'Then what happens to the money?'

'I take it home, then bank it the next day.'

'You take it home?' Disbelief grew with every word Henry said.

'Your ears definitely need de-waxing or perhaps you need a couple of these?' Veronica tapped her hearing aids.

'You take, what, thirty grand home?'

'Usually more than that. Once I had fifty-two thousand.'

'And where do you keep it when you're at home?'

'Hidden in the bread bin . . . haha! I'm old, maybe naive, but I'm not stupid,' she insisted. 'No one would ever find it there.'

Henry recalled a number of property searches he'd made as a cop when he'd found loot, drugs or other things in bread bins. He'd also lost count of the number of house burglaries he'd attended when the intruder had stolen money hidden alongside the Hovis.

'So that accumulates in your house over three nights?'

'Sometimes longer,' she admitted. 'Depends when I can get somebody to take me to the bank. As you know, I don't have a car.'

'Who would that somebody usually be?'

'Dr Lott or Dave Darbley.'

The local GP or the local butcher.

'And they are your security escort?' Henry asked hopelessly.

'Yes, I suppose they are.'

By this time, they had reached the bar and Veronica was less than gently nudging customers out of the way by crashing into their legs. Ginny leaned over and asked, 'Usual, Mrs Gough?'

'Yes, my dear. Could you bring it across?' Veronica smiled sweetly, then reversed the wheelchair back the way she'd come, spun it on a sixpence and headed for a table around which a few of the other committee members had clustered.

Henry followed.

'Not happening this time, not on my watch,' he informed her.

She braked suddenly, and Henry banged into her again.

'What is that supposed to mean?' she demanded.

'What I mean is that you – we – need to make better arrangements for the collection, handling and storage of that amount of money.'

'It's always been fine, Henry. I know you've got your crime prevention head on, but it'll be fine again. Trust me.'

'And then one year it won't be fine, Veronica. And the money will disappear and, God forbid, someone will get hurt.'

She shook her head stubbornly. 'Not happening.'

Henry took a breath, thinking it through quickly. 'Meet me halfway,' he said.

So as he entered *The Swamp* on the third day of the fair, this was the point at which they met in the middle.

She looked up at him from the money in front of her. 'Nearly done.'

Sitting in a chair alongside her now was Dr Lott, the ageing local GP who, though excruciatingly slim, was still capable of downing numerous pints of lager on a daily basis. He was now wearing a hi-vis tabard with the word *Security* emblazoned across his back. He gave Henry a nod.

Veronica dragged several stacks of pound coins into a plastic bag, wrote something on a piece of paper and said, 'Done! Anything more that comes in, I'll count separately.'

She stuffed the plastic bag into a medium-sized holdall, giving Henry a brief glimpse of the rest of the contents: many, many ten- and twenty-pound notes in bundles.

Veronica totted up her figures and announced, 'Twelve thousand, three hundred and fifty pounds, plus another thousand for the Ukrainian collection, although all of that is coin. Aren't people generous, Henry?'

'They are, indeed,' he had to admit. *As well as dishonest, fraudulent and violent*, he didn't add.

'So, all in all, thirteen thousand, three hundred and fifty pounds today.'

'Marvellous.'

This was the precise point at which Veronica met Henry halfway.

Henry had 'allowed' her to still have the tent on the village green on the condition that she had one of the stewards with her at all times. Henry knew that if he'd insisted on taking this away from her, it would have been too big a wrench and would have impinged on Veronica's pride and joy as she raked in and counted the charity money.

What he did insist on was that once the money was counted, he took it, also with his security guard Dr Lott at his shoulder, to be stored in the large safe in the office at The Tawny Owl. With that day's tally, he would have almost £40,000 stashed away from the fair, together with cash takings from Th'Owl that weekend, which meant there was close to £55,000 in there. He knew even that wasn't ideal, but it was far better than being in an old lady's house.

He thought.

He had also arranged that instead of the money being taken to the bank by car, a security firm was to pick it up the next day instead, at his expense.

Veronica had only reluctantly agreed to this, but Henry did not let her waver.

He hefted the holdall up with his right hand, his good side.

It was very heavy, and lifting it jarred his opposite side around his chest, making him wheeze slightly, which Veronica was quick to notice.

'Think you can manage?' she asked, concerned. She'd asked him that each day.

'I can,' he confirmed, although he knew that if someone tried to rob him, they would probably be successful.

He glanced at Dr Lott, who smiled. Once he was out of there, that was his responsibility done, and Henry could see his mind was focused on that long, very cold glass of lager. 'You ready to be my bodyguard, Doctor?'

FIVE

It wasn't such a problem for Ernest Lennox to punch the girl in the head just hard enough to stun her. Her fault, obviously, for wriggling about like a fucking fish, but he enjoyed it all the same.

Being small, scrawny and not just a little bit smelly growing up, he had often found himself on the wrong end of bullying as a kid. He knew he looked the perfect size, had the perfect looks and the perfect background to be picked on, but bullies targeted him at their peril. Although Ernest might have acquiesced to being pushed around in the middle of a circle of kids in the schoolyard (and he quite liked that in a way, going all rag-dolly, loose-limbed and vulnerable), he would bide his time and then pitch into the ringleader and deliver a punch to the side of his head that sent the other lad reeling. He knew this would incite the wrath of the bully's second in command, so he would put him down, too, and the other kids would back off, murmuring veiled threats that were never enacted.

This was how he was expelled from six secondary schools in a row, often facing teachers who had no idea how to deal with him or where to start.

But that was now ancient history to Ernest. The past. He was through with that.

Now he had got something he wanted, and his accurate punching skill had been put to good use to knock this silly girl into woozy oblivion and make her easy to manhandle while not spoiling her looks.

He and Benny dragged her out of the shower compartment and hefted her up the stepladder to stuff her into the sleeping area above the front cab of the motorhome – a space the width of the vehicle, just under two feet high and about six feet long accommodating a three-quarter-size bed with a very thin mattress. When not used as a bed, the space could be used to store items and locked.

Once the two lads had pushed Charlotte in, they hogtied her so her arms were behind her back, her wrists bound with a plastic tie and then fastened to her ankles, which were also tied together, ensuring she could hardly move at all.

Ernest refixed the tape across her mouth, winding it around her head, then he backed off down the stepladder and locked the flap into place with a small padlock so that Charlotte was now bound and gagged in a small, stuffy cell.

'What d'you reckon?' Benny asked.

'Trussed up like a Christmas turkey,' Ernest gleamed. Turkeys were something else he knew quite a lot about: in the run-up to each festive season, he and his dad targeted turkey farms across Lancashire, often stealing hundreds of plucked and prepared birds. Their criminal portfolio was wide and diverse.

'Guys!'

They looked around sharply at the word from Jimbo's lips, picking up on the warning behind the syllable. Jimbo was standing at the bottom of the steps into the motorhome, looking across the car park.

'You need to see this.' Jimbo jabbed his finger down the hill, across the roofs of the cars.

Ernest stuck his head out. 'What?' But even as he said the word, his eyes zeroed in on what Jimbo was referring to: the sight of a uniformed cop and a steward trudging across the field, zigzagging slowly between the vehicles but generally heading in a diagonal direction towards the exit gate.

The full implications of this hit Ernest immediately: they were going to be checking every single fucking car leaving, starting as soon as they got to the gate, and if he didn't get the Hymer off the car park now, he was in big trouble.

He weighed it up, then bent down and picked up a baseball bat which was wedged behind the driver's seat. He lobbed it to Jimbo, who caught it but looked at it mystified and said, 'What? You want me to go batter 'em?'

'No! Go that way with Benny,' Ernest said, jerking his thumb in the opposite direction to which the officials were walking, 'and start smashing car windows, yeah?'

It took a hazy second or two to dawn on Jimbo, but then he got it and nodded enthusiastically.

'Get their attention while I get this fucking beast off the car park, then leg it up through the trees and I'll pick you up on Caton Road, OK?'

'Yep.'

'What're you waiting for? Go, you numbskulls.'

It took another second for it to sink in, then both Jimbo and Benny bolted away, screaming and jumping, and within moments the first car windscreen had been smashed, followed by a shout of 'Oi! Coppers are cunts' and accompanied by a monkey-like dance of 'come and get me', and then a swift change of direction as the PC and the rather aged steward started to run towards them.

Ernest vaulted over into the driver's seat of the Hymer and fired up the unwilling old diesel engine.

As much as Henry was still six-two, his increasing age not yet having taken a toll on his stature, and apart from the triple knife wounds which were agonizing still and prevented him from moving with ease, he still maintained a reasonable level of fitness, the carrying of thousands of pounds in cash through a busy fairground did make him feel vulnerable. He was amazed that going home with similar amounts over the years hadn't fazed Veronica in the slightest, but he guessed that was mainly due to ingenuousness. Not to have been targeted, in Henry's estimation, was down to pure luck more than anything, because at the back of his mind something in his memory jangled slightly that a few country fairs had been hit by gangs before the pandemic and it was just chance Kendleton hadn't been one of them.

He wasn't particularly reassured by his security escort either. Dr Lott, Henry noticed, was limping quite badly and seemed to be in excruciating pain.

'You OK, Doc?'

'Gout. Big toe feels like a Bunsen burner is being used on it. Be
OK when I get to the pub and get a couple of pints and a handful
of paracetamols down me.'

'You're going to have alcohol and you're suffering from gout?'
Henry asked askance. 'Isn't that a bit, you know, silly?'

Henry knew that the affliction was caused by uric acid crystal-
lizing and settling in one of the lower joints, often the ankle or toe.
Uric acid was a by-product of alcohol, and either gout sufferers
produced too much uric acid or their bodies could not handle normal
amounts, resulting in gout and its accompanying agony.

'It is, and, as a medical professional, I agree,' the doctor said
with a grin, which turned into a wince as he placed his right foot
down. 'However, I need a pint.'

'Fair enough,' Henry said, reminding himself never to engage
Lott as his own GP.

A few minutes later, unmolested, they arrived at The Tawny Owl,
making their way across the front terrace, which was still awash
with customers, a sight that gave Henry a nice warm glow inside.
Inside, the pub was just as busy, and he had to do a lot of sidestep-
ping until he reached the door to the owner's accommodation area,
where he lived with Ginny, her boyfriend Fred and now, more or
less all the time, Debbie Blackstone. The safe was in one corner of
the office, tucked behind Henry's desk.

It was a sturdy old Mitchell multi-lock safe, operated by one key,
constructed from thick steel, fireproof and affixed to the wall with
hidden bolts. It was just about large enough to hold all the combined
takings from the weekend, though it was a squeeze.

Putting the money in gave Henry quite a pleasant feeling.

He opened up and stacked the fair's cash in, then locked it. He
returned the key to a wall-mounted key safe tucked away at the
back of the filing cabinet, the four-digit combination of which only
he and Ginny knew.

He went back into the bar, then bore across to the function room
where he found Blackstone talking to Charlotte Kirkham's mum and
stepdad. The parents were sitting side by side in two of the plastic
chairs while the sergeant was on another directly facing them, leaning
forward earnestly with her elbows on her knees, hands clasped.

Henry saw that Melinda West's shoulders were shaking as she
sobbed.

Blackstone looked across at him as he entered the room, a sort of hopeless expression on her face as she dealt with this distraught couple. It wasn't easy, however experienced a cop might be.

'Sorry, should I come back?' Henry asked, not wanting to intrude or break a thread.

Blackstone said, 'No, it's fine Henry, come in. We were just chatting.'

He crossed over and dragged a chair to join them.

'I was just telling Melinda and Dave what steps we are taking,' Blackstone explained. 'The searching, going to check cars leaving the site, and that we have extra officers on the way, who should be here by now,' she concluded impatiently.

Before Henry could comment, Blackstone's radio blared.

'*Assistance, assistance* . . . two lads smashing car windscreens,' came the voice of the constable who had been detailed to the car park. 'Making towards the woods at the back,' he said breathlessly. A rushing sound could be heard in the background as both his feet pounded on the grass.

Blackstone sat upright. 'That's all we need.' She looked at Henry, then at the couple. 'Look, sorry, I need to help out here.'

They nodded their understanding.

'I'll be back,' she promised, then she was up and gone in a flash, leaving Henry with the Wests.

Melinda's eyes were red raw; Dave looked a little bored by it all, Henry thought.

'How are you two doing?' he asked them.

'OK,' Melinda said with a snuffle, then blew her nose noisily, making her husband's eyes roll back in their sockets.

'The police are doing everything they can,' Henry reassured her.

'I know, I know,' she blubbered.

Dave sighed.

'That policewoman sergeant is very good,' Melinda complimented Blackstone.

'One of the best,' Henry agreed wholeheartedly.

'She told us you used to be a really good detective,' Melinda said.

'Once upon a time,' he said. 'Now I'm a really good landlord.'

That brought a slight smile to her lips for a moment, which dropped when she said, 'Do you think Charley will be all right?'

'I'm sure of it.'

'Gone off for a snog,' Dave, the less-than-concerned stepdad, murmured.

'Fuck you,' Melinda said.

Henry just blinked at him, annoyed by the attitude. He didn't even have his arm around his wife's shoulders, and Henry noticed his chair was a good three feet away from Melinda's. The atmosphere between them was brittle, and Henry knew this relationship was doomed.

'Do you mind if I just ask you something?' Henry said to Melinda, cutting Dave out of his eyeline.

'Yes of course.'

'Let me backtrack slightly,' he then said. 'Where do you live?'

'Blackpool.'

'Oh, OK. Does the name Ernest Lennox mean anything to you?'

'No, should it?'

'How about Leonard Lennox?'

Both shook their heads.

'Charlotte never mentioned either name?'

'Not to me,' Dave said, leaning into Henry's line of sight. He looked questioningly at Melinda who shook her head, then, to Henry, said aggressively, 'Why? Do you think she could be with these two? Are they brothers or something?'

'No, father and son. It's likely nothing,' Henry said, realizing he was probably stepping on Blackstone's toes now, getting involved in something that really wasn't his problem and planting seeds of hope in Melinda's mind. That was Blackstone's job, not his, and he didn't want to jeopardize any future line of inquiry by doling out names, which might motivate someone like Dave – who Henry had pegged as a hothead – to do something rash, even though his stepdaughter's disappearance seemed to be making him cross rather than worried.

The diversion caused by Jimbo and Benny worked well. At least long enough for Ernest to get the Hymer off the car park without being stopped and searched. As he turned down the road, which unfortunately led into Kendleton, he couldn't stop himself from cackling like a hyena and jumping up out of his seat to punch the cab roof, which was also the floor of the sleeping compartment above.

'We've got you now, bitch!' he shouted upwards, cupping his

mouth with a hand to form a loudspeaker, then he smacked the roof again.

By that time, he had driven the short distance into the village and had to negotiate his way slowly through the numerous people thronging the main street who seemed to think it was OK to step in front of cars without looking. It took all his willpower not to ram folk over.

The enforced snail's pace quietened him down, made him wary, especially when he came out of the village and was driving towards The Tawny Owl with the village green on his right, teeming with people, and he spotted a policewoman on the edge of the road, clearly in a hurry to cross, speaking urgently into her radio.

He slowed and beckoned her to go.

She gave him a quick wave of acknowledgement and dashed across, still talking into her radio.

Ernest smiled victoriously. 'Hey, if only she knew, eh?'

He punched the cab roof again and continued his journey.

Tony Owl, real name Jim Taylor, also known as the Millennium Falconer (which he thought was really neat), a kestrel clinging patiently to his leather glove, stood patiently in the queue at the burger guy's van.

The chestnut-backed bird of prey seemed to be revelling in the attention it was receiving from kids and adults alike, allowing gentle fingers to caress its head and wing feathers while its owner tirelessly answered the many questions put to him about the bird.

Tony had just finished his final display, using a wide ring of hay bales set at the far end of the village green. It had been spectacular, but the afternoon had just one slight failing: the golden eagle Elizabeth, which had been released at the start of the half-hour display and was expected to return with a spectacular fanfare at the end, having circled overhead for thirty minutes, did not come back. The audience found it highly amusing, and Tony laughed along, although Elizabeth seemed to have become quite headstrong lately and had done this trick twice. Tony wasn't too worried, not least because he had hand-reared her – legally – from a chick, and she did not have a clue how to hunt for herself. When she got peckish – and the display birds were always kept hungry – she would fly back.

Even as Tony glanced up into the sky while waiting in the burger queue, he spotted her gliding way above some nearby woodland to the south of the village about a mile away. Tony grinned. Little minx.

The burger queue moved on until Tony reached the serving hatch. He looked up and smiled, expecting to see the bonny girl, but instead found himself looking at Lenny Lennox who was flipping the burgers.

'Double cheeseburger, mate,' Tony ordered.

Lennox eyed him and the kestrel. 'Onions?'

'Absolutely.'

Lennox picked up a burger bun from the stack and opened it out flat, laying the burger on it.

'So what's your lad been up to?' Tony asked.

Lennox was about to spoon some fried onions on but stopped mid-application. 'What do you mean?'

'Uh . . . I saw him with that lass the cops are looking for. Nothing untoward going on, I hope?'

Lennox's bottom lip pouted as he did the mental calculation. 'No, nowt. Cops've spoken to him. Nothing to see here. Sauce?'

'Oh, OK. Brown, please.'

Lennox handed the burger over and said, 'Hey, uh, if you need any raw meat for the birds, got some stewing steak I haven't used today. It'll only get chucked cos of food hygiene and all that.'

'I'm always on the lookout for a free meal – for these guys, anyway.' He held the kestrel up.

'In that case, come back a bit later and I'll sort you. How does that sound?'

'Phenomenal, and cheers.' Tony Owl turned away, chomping into the fat-drenched burger which tasted amazing – in the way that one's last meal on earth tends to, even if you might not know it at the time.

'Two of the little gits!' the officer panted. 'They easily outran me into those woods.' The exhausted copper pointed to the trees into which the two criminals had disappeared after goading him and his sidekick, a steward who had a pair of bad knees and advancing age going against him. The PC was explaining this to Blackstone as they walked around a few cars, finding four with smashed windscreens. The young lad was still trying to get his breath back and his lungs were killing him.

'Ah, well, so be it,' Blackstone said philosophically and with a certain degree of sympathy. She probably couldn't have given any meaningful chase either. 'Take a note of the car numbers, put a note on the cars and wait for the owners to make contact with us, but don't chase them up for the moment. There's more important stuff going on. Get over to the exit and start searching cars leaving the site and record registered numbers and owner details.'

'On it, Sarge.'

Blackstone spun away and began to walk across the field, frowning deeply because of her thoughts of disquiet concerning this incident.

She phoned Henry.

Henry looked at the parents. The desolate mother. The indifferent stepfather. He toyed with the idea of offering them a room for free at The Tawny Owl. The place had been booked solid for the weekend, but that day, the last of the fair, guests were leaving, and the hotel side would be empty that night. Henry was reluctant to have anyone staying because he wanted to give his staff a breather the next day, so he zipped his trap. If they had asked, he would have said yes, although it would probably be better not to have them on top of the police investigation. They might start interfering, which would be a pain. They were better off at home.

There was an uncomfortable silence.

Henry had said his bit, made his reassurances, and now there was little he could add, plus he needed to get back to his Kendleton fair duties now.

His phone rang.

'Excuse me.' He moved out of earshot of the strained couple and answered it. 'Hi, Debs.'

'Know what I think?' she asked without any foreplay.

'I truly never know what you think,' Henry answered honestly.

'Distraction.'

'Distraction?' he said with a querying lilt, but he knew exactly what she was talking about: diverting attention, in this case by smashing a load of car windscreens. 'Occurred to me, too.'

'But for what purpose?' she asked. In the background, Henry could hear the noise of the fair, a steam engine hooting, kids screaming, Blackstone rushing.

'To get a car off the car park unscathed?' he took the punt.

'Possible. Or are we just making things up to shoehorn into our scenario?'

'Hypothesizing, you mean?'

'That's the fancy word, but I guess so.'

'It's what often drives investigations, especially when you've nothing else to go on. It's also called creative thinking.'

'Whatever,' she said, unconvinced.

Henry heard her collar number get called up on her radio.

'Got to go,' she said. 'The rest of the gang's arrived at last.' She hung up.

Henry assumed she was referring to the arrival of the remaining half of the Support Unit team, which, when deployed, would greatly increase the chances of finding Charlotte, if she was anywhere to be found. They were brilliant searchers.

However, this did nothing to alleviate Henry's bad feeling, especially since it was several hours since Charlotte's disappearance. Time flew in these sorts of cases. He turned back to the parents. Dave West just pulled a face, while Melinda looked at him as if he thought he knew something more.

He shrugged weakly.

Tony Owl transported his birds of prey around in what had once been a prison bus, which was ideal for the purpose. It didn't even need to be converted as it already consisted of a dozen 'cells' in the back, each one designed for a single prisoner and each with a secure door and hatch, with a walkway down the centre. All Tony had to do was fit a couple of perches in each cell and he could easily carry twenty-four birds if he had to, although a dozen was the usual number he took to displays.

After munching through the burger, which was a guilty pleasure, he started to transfer the birds from their wooden perches in the show area into the former prison bus.

Every bird was familiar with the routine and none complained, not least because they knew they would be on their way home soon and would be fed a proper meal – usually mice – before roosting time, so they were all content to be lashed on to their perches.

When all the display equipment had also been stored in the back of the bus, there was only one thing left for Tony to do and that was to await Elizabeth's return. He shielded his eyes from the glare again as he looked up into the sky as the sun dropped.

Finally, he spotted her eighty-inch wingspan as she drifted lazily on air currents above the nearby woods, still a good mile distant.

'Taking the piss, you are, Lizzy,' he said with a grin. She was a wonderful, beautiful, challenging bird, the absolute pride of his flock, and he loved her to bits and was happy to indulge her sense of freedom occasionally. She would be back.

In the meantime, he thought he might take up the burger guy's meat offer. Keeping these birds in the manner to which they were accustomed was an expensive business, and the pandemic had decimated his savings because of a lack of displays, so anything free was always welcome. With one last rueful half-salute to Elizabeth up on high, he walked across the showground on which stallholders and exhibitors were now wrapping up their wares as the fair came to a close, all having made a decent wodge over the weekend. When he got to the burger van, he wasn't surprised to see the shutters up, business done for the day.

He walked around the back and found the burger guy at the open side door of the Transit van behind. He was working on a chopping board on a small table with something resembling a washing-up bowl next to him, in which was a stack of meaty chunks on the bone.

The burger guy was busy slamming down a medium-sized meat cleaver into the shin of something, possibly a lamb's leg, and did not seem to notice Tony Owl's appearance.

'Hey, man, thought I'd take you up on that kind offer,' Tony said.

Leonard Lennox stopped the cleaver in mid-air, halfway through a downward chop. He turned slowly to Tony. 'Great stuff, no problem. Just give me a second.'

Lennox continued to hack the shin to pieces, one of the lesser-known, sub-standard ingredients he used in his burgers.

'No probs, mate.' Tony stepped away, turned his back to Lennox and looked up into the sky to see if he could still spot Elizabeth.

Unknowingly – and much to Lennox's glee – Tony had presented a perfect target: facing away, head tilted back, showing the perfectly circular bald patch on the top of his cranium, into which, with precision honed by chopping and dissecting meat for many years, Lennox plunged the blade of the cleaver.

SIX

Maude Crichton had not enjoyed her day at the fair.

She and her late husband – who had made oodles of money (which was still accumulating) in software based around the collection and dissemination of mobile data (Maude, incidentally, wasn't dim, but she didn't have a clue what that meant) – had been generous sponsors of the annual bash for a few years, and she had continued to put money into it even after he had passed away suddenly on a business trip to Thailand.

Normally, she loved the fair.

She wasn't on any of the committees that ran it these days, preferring just to enjoy the weekend, leaving its organization to others like Veronica, who had been doing it for so long she knew every nook and cranny.

But today, unusually for Maude, was the first day of the three she had ventured down to the village green and showground, and she found she could not get into it at all, especially after 'accidentally' bumping into Henry Christie. Not accidentally at all if truth be known. It was a deliberate act, but it had all gone awry because of Manderley, her feisty Bichon Frise, whom she adored, wrapping the extendable lead around Henry's legs – which infuriated him – and when all that had been sorted, immediately humping his leg. Nor did it help that Maude knew Henry wasn't very keen on the dog anyway, and Henry had been pretty much avoiding talking to Maude over the last few months, so being almost tripped up and then shagged by her dog did not open the floodgates to a line of dialogue between Maude and Henry who – *for some fucking annoying reason* – she could not get out of her mind!

Fuck the man!

It wasn't that she was a desperate widow. Far from it. She had a massive stash of money, now in excess of eighteen million and growing daily like some uncontrollable weed, and lived a fairly frugal existence in a village she adored. She wasn't bad looking for a slim sixty-year-old, had no pretensions or airs and graces, was popular and didn't shove her wealth down folks' throats. She'd had a few liaisons since her husband's death, but none of them did anything for her, whereas Henry Christie, in spite of him trying to keep her at arm's length, did. And she could not really explain why.

He was pretty decent in the looks department. She found him funny, and when their relationship was going through an 'on' phase, she just felt right in his company and in his bed. Yet, for some reason, he somehow could not bring himself to commit to her.

She thought she half understood this.

He'd lost his first wife, Kate, to cancer – suddenly and brutally – and then tragically lost his fiancée, Alison, the owner of The Tawny Owl. He had not been burned by love as such, but by the loss of the two women he had truly loved, and now he was wary of commitment again.

At least that was Maude's theory, even though she had never really been able to get him to admit that.

The other pretty big – nay, huge – issue Henry had with her was her children. To start with, they had an issue with him because both her son and daughter had picked up Maude's strong feelings for Henry, which in turn made them feel vulnerable. Her son, Will, believed Henry was just a gold-digger, ready to step in and steal their massive inheritance from under their noses. What they could never accept was that he wasn't interested in money. Maude had been at great pains to explain this, but they weren't having it. They were certain he was in it for the dosh, that he was playing her, toying with her emotions and alienating her bit by bit from them.

The upshot had been that Will had gone face-to-face with Henry, confronting him in Maude's kitchen after an evening meal at her house which should have been a getting-to-know-you occasion of pleasantness, and Will had straight accused Henry of wanting his mother's money and personally insulting him into the bargain.

Henry had walked out.

The next upshot was that when Henry had been stabbed on the church steps, he was convinced Will was his attacker.

There was no evidence to substantiate this, and Will vehemently denied it, but Henry was resolute, and this had resulted in a further deterioration of the relationship between him and Maude.

At least Henry had agreed to a chat later that evening after the fair had finally ended, and that was something Maude was thankful for. It would give them both the chance to air their views and, if nothing else, be friends. One thing Maude would not do was plead, because life was much too short for crap like that.

So although she hadn't enjoyed the fair that day, at least something positive had come of it.

Following her encounter with Henry, Maude had left the fair and decided to take Manderley for a stroll into the woods on the opposite bank of the stream, where there were a couple of decent paths for dog walkers and Manderley, despite being and looking like a pampered pooch, could have a run off the lead and get a bit grubby. Maude's plan was to emerge on the far side of the trees, walk up the road to her house and then, despite herself, make sure she looked and smelled great for the evening ahead.

'Weak bint,' she chided herself as she released the dog from the lead. He ran off wildly into the woods, but not too far. Manderley knew his limits.

As Maude approached the road, Manderley was by her side, back on the lead again. There was a rushing noise behind her. She twisted round to see two teenage lads hurtling up the path towards her. She attempted to avoid them, but the scrawny lads barged her out of the way, calling her a bitch and laughing raucously as she sprawled backwards and they carried on running up the road.

Maude hadn't been hurt and picked herself up angrily, brushing her arse down where she'd thumped heavily into the undergrowth.

She stepped out on to the road as a large vehicle sped past, almost colliding with her, making her cower. The vehicle – it was a mobile home of some sort, an old one – swerved to a halt about fifty yards ahead by the roadside next to the two lads who had flagged it down. They opened the side door and jumped in.

Maude glared at it, expecting it to set off, but it remained stationary. From where she stood, just on the road, she could see the reflection of the face of the driver in the wing mirror and then the squashed-up faces of the two lads who had shoved her aside against the rear window.

The fact that the motorhome did not move away was creepy and unsettling, as the faces of the lads all looked back at her for too long.

Not nice. Disturbing. Worrying. It gave her a bad feeling of defencelessness. Her legs went weak.

She quickly scooped up Manderley, who was as light as a feather, then dashed across the road into the driveway of her house, where she paused and looked up the road.

The motorhome was still there.

'Shit.' A lot of people thought of her as classy, but she knew some pretty filthy words, mainly because she had been brought up on the streets of Burnley in a no-frills family and been lucky enough to meet and fall in love with another Burnley inhabitant, an entrepreneur who went on to become her husband, then a millionaire. So if circumstances required, she had a dirty mouth. She shouted, 'Fuck you!' at the back of the motorhome, jerked up a middle finger, then turned and fled into the safety of her house.

Ernest Lennox adjusted his wing mirror to get a better view of the woman Benny and Jimbo had knocked out of their way.

A lone, middle-aged woman with a dog in her arms. A Bichon Frise.

Ernest knew his dogs because he had stolen so many of them over the past two years, mainly to order, some just on the hoof, for 'clients' (as his father liked to call them) all across the UK and Ireland. Dognapping had been one of the most lucrative of their sidelines – easy money, little effort.

He knew of someone who wanted a Bichon Frise.

'Oi, fuck you waiting for?' Benny shouted down from the back of the Hymer. 'Cops are after us in case you didn't know.' As much as it had been a blast doing the car windscreens and knocking the skinny bitch off her feet, Benny knew they needed to get out of there.

But Ernest watched the woman shout at them and jerk up a finger before disappearing.

'Just thinking,' he said.

'Yeah, well, think and drive, mate,' Benny urged him, then started to giggle at his own wit. 'Think and drive – haha! Get it? Think 'n' drive, like drink 'n' drive.'

'Highly fucking amusing,' Ernest said as Benny and Jimbo collapsed into hysterics on the sofa. Ernest crunched into first gear and set off with a few kangaroo jerks and something churning in his mind.

From the front terrace of Th'Owl, Henry watched the exhibitors troop away in their vehicles or in the air, as an old USAF helicopter had also been at the fair. Customers at the pub were less keen to disperse, but that didn't bother him too much.

As he sat there, he thought about how he felt.

This weekend had been his first sustained physical test since the stabbing. Not in the sense he was doing push-ups or throwing a medicine ball around, but in terms of his ability to keep going for three days on the trot, morning to night.

And he'd done it.

Yes, he was completely shattered and his back hurt like hell, as though it was on fire, but he had kept going and thought that once he'd had a bit of recovery time, he would be OK for the next hurdle, whatever that might be.

So as he watched the exhibitors trundle away, he felt fairly happy and knew he would sleep well that night. What concerned him more than anything was the missing girl, Charlotte Kirkham, and the desire he had to cast a magical spell to be able to freeze time so the police could go through everything.

But that wasn't going to happen, and he sighed as cops in uniform moved among all the people packing up and leaving, hoping to uncover something.

'Shit,' he breathed.

'Hi, Henry.'

His bleak thoughts were interrupted by Ginny pulling up a spare chair next to him.

'Sweetie,' he said.

'Still nothing?'

He shook his head. 'Not as far as I know.'

'Damn.'

'Damn indeed.' He gave her a wan smile. 'Not good, but Debbie's on the case, and if anyone can get a result, it's her.'

'Absolutely.'

'Are the parents still inside?'

Ginny nodded. 'Debbie's with them again, but I think they're getting ready to go home.'

Henry's face screwed up. He was still a bit conflicted, not a hundred per cent sure if it was in their interests to be packed off home. Practically, for police purposes, it probably was, but for them maybe not so. He was still half considering offering them a room.

Ginny said, 'If I were them, I wouldn't want to go home. You'd want to be on hand, wouldn't you?'

'Maybe so. On hand but not interfering,' he said, then added, 'I

don't have a definitive answer, but it's not my decision to make or
even suggest, really.'

'Thankfully.'

Henry turned to look at Ginny. Although she was only Alison's
stepdaughter, not a blood relative to her, she seemed to have
inherited many of Alison's traits, which Henry loved to see.
She was an incredible reminder of the second big love of his life,
the first being Kate, whom he had treated badly on too many
occasions. She had been taken from him just when, in his mind
at least, he'd got his act together. Alison had also been taken
tragically, violently, murdered by an obsessive ex-husband, Ginny's
father, who could not handle her moving on. From there, Henry
and Ginny had seemingly inherited each other, helped one another
through shared trauma and grief, and gone on to develop a loving,
almost father/daughter and working relationship. Henry had been
left The Tawny Owl in Alison's will, unbeknown to him until it
was revealed, and had subsequently given fifty per cent of the
business to Ginny. They had then continued to build the enterprise
in Alison's memory.

Looking at her now, Henry knew Ginny well enough to know
she had something on her mind.

Her eyes narrowed. She leaned forward with her elbows on her
thighs and the tips of her fingers steepled under her chin.

Glancing past her, he spotted Fred, Ginny's fiancé, approaching.
Henry smiled at him. He was a good, gentle guy, and he and Ginny
made a cracking team.

'Hi, Henry.'

'Fred.' Henry nodded, seeing the young man's eyes flicker uncer-
tainly between Ginny and himself. Henry also knew Fred well
enough to know when he had something on his mind.

Fred crouched down next to Ginny. 'Have you told him?' he
whispered loud enough for Henry to hear.

She shook her head.

Henry's insides did a double somersault. This didn't bode well.
Tentatively, he asked, 'Told me what?'

He was already fearing the worst. Did they want out of the business? To sell up, cash in? Henry knew that running The Tawny Owl
was like keeping a supertanker on course. It was a huge undertaking,
and he knew that he sometimes left Ginny at the helm for long
periods when he was co-opted into chasing villains. Although she

never admitted it, this may have pissed her off mightily. She was far too polite to say so even when asked.

Ginny didn't respond immediately to Henry's question, which deepened his concern. 'Ginny?' he prompted her.

She sighed.

'Have you had enough?' he asked.

'Eh? Of what?'

'Er . . . me, The Tawny Owl? All this. I know it's a hell of a commitment, especially for a young couple . . .'

'Henry!'

'What?'

'Shut up! It's not that at all. We love this place and what we do, don't we, Fred?'

Fred nodded as though he had no choice.

'It's our home. It's our life . . .'

'What then? Something's bugging you,' Henry probed.

'Well, clearly it is something,' she mimicked him, and then her face changed completely, all traces of worry dissolving as she reached for Fred's hand and made the announcement. 'We want to get married soon, here.'

Henry's head bobbed as though to convey he was thinking about it until he couldn't hold it much longer. His face cracked into a wide, beaming smile and he said, 'That's brilliant news. At last! When?'

'Very soon.'

The Tawny Owl had a licence to conduct weddings, and the year ahead was virtually fully booked as all the weddings cancelled due to the pandemic had now been rescheduled.

'We just want it plain and nice. I'll find a date in between all the others if that's OK?'

'Course it is,' Henry said enthusiastically.

'Plus there's something else.'

Henry's lips pursed. 'Go on.'

'Will you give me away?'

Henry's throat constricted and a strange breathless feeling came over him. 'I'd be honoured – oh God, would I be honoured!' He exhaled slowly as he wrestled with his emotions.

'And so would I,' Ginny said. She released her hand from Fred's grip, twisted around and embraced Henry where he sat. He patted her back and rested his chin on her shoulder, looking at Fred who he winked at. Into his ear, Ginny said, 'Love you, Dad.'

Henry almost dissolved where he sat. 'Love you, too, Daughter,' he said, and it was all true. Although he did have two other grown-up daughters who lived away and with whom he had great relationships, since Alison had died, Ginny had looked on him as her father and asked if she could call him Dad. That had been one of those heart-exploding moments, too.

Finally, Ginny disengaged and looked at him. 'And I'd like Debs to be my bridesmaid. Do you think she'll say yes?'

'Certain of it,' Henry said, knowing that the outwardly brash, tradition-bashing Blackstone also had a soft, gentle side and would revel in all the pomp and circumstance of a wedding.

'Best man is Phil, Fred's best pal.'

'As he should be.'

'There is something else,' Ginny said mysteriously.

'Oh dear.'

'It's a good "oh dear",' Ginny said with a smile.

She tilted forwards and reached behind her to pull something out of her back pocket about the size of a postcard. At least that is what Henry thought it was at first until she turned it slowly over and showed Henry a grainy, indistinct black-and-white photograph which had the effect of making his heart race again.

An ultrasound scan. Of a baby. In a womb.

'Oh my God,' Henry gasped, looking from it to the beaming, deliriously happy faces of the couple. 'Congratulations.'

This time he stood up, brought Ginny to her feet and embraced her; then he hugged Fred and resisted the urge to tease him by saying, 'I didn't think you had it in you,' into his ear in jest. Then he shook Fred's hand heartily, clasping it and saying, 'You'll make a brilliant dad.'

Modestly, Fred coloured up in embarrassment. 'Thanks, Henry.'

Henry patted his shoulder. 'You're a good guy.' Then he turned his attention back to Ginny. 'Awesome news, this,' he said, having to choke something back and fighting the kind of tears he hadn't wept for a long time. 'And you'll be a great mum.'

'Like my mum was,' she said, meaning Alison. 'We wanted to get married because we are old fashioned like that, and the baby will be born in wedlock.'

'Nothing wrong with that,' Henry assured her.

'And we also wanted to know what sex it is, so we asked.'

Henry swallowed again. Dry throat.

'It's a girl,' Ginny revealed.

'Oh, that is brilliant news.' Henry liked baby girls.

'And we know what we want to call her.' Ginny eyed Fred, who nodded. 'Alison Katherine.'

Once more, time stood still for Henry.

'But we'll know her as Alison Kate.'

'Bloomin' 'eck. Almost too much to take in. I'm speechless. So proud – and your mum would be, too, and so would Kate.'

'I'm delighted you think so. Something else, too,' Ginny said.

'Do I need to sit back down? This is all getting a bit too much for an old guy.'

'Maybe.'

So he did – just to be on the safe side.

'If it's all right with you, we want her to know you as Grandad.'

All Henry could do to this was nod.

He was already a grandfather to his daughters' children, so the epithet didn't faze him, but the circumstances did. Finally, he said, 'I accept.'

'And we also want her to be your goddaughter. So, will you?' Ginny asked.

'An offer I cannot refuse.' He didn't dare to say anything else for fear of becoming a blubbering idiot. Through watery eyes, he looked out across the village green, trying to hold it all in. He spotted Elizabeth, the golden eagle, still soaring and circling on the air currents way above, not having yet returned. Distractedly, he thought Tony Owl must be getting a bit concerned.

Lennox cheekily leapfrogged the line of slow-moving vehicles pulling off the showground, causing a few people to scowl at him and one or two to blast their horns, but he did not care. He knew he had to put some distance between himself and Kendleton for a few hours, not least because he was transporting a dead body in the back of the Transit van with a very deep ravine in its skull. Lennox needed to dispose of the body properly before the next stage of proceedings began. Jumping the queue might have been pushing his luck, but he knew everyone else was knackered and unlikely to physically confront him over his manoeuvre. They all just wanted to get to their homes, many of which were some distance away.

As he passed The Tawny Owl, he spotted Henry Christie out front talking to a couple, and he wondered if they were the parents of the missing girl, although they looked a bit young, and Lennox knew for sure they weren't when Christie embraced the woman.

Lennox settled behind the wheel with the girl alongside him.

Her name was Ella, as in Cinderella, her birth name. She looked like a little princess but was actually a devil in disguise, one of the best pickpockets and opportunist thieves Lennox had ever encountered, and she could also flip a burger, which is what he had insisted she did that day. She was also not averse to violence, particularly of the knife variety, and was more than happy – delirious, even – to help load Tony Owl's brutally murdered body into the back of the Transit. She did it with a grim smile and without a murmur.

A good lass, Lennox thought.

But not one to be trifled with. He had once tried to grab her cunt, but she had kneed him ferociously and he had respectfully heeded the warning. She controlled who touched her after a childhood of abuse at home and in care homes. Lennox knew that Jimbo was screwing her, even though she was only fifteen. He knew because he had watched them at it a few times, unbeknown to them, thinking how lucky Jimbo was.

Lennox's thoughts returned to Henry as he wove the Transit and the burger van in and out of the long tailback to the main road.

Henry Christie.

The cop who had sent him down for that stretch. Ten very valuable years in terms of the time of his life they covered, nineteen to twenty-nine. The prime of his life. Years that should have been well lived, ones he would never get back.

For doing nothing!

Lennox hated Henry, a simmering rage that had festered in his soul for many, many years. He had known that if there ever had been the remotest possibility of taking revenge on the smug bastard, he would have taken it, but he had accepted that, as the years rolled by, there was little chance of that happening. Now, unexpectedly, Christie was back in his life, and it really gnawed at him that he wouldn't be able to make the most of the opportunity.

But there might yet be a way. Lennox was going to be returning later that day to the village, and maybe that would provide the means to revisit the ex-detective who had stolen his life and teach him a lesson he would never forget. Even as he drove away, there was a plan forming.

*   *   *

With most of the vehicles having left the site, Henry walked across from The Tawny Owl on to the village green and showground, his chest still pumping with pride and happiness and the generosity of spirit of Ginny and Fred regarding the names chosen for their baby girl.

Alison Kate Livingstone.

A fine name by any standards, he thought as he wandered and saw Veronica Gough rolling towards him on her super-powered wheelchair.

'Hi, Ron.'

'Is all that money locked away?'

'Safe and secure,' Henry assured her.

'Good boy.'

Henry saw that the former prison bus used by Tony Owl to transport his birds of prey was one of the few remaining vehicles still parked up, and if he was right in his identification of it, the golden eagle was now standing on the roof of the bus looking a tad forlorn.

'Have you seen the bird man?' Henry asked Veronica.

'No.' She squirmed around in the wheelchair to look. 'The door's open, maybe he's inside. I know that bird on top did a bit of a runner . . . or would that be a flyer?' she said, chuckling at her humour.

'Good one, Ron,' Henry congratulated her. 'I'll go and see,' he said, but before setting off, he asked, 'Long weekend, good weekend?'

'One of the best ever, although 1965 was amazing,' she said. 'But now I'm whacked, so I'm setting my autopilot for home where a Sainsbury's ready meal awaits, a shower, then bed.' She paused and gave Henry a critical once-over. 'How are you faring?'

'Bushed, too. The lion will sleep tonight.'

'And your stab wounds?'

Henry rolled his left shoulder. No doubt it hurt, ached, but not enough for him to call it a day just yet. 'Not so bad.'

They held each other's gaze for a moment, their recent history a bond that would remain unbroken.

Henry cocked his forefinger at her. 'You get yourself home, and I'll come and collect you in the morning and you can wave the takings off in the security van – how about that? Then we'll go for breakfast somewhere.'

'Sounds wonderful.'

He watched her trundle away. She might have been confined to a wheelchair and she was more than thirty years older than him, but she dwarfed him energy-wise.

Henry turned and went towards Tony Owl's vehicle. This was the type of bus in which Henry had spent quite a lot of time in his younger days as a uniformed PC, travelling in and conveying prisoners on remand from magistrates' courts to prisons, not a job he relished. When the responsibility of prisoner escorts was finally given over to private security firms, a lot of police officers had moaned about jobs being taken away from them, but Henry had been pleased. It was time-consuming, didn't require specialist skills and could occasionally be dangerous. Cops should never have been doing it.

As he looked at Tony's bus, he wondered if he had ever travelled in it himself.

The golden eagle's piercing eyes watched him approach over its aquiline hooked bill, flexing its talons on the roof of the bus to keep a grip, occasionally flapping its magnificent wings to keep balanced and making threatening squawks.

Henry smiled to appease it.

The side door of the bus was open, and Henry wondered if Tony was still waiting for the police to recontact him over the ID he had made earlier.

At the foot of the steps, Henry called, 'Tony? You in there?'

No reply. Henry climbed in to check. Tony wasn't there, but the other birds of prey were all housed in their own little prison cells. Tony wasn't in the driver's cab either. Henry was starting to find the situation slightly odd; he knew Tony Owl was a complete professional where his birds were concerned and would never have left them unattended for any length of time. Henry backed out of the bus and walked around to the driver's door and hauled himself up into the seat.

He frowned at the sight of the keys dangling in the ignition and Tony's bush hat on the passenger seat. Various scraps of paper were screwed up and chucked into the passenger footwell together with a couple of screwed-up napkins. He picked them up and saw the logo on them: they were from the burger guy. Lennox.

Above him, he heard the golden eagle scratching on the roof and making a loud, plaintive wail.

Henry could not help but put two and two together.

Where the hell was Tony?

Frustrated, he lowered himself out of the cab. Behind him, he heard a merry voice approaching.

'I'm going to be a bridesmaid, I'm going to be a bridesmaid,' Blackstone sang tunelessly as she shimmied towards him.

'You've heard the news, then? Congratulations.'

'Yep – how good is that? Preggers, in love, gonna get hitched.'

'A perfect storm,' Henry agreed.

'And you a godfather.'

'A role I was born for,' Henry said. Then, even though he did not want to bring Blackstone back to reality, he said, 'Have you seen the bird guy anywhere?'

'Uh, no.' She looked up and saw Elizabeth staring piercingly down. 'Should I have?'

With a sweeping gesture, Henry said, 'This seems odd because he isn't here and that eagle up there is still free.'

'Phone him. Maybe he needed the loo.'

Henry looked at Tony's logo and mobile number on the side of the prison bus. He pulled out his phone, called him. He shook his head at Blackstone. 'Straight to voicemail.'

He eyed the eagle, then had an idea which was usurped by Blackstone who said, 'One of my constables does this as a hobby – you know, falconing or whatever it's called. He might be able to entice the big bird off the roof. I'll shout him.' She brought her PR to her mouth.

Henry walked around the bus, stooping to look underneath, but there was no sign of Tony Owl. Looking around, he saw that almost all the exhibitors had now gone. A few remained in their caravans to have an extra night here.

Blackstone caught up with him just as he was climbing back into the driving cab and reaching across the seats. 'He's coming to see what he can do but makes no promises.'

Henry eased himself back out having grabbed what he was after, which he showed to Blackstone.

The scrunched-up napkins from Lennox's burger van. He unfolded them and showed them to Blackstone and said with a shrug, 'Probably means nothing . . .'

SEVEN

Blackstone's constable found a leather glove in the back of the prison bus, plus a dead mouse in a cool box, and coaxed Elizabeth down from the roof. In fact, the huge bird didn't need much encouragement. Once she'd spotted the unfortunate rodent, it was game over. She flapped down like something from a horror movie on to the constable's wrist, gripping tightly with her talons and ripping the mouse to shreds with the long, hooked bill.

'Biggest bird I've ever had on my arm,' the officer quipped. 'Poor babe's starving.'

Henry watched the short display with admiration and respect – and from a safe distance. He would not have liked the bird to land on his arm, leather-gloved or otherwise.

Speaking soothingly to the bird, the officer climbed slowly into the bus and gently transferred her on to a perch in one of the vacant cells, then closed the door.

'They all need care and attention,' he told Blackstone. 'They're all delicate creatures, however scary they may look, and they could easily die.'

'Any ideas?' Blackstone asked.

'There's a garden centre near Garstang that has a display of birds of prey,' he said. 'They might be able to help short term.' He checked his watch. 'Be closed now, though. Foxton's I think it's called. On the A6.'

'OK,' Blackstone said. 'Can you drive one of these things?' she asked the officer and pointed to the bus. He nodded. 'Good. Jump in and start making your way and I'll get comms to turn out a keyholder and persuade them to help out.'

'Will do, Sarge.'

'And nice one, Duncan, with the eagle and the mouse.'

He gave her a grin. 'I'll get my gear.' He gave her a thumbs-up.

Watching him go, Blackstone turned to Henry. 'Thoughts?'

He shrugged. 'Just very odd.'

'Or' – Blackstone looked at the napkins Henry still had in his hand

- 'linked to Charlotte's disappearance? He was a witness, saw her – supposedly – with Lennox's lad, who we have yet to trace.'

'I see that, although it's all a bit vague, and who would know he was a witness, a witness who didn't see all that much?'

'Unless he blabbed to Lennox. He could have opened his trap.' Blackstone pointed to the napkins. 'I'm now not happy we let Lennox go.'

'Nothing to detain him for, unfortunately,' Henry pointed out.

Blackstone shook her head with frustration. Her lips tightened across her teeth, and she pinched the bridge of her nose. 'Migraine forecast,' she said, then, 'Where the fuck is Charlotte?'

'And where the fuck is Tony Owl?'

'At least as the site clears, it'll give the Support Unit a good chance to sweep the place before night starts to set in.'

Henry nodded. 'But don't forget, we need to know more about Charlotte, too. She's from Blackpool, and Lennox and his lad are from there, historically anyway, so it is possible she already knew him and has hooked up with him voluntarily just to stick a middle finger up at Mum and Dad? So as much as it's worrying and I don't like it – particularly finding her phone, which she might have jettisoned deliberately – there is no evidence yet of a crime being committed.'

Blackstone scratched her ear. 'I need to speak to Mum and Dad again, and probably get into Charlotte's social media accounts, Facebook and suchlike. The answer could be there.'

'Which still leaves Tony Owl.'

'Coincidences?' Blackstone put out there. 'Your favourite saying?'

'Coincidences is clues – yep, exactly that.'

They called it the headquarters. In some way, that was accurate because this was the location from which Lenny Lennox ruled his small but perfectly formed organized crime group, which consisted of him, his son Ernest, Ella and Benny and Jimbo. Other non-family members had come and gone, but this was the current line-up, and it had worked well for about eighteen months. On the face of it, to passing motorists, this was just an old garage premises, once a small petrol station with a forecourt, now crammed with a variety of cars and vans in various stages of decay; behind was a large bungalow with a driveway up the side, leading to a long track at the rear on which were open barns used as workshops, plus other outbuildings used for storage, mainly of stolen goods in transit.

The whole site was in a quiet location just off the A6 near the village of Scorton, to the north of the old market town of Garstang. It was surrounded by open fields, was not overlooked – with the possible exception of the bungalow on the road opposite – and did not stand out. Lennox was able to go about his activities very much under the radar. The property was close to the M6, plus had easy access to Blackpool and Morecambe, locations that predominantly funded his enterprises, and was therefore ideal for Lennox and 'his lads', as he liked to call them.

So it wasn't too far for Ernest to reach in the Hymer motorhome, and within half an hour of leaving Kendleton, he was turning into headquarters and driving slowly past the bungalow, rattling over a cattle grid on to the track, continuing up past a large workshop, an industrial unit and an open barn, and finally up to a single-storey unit with a roller shutter door at one end. There was a gravelled turning circle in front of it where Ernest U-turned the Hymer, then backed up to the shutter door. Benny leaped out, entered the unit through a personnel door and hauled up the door with a chain. Ernest then reversed so the Hymer was completely inside the unit and Benny was able to let the roller door clatter shut by allowing the chain to slide through the palms of his hands, letting gravity do its job.

Ernest dropped out of the cab and walked around to the side door, which had already been opened by Benny. He glanced around the interior of the building and the glimmer of a smile played on his face as he rubbed the tufts of hair around his chin and the weedy moustache over his lip.

Along the back wall were half a dozen enclosures – kennels – all six feet by four feet, made of strong mesh, each with strengthened steel doors. Each enclosure had an actual kennel inside it with a trough or bowl for food and water.

Four of the enclosures had undernourished dogs in them, chained to the back wall, none of them making noise above a whimper, because in the short space of time they had been incarcerated, any barking had been punished by one of the boys cracking them with a riding crop, plus each dog was tightly muzzled. The dogs learned quickly. Not that it would have mattered too much as most of the inner walls of the building were lined with cardboard egg boxes, literally thousands of them (all stolen from a nearby farm) and they absorbed and muffled sound, effectively making it impossible to hear anything outside from more than thirty yards.

Each of the dogs was a pedigree, stolen to order. Two cocker spaniels, one French bulldog and a Staffordshire bull terrier. All had been microchipped by their owners, but one of the services offered by Leonard Lennox to would-be customers was the surgical removal of the implants, although the term 'surgical' was somewhat of a misnomer: Lenny had lost four dogs recently through infections caused by his inability to properly sterilize the scalpel he used to dig out the chips.

So, cowering in the kennels at the reappearance of Ernest, whose task it was to look after the dogs, was almost £5,000 worth of dogs, all due to be taken abroad soon.

'Hello, boys,' Ernest called to the dogs. In response, each one either cowered in the back corner of their enclosure or slunk into the kennels as far as the chains would allow. Ernest didn't care about the spirit being beaten out of the animals. They were resilient beasts and their new owners would probably retrain them if they could get them through their psychological issues.

Again, not that Ernest cared.

The dogs were already paid for, and it was unlikely he would ever meet a disgruntled customer.

He grinned again.

Lenny had said he needed one more dog for the next trip abroad, and Ernest now knew exactly where such a dog could be sourced.

He turned back to the motorhome. 'Time to get her out.'

Benny unlocked the hatch to the overbed and slotted the stepladder into place, gesturing for Ernest to go up. 'You want the pleasure?'

'Nah – you guys drag her out for me, eh?'

Without having to be invited twice, Benny stepped up two rungs of the ladder and reached into the space, grabbing Charlotte's ankles even though she was curled up and terrified in a foetal ball. She had no means of stopping herself from sliding out and into the arms of Benny and Jimbo who roughly dropped her on to her backside in a sitting position so she was facing Ernest who was standing outside the motorhome.

Ernest smirked triumphantly. 'Bit of a coincidence us meeting up like that, eh?'

Charlotte, her mouth bound closed by the tape, tried to scream and lash out with her feet, but Ernest doubled back so he was just out of range. He laughed pitilessly.

'You should never have dissed me, you little bitch!' On the final word, he lurched forward, grabbed her ankles and ferociously yanked her out of the door, smacking the back of her head on the threshold, then on the steps and finally on the shiny concrete floor of the unit, splitting her scalp open with a nasty gash as her skull hit the ground. Blood ran. 'Fate,' Ernest said, 'that's the word: fate! Right.'

Ernest dragged Charlotte across the unit, making her short skirt and top ride up, scraping her flesh, and completed the journey by bundling her into one of the empty enclosures and rearranging her into a sitting position as he strapped a leather dog collar around her neck which was fixed to the wall by a chain. He checked to see her wrists were still tightly fastened around her back, then he leaned into her face, breathing unpleasantly into her nostrils.

'Won't be long until I'm back,' he promised her.

She mewed, terrified, behind the tape, but also stared at him with defiance.

Ernest tapped her cheek, winked and stepped out of the enclosure. He padlocked it from the outside, rattling it so Charlotte got the message: she wasn't going anywhere.

'Ron? It's Henry . . . hi, you back home now?' He was speaking to her from his mobile and was currently on the front terrace of Th'Owl.

'I am, Henry.'

'Can you do me a favour?'

'Yes,' she said instantly.

'You don't know what it is yet.'

'If it gives me one in the bank, then it doesn't matter.'

Henry smiled. 'Tony Owl, the falconer guy, still hasn't turned up – just seems to have vanished into thin air.'

'Bit worrying.'

'I know you've got all the paperwork for the show. I was wondering if you have an address for him. We could do with sending a bobby around, just to make some enquiries.'

'I'll have a look. I don't know it off the top of my head,' Veronica said, 'but I'm pretty sure he lives alone somewhere in Cumbria. Give me a minute or two and I'll get back to you, although the address could be on his website.'

'Thanks, Ron.'

'Is that golden eagle still free?'

Henry explained they had managed to recapture it and to where the deserted birds were now being taken. Before he hung up, he said, 'Another favour, Ron – can you also get me the address of the burger guy, Mr Lennox, from the paperwork?'

She said she would.

'Henry!' Blackstone called from behind him. He spun and she beckoned him. 'Will you speak to Charlotte's parents again for me? They're getting arsy, and I'm also getting some earache from my team who, apparently, are still dealing with a whole bunch of people who've had things nicked from them and their vehicles today.'

Ernest and the other two lads busied themselves unpacking the motorhome, stacking up the catalytic converters in the corner of one of the outbuildings on top of a large pile of others they had stolen previously. They made certain all the mobile phones stolen that day were switched off and their batteries removed. These were then stashed in an aluminium-lined box crammed with other stolen phones. The cameras they had stolen were kept separately in a small office; they had now amassed more than twenty high-quality cameras, each worth in excess of £500 even on the stolen-property market.

After this, the trio closed up the unit in which Charlotte had been secured and made their way back down the track to the bungalow, shouldering each other and playfighting as they went in through the side door.

They each grabbed a chilled beer from the fridge and lounged on the two battered old settees in the living room, eating crisps and salted nuts as they waited for Lennox to arrive back. It was in this room that the lads stacked up the wallets and purses they had managed to steal that day. They began to unpack the contents. Today was cash-rich because many people attending the fair came armed with actual dosh because they knew it would be easier to pay with cash for stuff at a country fair rather than with cards.

Finally, they had a pile of Bank of England notes totalling around £900, also a stack of debit and credit cards, several driving licences and even a couple of hundred euros and someone's passport.

They divvied up the cash between themselves. Lenny always allowed this, but he got to keep the cards and licences which he knew he could get a good price for on the criminal market where such things were in constant demand. Fraud was like a pandemic, and no matter how the authorities responded, it always came back like whack-a-mole. Identity documents were often the key to bank accounts and life savings, and although Lennox did not have the IT skills to commit these sorts of crimes, he knew people who did – people who would pay well for the right documents.

After the beers and the celebrating of a day's work well done, the lads all showered and changed into black jeans, black T-shirts, black jackets, black trainers, ready for Lennox's arrival home.

So far the day had been fun.

But now it was about to move up a level on the serious scale.

'This is just not fucking good enough!' Dave West shouted. 'Just another police fuck-up if you ask me.' He slammed the side of his fist down on the bar-room table. 'Not good enough!'

Henry let him have his say. Charlotte's stepdad had been back and forth to the bar in Th'Owl and had probably had more than a few drinks. Henry could smell the reek of alcohol on his breath, and although he would not have said the man was drunk, the booze had affected his mood and he'd become belligerent.

Melinda remained stone-cold sober.

'Dave, shut it,' she said, squirming with acute embarrassment on the chair alongside him. Both were sitting opposite Henry, who had replaced Blackstone as a target for Dave's ire and, as she'd called it, arsy-ness.

'I really do understand your worry and frustration,' Henry started to say apologetically.

'Oh? How would that be? How could you?' Dave demanded, having become the concerned parent under the influence of a few beers and a chaser. He slurred some of his words, and Henry thought that, possibly, he had underestimated the extent of Dave's drunkenness.

'Well, let's say I do,' Henry retorted firmly (one rule he had adhered to throughout his police service was never to argue with a drunk). 'The fact is that the police response has been pretty damn good in such a short space of time, and it concerns them greatly that Charlotte hasn't turned up yet, although it does remain possible she is doing something of her own volition . . .'

'And yet you found her smashed-up phone!' Dave blasted him.

'Very true, and that is a concern,' Henry conceded.

'And what about those names you mentioned?' Dave asked.

'The police are following them up.'

Melinda gave Dave a pacifying gesture, and he sat back, his lips wriggling angrily and his eyes rolling with great exaggeration. Melinda leaned towards Henry. 'Bottom line, Mr Christie, bottom line? Based on your experience. Tell me.'

Henry sighed and scratched his nose. 'OK, every missing person is just a bit different in their own way, but there are common characteristics and, to be honest, statistics show that most turn up unharmed.'

'And in this case? Charlotte?'

'I would honestly like to think she's just doing this to make you angry, Mrs West, but I am worried, as is PS Blackstone.'

Melinda sucked in her breath and covered her mouth in shock, making Henry wish he hadn't been drawn into giving an opinion.

'But the police will find her, I'm sure,' he said quickly, backtracking slightly.

'Rubbish!' Dave blurted.

Melinda shot him a hard scowl which closed him right down, and suddenly Henry felt sorry for this couple on two counts: first because Charlotte had gone missing, and second, because of that, the problems in their already fragile marriage were starting to grate like tectonic plates before an earthquake.

'It's out of my hands, though, as it is a police matter. Our stewards and volunteers will all stay on a little longer to do another sweep of the area, but I can't make them stay and they're doing this out of concern for Charlotte. They've worked hard all weekend and they're knackered, but they'll all put in extra for you.'

Henry watched a tear form in her eye, then dribble down her stressed face.

Dave just shook his head.

'And in the meantime, you should go home, get showered, freshen up and try to chill.'

Dave snorted again. Henry resisted the urge to punch him.

'I'll keep on to the police to keep you updated. Sergeant Blackstone is on it and she's like a terrier with a bone. She won't let it go, I promise you.' He looked pointedly at Dave. 'I hope you won't be driving.'

'Why, will you tell the cops to breathalyze me?'

'In a heartbeat,' Henry assured him.

'Fuck you!' Dave snarled under his breath.

'I'll drive,' Melinda said. 'And you're right, we should go home, but it feels wrong to do so.'

'I understand that, but you must, for your own sanity,' Henry said.

'But she might be out there, somewhere, needing me – us,' Melinda cried, starting to lose it.

'And when the police locate her, they'll bring her straight back to you,' Henry said, now finding this tedious and draining. He was relieved when Blackstone came back in. He was getting far too old for shit like this.

Blackstone made her way directly to Henry, smiling at the Wests. To Henry, she said, 'A word, please.'

'Is it about Charlotte?' Melinda demanded.

'No, something else.' She jerked her head for Henry to follow her out of the pub, where she turned to him. 'I kid you not, Henry, there has been a frickin' crime wave at the fair today. So far, eight owners of four-by-fours have come to report their catalytic convertors gone while they were in the car park. There may be more yet. At least a dozen people have either lost or had their mobile phones nicked. At least four decent cameras gone, too.' She sighed. 'And wallets galore, for eff's sake. One minute there, next gone! There may be more.'

'Definitely a team, then.'

'A skilled team working the crowds, and no one saw or felt a damn thing. They were – are – very good.'

Henry frowned.

'What?' Blackstone said.

'I wonder if it's worth checking out previous country fairs and the like around the country pre-2020, see if there's a trend, or some intelligence that might be helpful,' he suggested, recalling his earlier thoughts on the subject.

Blackstone sighed dramatically. 'Suppose so, but only after we finish dealing with our missing person, which takes priority.'

'Your shout, but I agree,' Henry said. He lowered his voice slightly and almost whispered, even though the Wests were well out of earshot, 'I think they're ready to go home now, but if the stepdad drives, bag him because he might be over the limit – and I don't like him.'

It felt like a very long journey, although it was perhaps twenty miles at most, but a dead body in the back of a van doubled the length of any journey, Lennox guessed. Especially with a head that had been meat-cleavered. The traffic coming out of Kendleton was pain-fully slow, made even more dodgy by the sight of cop cars blue-lighting and two-toning it in the opposite direction, undoubtedly heading for the village.

Once on the M6, he went south from junction 34 and exited the motorway at the next junction, 33.

From there, it was only ten minutes to headquarters, the former petrol station not far from Garstang. Of course, when Lennox referred to it as his, it wasn't really, but it had fallen legally, more or less, into his hands a couple of years after he'd been released from prison in the early 2000s. At that time, he had been on the lookout for a more rural place from which he could operate unseen. He owned four properties in Blackpool – three bedsits and a terraced house divided into flats – and two in Morecambe, which were both shitty bedsits. All of these properties made him a sound income from social services mental health and youth offending teams, keen to place patients and young adults back into the community to lead 'full and meaningful lives', as the slogan went. Or, in Leonard Lennox's case, into his uncaring, manipulative, exploitative mitts, where he could take full advantage of vulner-able young men and women without fear of discovery, mainly because social services did a terrible job of supervising the young-sters in their charge and were just happy to get them off their hands without proper, in-depth checks. Out of sight, out of mind. A tick-box win.

And good money, Lennox discovered. Steady, a blanket from which he could carry out other lucrative crimes, with the ever-changing personnel, which had to be wisely chosen to be his 'little soldiers' as he called them. Youngsters like Ella, Jimbo and Benny. His gang.

Then he had found the former petrol station.

It was advertised in a business sales newspaper. As Lennox looked into it, he found it hadn't been open for years and was owned by a decrepit old man who was losing his mind and did not have anything in his armoury to stop Lennox moving in, 'cuckooing' him, accessing his money – which was plentiful – discovering he had no family and drawing the old man's pensions. After a few years, the guy had died and left everything to Lennox, not knowing what he was doing.

Now the old petrol station was in Lennox's sole name, and he had a great base from which he could operate his diverse criminal activities without scrutiny, other than from the slightly weird guy opposite who occasionally reported him to the council.

More or less, then, this was like having a secret hideaway; his 'official' residence was a semi-detached house in Bispham to the north of Blackpool, where he had lived briefly with his wife and son, though he rarely spent any time there these days. He enjoyed the privacy the old petrol station afforded him, without the daily pressure or worry of cops knocking on his door.

As he pulled into the driveway in the Transit pulling the burger van, he drove slowly past a large lorry – a former Post Office box van – parked on what used to be the petrol station forecourt, knowing that very soon it would be full enough to make its usual six-weekly journey. Then he stopped and parked just beyond the bungalow, glancing in through the side window to see the three lads in the lounge, having changed into their evening attire.

Ella glanced at him.

'Open the side door,' he said to her.

Lennox walked to the kitchen door of the bungalow, leaned on the door jamb. The lads all looked at him from the settee. He did not speak, but his face showed anger.

'What, Dad?' Ernest asked.

'Get up off your backside and come here, you little shithouse.'

'Oh Gawd, here we go again,' Ernest said, rolling his eyes and trying to make light of the summons. Reluctantly, he shoved himself up on to his feet and sloped across to his father, who, once again moving more quickly and unexpectedly than Ernest could react, smashed an open hand across his son's face. Lennox wasn't the most physically violent of men other than when he totally controlled a situation, but a lifetime of dominating and oppressing Ernest made hitting him easy.

With his face reddening fast not for the first time that day, Ernest wavered but held his ground, glaring at his father with a hand over his cheek.

Lennox's right hand then snaked out and grabbed the front of Ernest's black T-shirt and dragged him outside, snarling, 'Come with me.'

Behind them, the other two followed, frightened, curious.

Lennox pulled Ernest around to the side of the bungalow to the Transit van. Ella was standing by the open side door of the vehicle.

Lennox spun Ernest around and grabbed him by the scruff of his neck, holding him so he was forced to look inside the van.

'That is what I had to do to save your scrawny, pathetic little neck.'

Behind them, Benny and Jimbo rubbernecked to see what was happening, their heads bobbing to get a look at Tony Owl's dead body with a skull split cleanly in half.

He released Ernest who, horror-struck, turned slowly to his face. 'Why?' he asked.

'Because he could identify you, and if he identified you, he identifies us and we get the cops crawling all over us, and everything we have and do will fucking disintegrate, you little prick! And I couldn't allow that, and all because you want to jack off in a girl's mouth!'

'But—'

'What have you done with her?'

'In one of the kennels, shackled up like the dog she is. She in't going anywhere.'

'OK – but she's seen your face? And everyone else's faces?'

Ernest nodded.

'And what *are* you going to do with her?'

'Have fun.'

'Then what?'

'Pass her round to the guys.'

'Then what? Pat her on the arse and send her on her way, tell her to keep her mouth shut like a good girl?'

Ernest swallowed, didn't have to say anything.

'Exactly,' Lennox said. 'I fathered a halfwit.'

'Sorry, Dad,' Ernest whimpered pathetically.

The other three sniggered at his humiliation, but when he scowled at them, the venom in his eyes stopped the tittering instantly.

Lennox pointed at Benny and Jimbo. 'You two – get this dead man into the freezer in the big shed to keep him from stinking. We'll decide on his fate later after we've done what we have to do – that's if you're all still up for it and won't wimp out.'

The muted chorus was 'Yeah,' 'Yeah, course,' and 'Yep.'

Lennox eyed them. 'You sure?'

The next response was much more positive, especially when Ernest piped up, 'Dad, I've thought of something we might do!'

*   *   *

Jimbo uncoupled the Transit from the burger van, then drove it to the unit right at the back of the property with Benny and Ella following on foot.

Ernest stayed with his father at the bungalow, still cradling his swollen cheek pitifully, wondering if his father had broken his cheekbone with the blow.

Lennox walked into the short hallway that led to the front door. A length of metal with a hook stuck on one end of it was propped up in a corner. Lennox took it and hooked it into the latch on the loft hatch, easing the door down carefully, then pulling down the extending loft ladder which clicked into place.

Lennox climbed up and hoisted himself into a sitting position on the edge of the hatch, his feet dangling.

He could see Ernest looking up at him.

'What have you got to tell me, boy?' Lennox asked.

'Sorry, Dad,' he mumbled sullenly.

'We cover our tracks, boy,' Lennox said. 'That way we don't get caught. We don't do stupid things like kidnap girls where we're operating. That draws attention – the kind we don't fucking need, like cops crawling around and people seeing things they don't need to see.'

'I get it, OK?' Ernest said crossly.

'Whatever. What's done is done. We've got to move on, and tonight's very important to us.' He rubbed his finger and thumb together for Ernest to see – the gesture that said *money*.

Lennox raised his legs and twisted himself into the loft on all fours, crawling along a board until he reached a gap, then peeled up a section of the earth wool insulation between two of the rafters.

As he did this, he called back to Ernest. 'So, what else do you have to tell me, laddo?'

Ernest, who had climbed a few rungs up the ladder and was peering into the loft, watching his father, explained his idea as Lennox slid his hand under the insulation and extracted four handguns and two small ammunition boxes, after which he relaid the insulation and backtracked towards the open hatch as Ernest stepped back off the ladder. Lennox sat on the edge again and handed the items down to him, just as Ernest drew his little idea to a conclusion.

As Lennox twisted on to the ladder, he said, 'That is not a bad idea, lad.'

Words that were like gold dust to Ernest. Praise from his father.

* * *

The fact that the contents already in the chest freezer in the unit freaked out Benny, Jimbo and Ella did not prevent them from following Lennox's instructions, which also freaked them out. But the three of them were used to blood.

Between them, they had caused many people to bleed on many occasions, often with unprovoked attacks leaving their victims badly injured, bleeding profusely, in alleyways and gutters. That kind of violence gave them a high like an actual drug and was often a release for them as they had all suffered physical abuse when growing up.

Tony Owl's dead body was on quite a different level, though.

And instead of giving them a buzz, it made Benny and Jimbo take stock of the nature of the man who currently controlled their lives, Lenny Lennox. He had the ability to take everything just one step further, and the lads knew they could never cold-bloodedly attain such heights of violence. They had seen him do it a couple of times before, and it served to keep them on a tight leash of fear.

The victim of one of those occasions when Lennox had lost it – although this was before their time in his 'care' – was still in the chest freezer, a solid block, folded up in the bottom, covered by a clear polythene sheet.

Now and again, the lads would creep in and have a look, usually when they were on dog-feeding duty. They would unlock the freezer and peer into it as if looking into an abyss and see the frozen face of the 'folded-up woman', as they called her, looking up at them. They were pretty sure she must have had a broken neck for her head to be in that awkward position.

Then they would close and relock the freezer, placing the key in its hiding place.

At the van, Benny slid open the side door and looked at Tony Owl's body, weighing up how best to transfer it into the freezer.

'I'm not taking his head,' Benny said.

'I'm not, either!' Jimbo said. He looked at Ella, whose face remained impassive and a little contemptuous of the lads. Unlike them, bodies did not freak her out. She kind of liked them.

'Just drag him out. One of you take one leg, one take the other, and I'll pick his head up, you losers,' she said.

They didn't argue.

They had to manoeuvre him into position first so his legs stuck out of the van door, which was like wrestling with a big, loose-limbed dummy as it was still too early for rigor mortis to have set in. The lads took a leg each under their armpits, counted to three and dragged Tony Owl out. His head crashed to the gritty ground, but Ella did not even try to pick it up, just laughed uproariously at the lads who told her what a cunt they thought she was and then pulled him into the unit through the door, leaving a trail of blood and brain matter.

Once inside, they paused to get their breath back and looked across to the kennels where they could see Ella kneeling in front of the one that housed Charlotte, who was huddled down with her face pushed into the corner.

Ella was whispering something the lads could not hear through the mesh of the enclosure. When she became aware that Benny and Jimbo were watching her, she turned to look at them, and both lads swallowed at the sight of her face which could have been the mask of a devil.

By mid-evening, the village green and showground were almost empty of exhibitors and stallholders, except for those staying an extra night. All the old steam engines, classic tractors and old service vehicles had eventually left. A team of volunteer litter-pickers had descended and quickly collected all the rubbish in a well-drilled operation.

Like most people who had only ever experienced the sharp end of such events, Henry had been amazed to see what went on behind the scenes, the huge amount of concerted effort from people like Veronica and other dedicated individuals (he did not count himself among their number) to pull the whole shebang together.

He was impressed.

It was after nine now, and Henry decided it was time to start closing down The Tawny Owl. The staff deserved an early dart before their day off tomorrow.

As it was, there were only the usual diehards in the bar, including Dr Lott – who had quenched his thirst probably more than necessary – Dave Darbley and a few others. Henry gave them the 'one pint' notice that the place would be shut by ten. This brought groans of disapproval, but because almost all of them had been involved in the fair in some capacity, he said the last pint was on the house. That brought a cheer.

'Too bleeding generous by half,' Henry muttered, going behind the bar and helping himself to a very cold pint of Stella Artois, glugging a third of it back in one gulp as he came out from behind the bar to find an empty seat which he settled down on, then suddenly remembering something.

'Maude! Jeez!'

Ginny came out of the owner's accommodation and made a beeline for him.

'Did Maude turn up?' he asked her. 'She said she might.'

'Nope.'

'Not been and gone?'

Ginny shook her head.

'Ah, OK,' Henry said, feeling a slight sense of relief that she hadn't turned up and he'd missed her. Maybe she had simply changed her mind about coming in for a chat. Fingers crossed.

Henry reached for Ginny's hand. 'How are you doing?'

'I'm doing fine because I'm a bundle of energy at the moment, though that probably won't last.'

'Well, I need to start looking after you better from now on,' Henry said. 'No more crime-solving jollies for me for a while, maybe forever.'

'Not necessarily.'

'Well, y'know, let's do some planning – you, Fred and me – get things in place.'

'Sounds good.' She squeezed his hand. 'Anyway, things to do, glasses to collect.'

'Oh, by the way, ballpark figure for the weekend?' he asked. Ginny was in charge of accounts.

She pondered. 'Sixty grand – about a quarter of that in cash.'

'Brilliant,' Henry said. 'You've done good.' He knew Ginny had been the driving force to get Th'Owl up and ready for the fair, and there had been no shortages of anything.

'And that doesn't include the hotel side, although we are empty tonight as agreed.'

'Wow, nice.'

'Glasses,' she said, and broke away from him just as Blackstone marched in through the door looking harassed.

EIGHT

Maude knew it wasn't really important, but she did want to look her tip-top best for Henry because she realized this was probably the final chance for them. Whichever way it went, she still wanted them to be friends. Living in such close proximity in a small village like Kendleton meant there was no way she and Henry could avoid bumping into each other regularly. Their relationship, whatever it might be, needed to be cordial for both their sakes. And to be honest, she had got it into her head that it was truly over. But one last conversation . . . Who knew?

Thing was, Maude knew the end wasn't completely down to Henry being stabbed, although it didn't help matters that he thought her son had done it. Maude knew that even if Henry hadn't been stabbed, it was pretty rocky between them.

She wondered if he wanted a younger woman. The one he'd been seeing, Diane Daniels, had been quite a bit younger than him, but that was now over.

And this Debbie Blackstone, who seemed to have taken roost at The Tawny Owl, was also a lot younger than Henry, although Maude wasn't certain if Henry was doing any messing with her. She got the impression it was a friendship thing. At least that's what Maude hoped.

She spent some time getting her head around what she should wear that evening.

That snazzy trouser suit? A plain frock? Or just a simple blouse and cut-off jeans which she knew she looked pretty hot in.

That would do.

But before all that, some tarting up needed to be done. The foundation on which everything else was layered. First was a long, lazy, smelly bath, followed by a makeup-and-nails session. Nothing too outrageous – just cool elegance topped off by her favourite perfume by Jermaine.

But as she slid into the soapy bath, Maude acknowledged that deep down, or maybe not so deep down, she wanted Henry to find

her too damned attractive to turn down. She wanted him to gasp
when he saw her . . . and a little later, gasp again.

'Well, I can dream, can't I?' she asked Manderley, who watched
her slither into the bath. 'Can't I?'

The little dog gave a sharp bark in reply.

Blackstone was almost undressing as she came into the pub, swinging
off her stab vest, unbuttoning her epaulettes and unstringing all the
wires relating to her radio, then dropping the lot at Henry's feet.
She then removed the heavy utility belt from around her waist and
dumped it, contents and all – handcuffs, baton, incapacitant spray
– on top of the stab vest. Underneath all that, the white short-sleeved
uniform shirt was drenched in sweat and clung to her contours.

Henry averted his eyes.

'I'm off duty,' Blackstone declared. 'And I need a long, long,
cold, cold drink, then I might have a shower and some decent food
after a day of takeaway chips and mayonnaise.'

'Drink's on the house,' Henry said. 'Every other bugger here's
taken full advantage of that.'

'Be rude to say no.' She headed for the bar, pushed through a
small crowd of locals and demanded a pint of lager.

The barman, a young lad called Mark, asked which she preferred.

Blackstone pushed her sweaty hair back and said, 'Do I look like
I give a shit?'

She returned with the same as Henry and plonked herself down
heavily beside him and began to remove her work boots, then her
socks, revealing sweaty feet and gaudily painted toenails. She rubbed
her feet with her free hand while tipping the pint of lager into her
mouth with her other.

'You'll never get me to say a woman can't multi-task,' Henry
said. 'It's a miracle to watch.'

She pulled her face at him. 'Sexist.'

'How's it going? Any updates?'

Blackstone released her foot and sat back. 'As a result of Veronica
getting Tony Owl's address, we got Cumbria Police to visit his
place, which is a sort of smallholding. No one's there, and from the
voters' list it looks as though he lives alone with his birds. On
the plus side, the people who own the garden centre near Garstang
and bird-of-prey display have agreed to look after Tony's birds
overnight or until we see where we are with things. Only problem

is that the patrol in Cumbria who visited Tony's address reports there are at least half a dozen other birds up there which need looking after. We're on to the RSPCA for some help.'

'OK.'

'I've just spoken to Charlotte's parents – they're at home now, thankfully, and they're going to speak to some of her friends and let me know if she has been in contact with them today. They'll also give me details of all the social media accounts she's on . . . basic stuff, I guess.'

'Could be valuable, though.'

'Agreed.' She took another swig of her pint. 'Now for the really odd bits.' She wiped her lips with the back of her hand. 'Veronica also gave me the details she had for Lennox which he had to provide in order to get on to the fair to sell his burgers.' She paused. 'All false.'

Henry sat upright.

'He gave an address in Morecambe on Westminster Road. The address exists but a family of three live in it and have never heard of Leonard Lennox.'

'Is that for sure?' Henry asked.

'I spoke to the cop who visited the address when he was actually there. The family seem totally legit.'

Henry sighed.

'Lennox also provided an email address but that doesn't exist. I don't know enough about tech to check it out, but I'll get on to Tech Support to follow that up tomorrow.'

'What about phones? There was a number on the side of the burger van, if I recall,' Henry suggested.

'Duds. Don't exist. Made-up shit.'

'Wow!'

'Wow, indeed.'

'What about PNC checks on Lenny?'

'His conviction in 1991 is recorded, as is his release in 2001. After that, nothing.'

'What about the son, Ernest?'

'No convictions as such. However, he's been locked up a few times for pestering girls and, being the weak-kneed fuckwits we are, he got his wrists slapped twice and bugger-all else. So, how shall I say this? He likes the ladies.'

'Address?'

'I got Blackpool to go round to his address on file. Empty. We do have an intel file on him, though, and a couple of his associates were listed who we're trying to check out now. Could be the lads he was with today, or not. But don't hold your breath on that.'

'Hm, a complex web,' Henry pondered out loud. 'They seem to be living off the grid. What about bank accounts? Did he pay Veronica via a bank?'

'Apparently not. He paid cash on arrival on Friday night. As you know, cash is king with these sorts of events, but it was a good thought, Batman,' Blackstone said.

'But everything that can be done is being done as night falls?' Henry asked. He pointed out of the window where the day was drawing to a close. Once it was dark, there would be little the police could do in terms of searching, although other enquiries could continue.

'I guess.' Blackstone shrugged.

'So how do you feel about it all now?' Henry asked her.

Blackstone considered the question. 'That she's with this Ernest Lennox, but whether it's a voluntary thing, who knows as yet? She's at that age, attracted by bad boys, no common sense. Been there, done it . . . remember it well,' she said wistfully. 'She could just land home as if nothing's happened and live with the fallout from her mum and dad, fait accompli. Just a pity we couldn't hold on to Lenny Lennox,' Blackstone said. 'However . . .'

'We are where we are,' Henry concluded her sentence. He looked at his watch and wondered where Maude was.

By ten thirty, The Tawny Owl had closed for business. Henry and Ginny had ushered the final locals out and the doors had been closed. After a short flurry of cleaning up, all staff had been given the nod to either stay for a couple of drinks on the house or go home. Exhausted, they all chose the latter option but left with cash-in-hand tips of seventy-five pounds each.

It had been a good weekend.

Henry and Ginny thanked them all individually and finally turned to each other for a hug.

'Congratulations again,' Henry said, holding Ginny at arm's length and surveying her with pride.

'Thank you. We're thrilled.'

'And so you should be.'

'Time to chill in a minute or two,' Ginny said. 'I know we've decided not to open tomorrow, but there are still one or two things to do.'

'Leave everything,' Henry told her.

'OK.'

Henry's mobile phone rang: Rik Dean, head of FMIT.

'Ricky Boy,' Henry said.

'Henry, have you closed for the day?'

'Yep, why?'

'Because I'm standing outside Th'Owl and the door is shut.'

'Have you tried the handle?' Henry suggested. 'It's still unlocked.'

Henry looked towards the front oak-panelled door which creaked open, and Rik Dean entered. At the same moment, Debbie Blackstone came out of the owner's accommodation behind Henry, towelling her hair down, having changed into tracksuit bottoms and T-shirt.

She saw Rik Dean. He saw her. At exactly the same moment.

Both, unprofessionally, pulled faces.

Henry's head pivoted from one to the other. He saw and logged their expressions and said quickly, 'Play nicely, children.'

The towel in Blackstone's hand rubbed furiously.

Rik Dean said over Henry, 'I want to speak to Henry, alone,' to Blackstone, who snorted like an enraged bull in Pamplona and said something under her breath which had the whiff of the word 'cunt' in it, although Henry couldn't be certain. She spun around and disappeared back into the private area.

'Is she still living here?' Rik demanded. 'If so, she's breaking police regulations by living on licensed premises and also not keeping her personal details up to date as regards her address.'

'Is that what you came for? To get one over on Debbie?'

'No, I came about a missing person, Charlotte Kirkham, whose parents have been phoning us every bloody half-hour. The comms room operators are getting mightily peed off.'

'I assume they're worried about their daughter.'

'Clearly . . . Hey, do I get a pint?'

'We're closed,' Henry said. 'And I'd get a fine for providing alcohol to a police officer on duty and you, being said officer on duty, would get disciplined.' He tilted his head and raised his eyebrows. 'So get off her case and tell me why you're here, Ricky Boy, brother-in-law and the person who now has my job.'

'Like that, is it?'

'I've had a long weekend, a pretty shitty day, I'm knackered, and the police still haven't arrested whoever stabbed and almost killed me – so yeah.' Henry stopped abruptly and changed tack. 'If you're here why I think you're here, then I think I might get a tad cross with you.'

'Why do you think I'm here?' Rik sat down opposite Henry.

Henry's jaw rotated as he wondered if he should spin the game out or not. He decided not. 'I'm hoping you're just interested in a missing-person case, and you've simply come to ask Debbie for an update, even if, knowing her, all updates will already be online.'

'Almost.'

'What, then?'

Rik swallowed. 'There's been some argy-bargy about who should be running it as it seems to have the potential to be a serious job. PS Blackstone has put herself forward to lead it.'

Has she? Henry thought. She hadn't mentioned this to him, and it went against his earlier advice to push the job up the food chain just in case it went downhill.

'And that's a problem?' Henry asked, deciding he would back Blackstone even though he knew it was nothing to do with him. Why was Rik here? Why had he come all the way out from headquarters or Lytham, where he lived? Henry's eyes narrowed suspiciously. He said, 'It wouldn't be a bad shout. She's done all the right things, ticked all the boxes, been in it from the word go.'

'I agree, but she isn't a detective any more, as you know. She has a completely different job now.'

'You could swing it,' Henry pointed out.

Rik gave him a weary look, which had a hint of being very hacked-off in it. Then came his little bombshell. 'Diane Daniels wants the job assigned to her. She's the on-call SIO and it does fall under her remit.'

'There you go, then. Simples. Let her have it,' Henry said. 'Decision made.'

Rik pinched the bridge of his nose as though he had a migraine. 'Yeah, I get it, but if I'm honest, I'd rather Blackstone did run it.'

Henry repeated, 'There you go. Simples. Let her have it.'

'You are no fucking use, brother-in-law.'

'I don't have to be.'

'Anyway, thing is, there are two screaming women who want the job, and I'm in the middle of it and I can't handle the hormones,' Rik moaned.

Hearing Rik make such outdated remarks caused Henry's eyebrows to arch high. He hadn't heard such stuff since way back, even though he knew the attitudes of many male cops towards their female counterparts were still entrenched in the dim and distant past and often quite unpalatable.

'You'd better not let anyone hear you rant shit like that,' Henry warned him.

'I'm not that stupid,' Rik said, affronted by the very idea he might let his true prejudices seep out. 'I know how to play the game. All I'm looking for here is a middle ground where no one's nose gets put out of joint or their knickers get in a twist.'

'Put them both on it, then,' Henry suggested naively. 'Diane's a DI and Debbie's a sergeant – the natural order of things?'

That brought a chortle from Rik who then went on to almost choke. He leaned forward. 'Let me let you into a little secret – those two wenches will never, ever work together again, not ever.'

Wenches? Henry thought. *OK, Rik really has regressed into the Middle Ages. At least he didn't say 'bitches'.*

'So what was your thought?' Rik asked Henry as though he expected him to understand the question.

Henry shrugged. 'I don't get you. Put either or both on it, make a decision. You know, that thing that comes with rank – making decisions.'

'No, no, no, you misunderstand. Maybe I haven't made myself clear.'

'Currently, I'm plaiting fog,' Henry admitted.

'Well,' Rik began tentatively, looking almost coyly at Henry, which Henry found cringeworthy. 'Technically, you are still on the books . . .'

'Woah! Stop right there,' Henry cut in dramatically. 'No way.'

'Normally I wouldn't ask, but this has the potential to be a serious case. You, like Blackstone, have been in this from the get-go, you're an ex-SIO, the only one with the skills—'

'I'm still recovering from a serious assault, Rik. I can't even raise my left arm over my head and I feel like I've been stuffed with tinfoil. Now if you'd asked me to run the investigation into my stabbing, I'd say yes, mainly because you lot don't seem to have got anywhere with it. But not this. It's got to be either Diane or Debbie, or both, or let the division run with it. You make the choice.'

'Bugger! Not even for a load of dosh?'

'Not for anything, Rik. So what's it going to be? Debbie or Diane? My gut says Debbie.'

Rik shook his head as Henry spoke. 'No way.'

'Then fine, make your decision and stick with it.'

Rik blew out his cheeks. 'It'll have to be Diane,' he said finally. 'She's FMIT and that's the end of it.'

'There you go, then. Easy.'

'I can't tempt you?'

'I'm easily tempted by most things, but not today.'

'Fair enough. I'd best get home, then.'

Rik rose to leave, at which moment Blackstone came out of the owner's accommodation door again, hair dried, flat to her head, but holding her mobile phone and with a very evil smile quivering on her lips. Both men instantly knew what she had done and what she was armed with, confirmed when she said, 'And I quote, "Two screaming women" and "Can't handle the hormones".'

She had video-recorded the whole conversation between Rik and Henry from a crack in the door.

'Thanks for standing up for me, Henry,' Blackstone said. 'You didn't have to, but thanks.'

'I know, but you're a mate and also more than capable of doing the job.' Henry paused and looked into her wildly sparkling eyes. Henry knew she had the most iridescent blue eyes, but because Blackstone was Blackstone – damaged goods, he thought, currently in the repair shop – she was wearing bright green contact lenses which made her look startling. 'That said, mates talk to each other, and now maybe it's time you told me the reason why you were kicked off FMIT.'

Blackstone's nose twitched in uneasiness.

'Tell me it didn't have something to do with me,' Henry pleaded. 'Well . . .'

Henry closed his eyes. It was something he suspected, but he hadn't wanted to force the issue with Blackstone.

When Henry had first met her, she was a DS on the Cold Case Unit. She'd arrived at that post after a series of moves within the force following an assault on her by a man who had thrown acid at her, scarring her neck and upper chest, and subsequently affecting everything she did and was. She became difficult, almost impossible to supervise, which was why she had been shunted around various headquarters departments.

Henry knew the acid attack had deeply affected her. She'd withdrawn into herself, crippled by self-doubt and self-loathing, and her response had been to become a wild child, striking out at anyone and everything. The knock-on effect was that she terrified supervisors who didn't have a clue how to handle her, whether they were male or female. Clamp down? Allow her free rein? Criticize her? Mollycoddle her? None knew or were trained in how to deal with such a volatile person.

But somehow Henry had jelled with her. Initially, he'd been thrown off-balance by her appearance and attitude, but as he came to know her and give as much as he got, a genuine respect for each other began to blossom, and behind her harsh veneer, he uncovered a deeply troubled woman who despised her own scarred appearance, but was also a warm, loving, good friend – and an excellent detective.

This last trait led to Blackstone finally being transferred from the CCU on to FMIT, but her only problem there was the recently promoted Diane Daniels, her new line manager.

Diane had been Henry's lover, but the relationship had ended on a sour note when Diane humiliated Henry, albeit unintentionally, during a police briefing during which Henry learned rather publicly that she was seeing someone else.

Blackstone had also been present at that briefing and was furious on Henry's behalf, although Henry, hurt though he was, took the 'dumping' philosophically.

He sighed. 'Tell all.'

'Well, she was always asking about you, making snidey remarks about you – about *us*.' Blackstone waved her hand back and forth. 'She tried to insinuate we were an item. Huh! We ain't, never will be . . . no disrespect intended, mate.'

'None taken.'

'We *are* just mates, aren't we? You don't harbour any lustful thoughts or ideas about me, do you?' Blackstone asked distastefully.

'Be assured. No.'

'Well, good. Anyway, she just kept on and on, niggling away, like she was a jealous bint. Jealous of what, I ask?'

'Exactly.'

'Me and you? For fuck's sake. Hardly.'

'Methinks you do protest too much,' Henry teased her. He knew the only thing between them – including thirty years – was friendship, and he liked it that way.

'But no, she wasn't having it. *Why are you living there, then? Are you shacked up with him?* She kept on. I tried not to remind her that you saved her life and all that.'

'Best way.'

'Anyhow, she started sending me on shit jobs. Wouldn't let me on to the squad looking at your stabbing. I even ended up taking someone's statement in Nelson for some half-baked robbery out there, would you believe?'

'Did it need doing?'

'Well, yeah, but a local jack could have done it easily enough, not me traipsing on an eighty-mile return journey. Anyway,' Blackstone began, averting her eyes shamefully, 'I'd had enough. Nit-picking, meh, meh, meh. I cracked.'

'Please tell me you didn't.'

'Hm . . . not quite. I pinned her against the wall in the ladies' loo in the FMIT block, one of those nose-to-nose things with my elbow across her throat. I mean, I didn't hurt her . . . much . . . I didn't, but I crossed the line, and Ricky Boy just took her side and next thing I knew I was chasing kids who'd nicked quad bikes across farmland, as good fun as that is.'

Henry had once come close to decking a more senior officer years ago when he was younger and wilder, and his body language on that occasion had signalled to the officer that it had been a close-run thing. It ended up with Henry being ousted in a jiffy, and quite rightly so. He had learned a lot from that episode.

He shook his head.

'Fortunately, people think I've got a screw loose, so there's nothing more coming of it,' Blackstone said. 'But not a proud moment, to be honest.'

'And now you've got Ricky by the balls?' Henry pointed to Blackstone's phone.

She gave him a secret smile. 'Not really. Only if you're a lip reader. I didn't get any sound; even though I could hear him, the phone didn't pick it up.'

'He thinks you got every word.'

'Let's keep it that way for the moment, shall we?' She looked disconsolate. 'I wouldn't use it even if I had got every word. But you know what? I'm not bothered who runs this investigation, as long as it's run right and we find Charlotte sooner rather than later. I'd just like Ricky Boy to grow a set and make a choice.'

Henry exhaled. 'You cheeky mare.' He checked his watch.

'Are you expecting someone?'

'Maude said she'd come around. She's late.'

'Booty call?'

'Nah.'

'So, Henry, mate, when *did* you last get laid?'

Somehow, through the course of the evening, Maude gradually and painfully lost all her self-confidence, even after a long bath, a leg shave, a bush and armpit trim. She had hoped that by going through this process, smelling lovely, sorting her hair, dressing nicely, she would have the courage to face Henry and maybe, after a nice glass of vino or two, sort things out.

Instead, after all the pampering, the painting of nails, it all seemed to evaporate into the ether.

Frustrated with herself yet unable to get any motivation despite some brutal self-talk, she finally gave up and dressed no further than having a snuggly dressing gown wrapped around her. She poured herself a large glass of white wine, plonked down on the sofa and flicked the TV on, then flipped her legs up on the footstool, feeling utterly miserable.

She wondered if being miserable with eighteen million in the bank was worse than being miserable and poor.

Both were pretty shitty, she guessed, but having money cushioned the blow, although that was probably a big part of her problem at this juncture.

'Come on, Mandy.' She patted the dressing gown across her thighs which now formed a tempting, comfortable hammock-like space for the dog. He jumped up and spun instantly on to his back, paws in the air, wedging his backbone between her legs, and waited for his chest and tummy to be scratched.

'How could anyone dislike you, my lovely?' Maude cooed and she could swear he purred like a cat. 'But Henry Christie does. You really need to stop shagging him every time you see him,' she chastised Manderley.

She remonstrated with herself to get a grip, but she couldn't.

Finally, she even switched the TV off and sat there in silence, staring blankly at the wall for inspiration, sipping her wine sulkily.

Then she heard the sound of a car engine and the crunch of tyres on the gravel drive which looped around the back of her house.

Manderley's ears pricked up. He flipped himself right on her lap and gave a little yelp.

'Who's that?' Maude wondered out loud.

Manderley scrambled off and dashed into the kitchen at the back of the house from where the garden and detached garage could be accessed.

As Maude made her way after the dog, she heard a tapping on the back door. Crossing the kitchen, she saw an indistinct shape through the frosted glass.

She had a vague hope that this was Henry come to rescue her from the pits of despair, although the figure outside looked too small.

She unlocked the door and opened it, but before it was even inches wide, it was kicked open out of her hand. Someone barged violently in and punched her hard in the face, sending her staggering backwards into the fridge-freezer, which wobbled and its contents clattered within.

She slithered down, head reeling, sensing blood gushing from her nose, down her face and on to the dressing gown. She was aware of her attacker standing over her. She tried to look up, to focus, but the blow had made her brain a mush and her vision was blurred, and it was like looking through frosted glass. Then her head lolled sideways, and she passed out. The last thing she heard was Manderley squealing.

NINE

The subject for discussion had moved back to Lenny Lennox and his son, Ernest.

'How do people like him even have kids?' Blackstone asked incredulously. 'Creepy git, should've been castrated at birth. And how do they end up getting married?'

'People end up with people,' Henry said. 'Doesn't sound like the marriage lasted, though.'

'Just long enough for a sprog.'

'And look how he's turned out: a chip off the old block.'

'He's been a lucky lad. One thing I'll be looking at when this is over is why Ernest didn't get prosecuted for those allegations,' Blackstone stated.

'Witness intimidation springs to mind,' Henry suggested. 'Maybe the victims were approached and were too scared?'

Blackstone nodded and took a sip of a whisky sour.

They were still in the bar of The Tawny Owl, now closed, sitting in the front bay window, chatting a lot of things through. Henry had thought it would be prudent for Blackstone to compile a to-do list of enquiries to be undertaken the next day if Charlotte hadn't turned up – and if she wasn't going to be the lead investigator (which seemed to be likely), to give the list of actions to whoever was in charge (the professional thing to do). She'd been compiling the list on her work iPad as the two of them spitballed ideas. It was getting to be a long one.

Having got a second wind, Henry was quite enjoying this process, and he thought that if he had been in a better state of health, he might have taken on the running of the job.

His phone rang: Melinda West.

'Henry Christie,' he answered. 'Hello, Mrs West.' He looked at Blackstone and thumbed the device on to speakerphone. 'How are you?'

'Not good. My mind is in a twirl. It's so unreal, all this.'

'That's understandable. How is your husband?'

'Drunk, in bed, blaming himself for being a rotten stepdad, which has more than a ring of truth to it.'

'I hope you'll both be OK.'

'We will, I think . . . I was just wondering if you'd heard anything from the police, any update? I've rung them so many times it's verging on harassment, but I can't stop myself.'

'Again, understandable, but you do need to let them get on with the job. They'll keep you updated, I'm sure.'

She started to sob.

'Look, Mrs West, they will keep trying. They've got quite a few addresses to check overnight, and tomorrow they will move on to other stuff.'

'I know, I know.'

'So try to get some sleep, yeah? I'm sure Charlotte will turn up unharmed; it's usually the case.'

'OK.' She sniffed snottily. 'Thanks for your efforts, too.'

'You're welcome.'

She hung up.

Henry looked at Blackstone who had been listening, but Henry noticed she was also messing about with Charlotte's phone, which though working when Henry had found it, had since died. Blackstone was tapping it on the windowsill, trying to get it to come on. Henry saw a look of triumph on her face when she said, 'Bingo – back to life, would you believe?'

Henry sat back. He had moved on to sipping a Jack Daniel's with ice.

Then Blackstone's face changed.

'What?' Henry said.

Blackstone picked up her work iPad and scrolled through it until she found what she was searching for. She handed it to Henry and said, 'Mugshot of Ernest Lennox, taken at his last caution for indecently assaulting a female.'

Henry looked at the two side-by-side photographs of the sullen, thin-faced boy glowering at the camera, one shot head-on, the other a profile. 'OK?' he said.

Blackstone handed him Charlotte's newly resuscitated phone.

On the screen was a photograph Charlotte had taken. It looked as though it was in an amusement arcade and was of a young man leering at her, looking dangerous and nasty: Ernest Lennox.

'She's come across him before,' Blackstone said, 'and he looks none too happy.'

The phone then simply died in Henry's hand. He was about to swear and hand it over to Blackstone when both looked up through the window and spotted a man crossing the terrace at the front of the pub. It was one of the volunteer stewards for the fair who had worked all weekend. He had seen the pair of them in the bay and was making straight to them. He was one of Henry's regular customers, and Henry assumed he was hoping to catch one last beer.

Henry opened a window, one of the old sash type that he had to push upwards. 'We're closed, Robbo.'

'I know, but I need to talk to you. About the missing girl.'

*   *   *

'Might be something, might be nothing,' Rob Howard admitted. Henry had directed him to the front door which was still unlocked and met him in the foyer, with Blackstone hovering behind. Rob was the headmaster of a school in Lancaster. 'I just thought I'd have one last look around, y'know, nothing structured, so I did a few diagonal criss-cross walks across the car park field.'

'That's good of you.'

He shrugged modestly. 'I know from experience as a teacher how a missing child affects most parents. Anyway, I found this.'

He dug into his shorts pocket and pulled something out in his fist which he then opened. On his palm was a cheap-looking bracelet.

Blackstone moved in to peer over Henry's shoulder. He heard her intake of breath.

'Where was it?' Henry asked, swallowing back the nauseous feeling that was starting to engulf him.

'Bottom corner of the field, quite close to the exit,' Mr Howard said.

'Can you just slide it on to this tabletop?' Henry asked, indicating the table on which there was a rack displaying flyers promoting local tourist attractions and businesses. Henry did not want to touch the bracelet.

Howard did as requested, and all three gathered around the find.

Henry looked at Blackstone, whose face had become hard and brittle.

'Do you think it's something of interest?' the teacher asked.

Henry got his mobile phone and found the photograph of Charlotte, taken that day, sent to him by Melinda West. As Henry had previously noticed, it looked as if Charlotte had not posed willingly for the photo and had partly covered her face by bringing up her right hand. On her right wrist were several bracelets. One was a single line of leather, but there were five others: one with a love heart, another with charms, another with a heart, one was a chain link and, lastly, a turquoise braided leather bracelet with a seashell clasp – exactly like the one now on display on Henry's table.

Henry showed him the photograph. Howard nodded. 'I wasn't sure. I've deleted the picture from my phone as requested, but I half remembered seeing one like this.'

'Could you say exactly where you found it?' Blackstone asked. Henry could hear the strain in her voice.

'Yes. I shoved a marker pole in the spot.'

'Nice one,' Henry said.

'Could be a trail,' Blackstone said thoughtfully, then to Howard she said, 'I'll have to put this in a sealed evidence bag, and I hope you don't mind, Rob, but we will probably need to take a sample of your DNA in order to eliminate you. Hopefully, there might be more DNA on the bracelet – Charlotte's and maybe someone else's other than yours – but we need to get it looked at by forensics.'

'I'm fine with that,' Howard said. 'I just hope she's OK.'

Not for the first time – and it would not be the last – Henry and Blackstone regarded each other, knowing exactly what the other was thinking and knowing that each other's arse was twitching.

'This place is a fucking treasure trove!' Ernest Lennox said glee-fully, emerging from Maude Crichton's bedroom with gold and silver necklaces and bracelets and chains dripping from his hands, plus diamond rings shoved halfway on to his bony fingers. 'Reminds me of Ali Baba's cave. Open sesame and all that. This woman is rich, Dad.' He held up two watches. 'Bloody Rolexes, and there's loads more.'

'So it would appear,' Lenny Lennox said. He was on his knees peering into a closet on the landing. There was a small safe screwed to the back wall, hidden behind a shoe rack.

'Unbelievable,' Benny said happily, appearing on the landing, having gone through the drawers of a writing desk in the study where he'd discovered over a grand in fifty-pound notes. He flipped the wodge. 'A load of euros, too.'

Lennox looked at him. 'How many?'

'Maybe ten grand. I gave up counting at seven-ish,' Benny admitted. 'There's other currencies, too – dollars and such.'

Lennox nodded. 'That's good; grab it all and bag it. I'm sure there'll be a supermarket bag somewhere.'

'What're you looking at, boss?' Benny asked.

Lennox pointed to the safe, and Benny peered into the closet.

Lennox pulled his ski mask back down over his head. 'I need to ask the lady of the house a few questions.'

He pushed himself up and went to the main bathroom.

Kneeling next to the bath was Ella, also wearing a hood; they had been instructed to keep them on.

Maude, with a small hessian sack pulled over her head and tied around her neck, had been dragged semi-conscious through the house, up the stairs, and laid out in the bath, dressed in only what she had been wearing underneath her dressing gown, a skimpy bra and panties. Her wrists had been bound in front of her and her ankles strapped together with tape.

Ella was leaning over the side of the bath, whispering something to Maude who was visibly trembling in terror. Ella had a long-bladed kitchen knife in her hand, and she was running the tip of it between Maude's breastbone to the top of her panties, pausing at the belly button to insert the tip and rotate it without actually cutting her.

'I could if I wanted,' Lennox heard Ella whisper. 'Slice you open like a pig, watch you bleed out, fill the bath with your guts.'

Maude whimpered.

'Oi!' Lennox uttered.

Ella had been so engrossed in causing terror that she hadn't seen Lennox enter the bathroom. She jumped at the word.

'Quit the shite,' Lennox warned her.

Ella's head rotated slowly and her eyes, even behind the mask, sent a shiver down his spine as he realized this girl truly was dangerous.

'Out,' Lennox said to her.

'But I was having so much fun,' Ella whined.

'Yeah, well, we're not here to have fun, are we?' Lennox said. Ella stood up peevishly, and Lennox then knelt in her place by the bath and looked at Maude who had now gone completely still. With a smirk, he placed the flat of his hand on her belly, and she jumped as if she had been touched by a cattle prod.

Lennox laughed, loving the power, then removed his hand.

'Now then, Mrs Crichton, I'm going to ask you a question and I want a truthful, direct answer, please. I know you've had your face bashed, but you can still speak, can't you?'

Maude said yes.

'Where is the key to your safe? Now don't be brave and say nothing or tell me a lie or whatever; otherwise, you're fucked and I will skewer you like a hog roast, understand?'

Maude nodded under the hood.

'If you tell me and cooperate, then you will not be hurt further. So, where is it? The key?'

'In the . . . there's a vase on the hearth downstairs, one with oriental figures on it. In there.'

'Good woman.' Lennox patted her belly, making her leap again,

and started to stand up. Ella had been watching the exchange while
leaning on the door frame, until Ernest barged her out of the way.
He had Maude's open purse in his hand.

'Dad, this bint has a ton of debit and credit cards.' He showed
the interior of the purse to Lennox.

'OK, get her to tell you the PIN numbers.'

'And there's about a hundred quid in here, too.'

'Take it, bag it.'

Lennox left the bathroom and went back to the safe in the closet,
going via the vase in the living room which he smashed on the
marble hearth and found the safe key within. Unknown to him,
the vase was from the Ming dynasty and had recently been valued
at just over three million pounds.

He opened the safe but was disappointed to see a stack of legal
documents, including a will and house conveyancing papers. No
money. Had there been, he might have been inclined to call off
the next part of the evening's proceedings – but he didn't want
to miss that fun. There were several more diamond and pearl
necklaces in boxes, though, to make up for the lack of cash.

'OK, guys,' he called. 'Get what you can, bundle it into the back
of the motor.' To Ella, he called, 'You gag the bitch, OK, but make
sure she can breathe and make sure she can't get out of the bath.
We're not here to kill her.' In his mind, he added, 'Though there is
someone else I might kill later.'

'It's one of those things you can put any interpretation on you want,'
Henry said, referring to the bracelet find.

Blackstone had just updated Charlotte Kirkham's missing-person
log online and ensured the uniformed patrol inspector was verbally
updated and also that the main comms room at headquarters was
aware of the development, which would also mean that Rik Dean
would be automatically informed.

'I know. I like it, but I don't like it,' Blackstone said as she
returned and sat next to Henry at the bay window. 'If she has been
taken, then maybe she's being cool enough to lay a trail for us.'

'Are you going to tell Melinda and drunken Dave?'

Blackstone shrugged. 'I probably should, but it won't be an easy
conversation.'

'Being a cop isn't about being popular,' Henry said, recalling
how unpopular he had been over the course of his service – and

not just with members of the public. Many of his work colleagues found him gruff and unpleasant, too.

'I know. I'll do it.'

Lennox had acquired a 'new' car for the job that night. He knew a guy who knew a guy with a chop shop in Blackpool, a squalid backstreet garage where stolen cars were literally chopped up into component parts to be exported to Ireland, Europe and the Middle East.

Occasionally, the guy made completely new vehicles from old, welding the back half of one to the front of another of the same model, and it was one of these Frankenstein creations that Lennox had borrowed for the night. A big Mercedes saloon, built in 2006 and 2009, but fused together almost perfectly and given a completely new registration number that, if checked by a nosy cop, would on the face of it be legit. It was only if the bonnet was lifted and that nosy cop started checking VINs, that anything untoward would be discovered or the welding line seen.

It was a big enough car for the five of them and fast enough to outrun most normal cop cars, although Lennox wasn't certain how strong it would be in a collision.

After Lennox ensured Maude was trussed up properly and going nowhere – they had even taped her ankles to the bath taps and re-taped her hands behind her back, making all movement, other than squirming, very difficult, they set off with a muzzled, abducted, terrified Manderley in the footwell of the front passenger seat, leashed to the gear stick.

The dog whined.

Ernest, in the front seat, gave him a few toe-cap kicks in the ribs to silence him.

Five minutes later, they had driven through Kendleton and were on the road towards Thornwell, stopping just short of their target's home.

'You sure it's here?' Ernest asked.

'Oh, yeah,' his father replied.

'Then we hit it, yeah?'

'Yes, we do – in, out, no dawdling, as discussed. Masks back on, please.'

Veronica Gough was about as exhausted as an almost ninety-year-old could be without actually being in a coffin, she thought as she returned home earlier that evening.

Yet even after a nice shower, then the promised quick curry in the microwave, she wanted to go to bed but didn't feel like going. The huge excitement and success of the weekend, the amazing efforts of all those involved and the money raised for charity kept her buzzing. The phone call from Henry about Tony Owl and Lennox had also kept her mind busy.

She knew she had to get some proper rest, though.

After watching a big chunk of her favourite film, *The Sound of Music*, she decided to make the effort because the next day would also be busy with supervising general clearing-up duties, ensuring the green and showground and car park were back to being spick and span as though nothing had ever happened on them.

Her all-singing, all-dancing electronic wheelchair had been left in the vestibule inside the front door, plugged into the mains to recharge the battery. Veronica could more or less navigate her way around her house without its aid, using a stick and a frame for balance, plus the many rails she'd had installed throughout the house. She did need a stairlift to get her upstairs where a small, old wheelchair was parked to transport her to her bedroom. She had considered moving her life downstairs completely but still loved getting in the big old bed she once shared with her late husband.

Following a recent house invasion, there had been talk of her moving to sheltered accommodation, but she was hesitating on that because it seemed to be the white flag of submission to her age.

The stairlift was at the top for some reason she could not recall. She accepted that her memory wasn't quite what it was and sometimes she did things she could not remember doing, such as sending the stairlift back up to the top without her in it when, clearly, she would need it at the bottom next time.

'Silly old fool,' she muttered. She pressed the call button and waited patiently for it to arrive, which, when you were very old and balancing with the aid of a walking stick, seemed to take forever. It was wasted time, she thought, that a woman of her age could use to do something more constructive.

When the chair finally arrived, the headlights of a car pulling on to her front driveway caught her eye through the glass of the front door.

She wasn't expecting anyone.

'Damn! Who can this be?' She looked at the grandfather clock in the hallway and screwed her face up. 'It's very late.' She began to make her way to the front door, using the walking stick to keep upright. Before she got there, someone knocked lightly on the door. 'I'm coming, I'm coming.'

Without even a thought for her vulnerability, and even though the time of day was very odd and she knew she should have learned from her recent experience of being targeted, suspicion never entered her head.

She unlocked the door and opened it.

TEN

ennox, in very rare moments of contemplation and introspection, sometimes thought it odd that he could stand by and witness the brutal overpowering of a person – in this case, a disabled old woman – and have no feelings at all. Other than pleasure.

Part of him knew he should have been disgusted and horrified, as a normal person would have been.

But he wasn't, and who the hell knew what a 'normal' person was these days?

He also knew he could not do anything about this state of mind, the way he thought and viewed things. God, he'd tried, on the face of it, as had others – counsellors, social workers, probation officers – when he had been in prison for *ten fucking years*. He had attended all the required sessions, sitting in the dreaded circle, experiencing the creeping death of being expected to give your personal input when it was your turn. Utter wank. He had said all the right, contrite things, but he saw the truth in the eyes of the facilitators that they did not believe a damn word that any of them were bleating, promising to be a reformed character, feeling oh-so terrible about past misdemeanours and changing their lives in the future. The look in the eyes that also said, *I'm just here for the payday, mate*. And the look in the prisoners' eyes that said, *I'm here, just saying what I have to say, to get released from this shit-hole sooner*.

Because nothing changed for Lennox other than an intense, gnawing, growing hatred for the man who had captured him, sent him to prison, broken his nose.

When he had eventually been released, he hadn't pursued revenge, but it had always been at the back of his mind, festering like a virus but kept under control. He knew he would never act on it – that was probably too dangerous a move – unless it became something possible to achieve, which he now believed it had.

Running into Henry Christie had reactivated everything. Every speck of hate.

And tonight Lennox had decided he would do something about it, but only after all the money from the fair was in his sack.

Which was how that almost random thought passed through his mind while knowingly, cold-bloodedly looking at the old lady sprawled pathetically on the floor of her hallway.

But Lennox did admire her pluck.

'You rogues, you vagabonds,' she cried as Ernest stood on one of her arms and Benny on the other.

Ernest laughed uproariously. 'We're not fucking pirates, you daft old bint.'

'No! You are disgusting people. Let me up. I'm going to call the police.'

Lennox moved to her side and squatted down. 'I don't think so, Veronica.'

'How do you know my name? How?' she demanded.

'It's called planning,' he smirked, then realized that he might have made a slight error by the admission.

'Take your masks off, you cowards. Look me in the eye!' she commanded, even though she was feeling utterly helpless.

'For your own good, that's a no,' Lennox said.

'Do I know you?' Veronica asked.

Lennox sighed. 'OK, enough is enough, you sad old bag.'

'What? Are you going to kill me now?'

'Don't even tempt me.' His right hand slithered behind him, and he drew out the knackered old revolver that was tucked into his waistband, one of the handguns he had brought down from his loft earlier. He ensured the old woman could see it, then he jabbed it hard under her chin, into the ragged, loose old flesh, and, using the muzzle, he shoved her head right back and then leaned forward to speak into her ear, noticing she had a hearing aid fitted.

'Nod if you can hear me,' he whispered.

She did.

'Good. Now. We don't have much time, dear, so just tell me where you've put the money from the fair.'

'What money?'

He screwed the muzzle into her flesh. 'Don't be a daft old woman or you'll be a dead old woman. The takings. The three days' worth of cash. Tell me where it is, and we'll be gone, my love. I know you have it because you bring it back here every year, don't you?' He tapped her chin with the gun barrel. 'C'mon, granny. I hear you keep it in the wash basket.'

'You hear wrong,' Veronica said defiantly.

'Oh, jeez, Dad!' Ernest had moved around to keep hold of Veronica's ankles. 'She's pissed herself, dirty bitch!' He reeled away in disgust at the sight of the spreading stain on Veronica's night dress.

'She's an old lady – what do you expect?' Lennox said, then saw the look on Veronica's face, the half smile. 'You did it on purpose, didn't you?'

'I'm not frightened of you,' she said.

'Well, you fucking should be. Tell me where the money is, or I will shoot you in the face.' He now jammed the muzzle into her forehead.

'No!'

'Last chance.' He thumbed back the trigger. 'Or you're dead.'

'There is no money.'

'Yes, there is. Now stop being stupid.'

'No, there isn't. Not this year. Not here.'

'What? Where, then? Where is it?' he screamed into her face. 'And don't lie or you are so dead.'

'That was a tough one,' Blackstone breathed out, coming back to Henry in the bay window following a harrowing conversation with the inconsolable Melinda West. There was really no positive spin on the news of the bracelet, a photo of which Blackstone had forwarded to Melinda's phone to confirm its identification.

Blackstone plonked down heavily by Henry. 'She kept saying, "She's dead, she's dead, isn't she?" It's pretty hard to pull a mother back from that one, but I hope I did.'

'Half the battle to keep them onside is to let them have their say, so they get it out of their systems for a while at least,' Henry said. 'Sounds like you did a good job. Might be worth suggesting a family liaison officer for the Wests tomorrow, depending on how the land lies.'

Blackstone nodded. 'Part of me wants to get back to chasing thieves on quadbikes,' she said. 'Easier and more fun.'

'But not what you're really good at, Debs, not what you were put on this earth to do,' Henry said. 'You are a detective, through and through, a seeker of the truth.' He meant every word.

Both then entered a short period of almost spiritual contemplation before Henry broke the moment and said, 'Nightcap, then bed, yeah? Whatever happens, I think you'll be busy tomorrow and I've got to get this place back shipshape.'

Veronica was actually appalled with herself for wetting her knickers, but the knock-on effect of disgusting the intruders was well worth it.

Truth was, she had been terrified. And now she could tell her mind was in a dangerous spiral and that she needed to get some control of it and her faculties, which is why she had gone all floppy when the gang dragged her down the hallway and, using the belt on her dressing gown, had tied her to the bottom banister rail, pulling the knot tightly. With the knowledge she had been forced to impart to them, they had quickly left her house.

And her. Still alive.

'Henry, Henry, Henry,' she incanted to herself at the moment she heard the front door slam and then the engine rev, and she started to twist and writhe her wrists against the cotton belt. The knot came loose easily. Breathless and near to exhaustion, she slumped back on the floor. Her old heart, which had had several stents inserted in various arteries over the years, was beating fast and irregularly, all over the place, and she was genuinely worried about it deciding to stop with a huge crescendo and a final flourish. But as she mentally ordered it to slow down, it seemed to respond slightly.

'Right,' she told herself as she lay flat, looking up at the hall ceiling. Her right hand slithered down the front of her nightdress between her breasts and her fingertips felt for the leather thong she always now wore around her neck, twisting it in her fingers and pulling out the plastic pendant alarm button on the end of it, pressing it three times in quick succession with her thumb . . . then a fourth time. With that, she breathed, 'Henry . . . please come.'

Lennox was at the wheel of the Mercedes with Ernest sitting along-side him (with Manderley still cowering in the footwell, his paws over his eyes); the other three were in the back seat, keeping their heads low as instructed.

'Right,' Lennox said, swerving backwards out of Veronica's driveway, 'slight change of plan – two birds, one stone.'

As the car came out on to the road, he swung it around and jabbed his foot on the accelerator, unaware that his plans would change again within a matter of minutes.

Veronica had fairly recently been the victim of a home invasion by a gang of feral youths seeking revenge on her because she'd had the temerity to stand up to them by trying to prevent them from running wild around Thornwell and Kendleton; they had subsequently attacked her in her house, and that had been a huge wake-up call for her. She lived in an old, crumbling house with little security other than a couple of iffy CCTV cameras on her front gate posts. They had broken in easily and terrifyingly, and this had led Veronica to make some huge decisions with her life. First was to try to sell up. This was a major wrench as she had lived there many years with her now-deceased husband, so it was still a place of cherished memories. Second, she had to find a place in decent sheltered accommodation. Both processes were underway, but the house sale had recently fallen through and there was some problem with the sheltered accommodation. All this meant she was, for the time being, still alone in the house, still vulnerable. This, in turn, had made Henry insist she must install some form of panic button, which, as an independently minded old person, she had baulked at vociferously. Like many older people, the physical exterior of ageing was just a cover for inner younger mentality. In her own mind, Veronica still thought like a twenty-two-year-old woman – it was just her body that thought differently – and she believed she could manage quite easily without a panic button, not least because of the expense. Over the course of some long and difficult conversations with Henry, a compromise was reached.

She had no desire whatsoever to have one of those 'old people's things', as she called them, much to Henry's mirth, referring to a panic button linked twenty-four/seven to an alarm company at some exorbitant monthly cost, but she was happy to have one that Henry and Blackstone found on the internet – a lanyard around the neck with a plastic button on it, linked to Henry's mobile phone. *That* she was OK with and, slightly reluctantly, Henry had agreed. He had warned her, 'No crying wolf, OK? You can't call me because you don't like the storyline on your favourite soap, or you've run out of biscuits.'

'I won't, I won't,' she promised him, rolling her eyes. As if she would.

And she didn't. Until now.

Henry had just handed Blackstone a smidgeon of his best whisky, which he kept hidden underneath the bar, when his phone began to bleat urgently.

It was on the bar top. It vibrated and twirled around on the spot and repeatedly called out, *Ronnie, alarm, Ronnie, alarm.*

He snatched it up and looked at the screen which flashed red and blue.

'Shit! Veronica.'

Without a second thought, he put his glass down. Blackstone did the same and said, 'My car.'

Both jogged towards the front door just as Ginny and Fred came out of the owner's accommodation.

'What is it?' Ginny asked.

Henry waggled his phone and looked back over his shoulder. 'Veronica's panic button.'

Ginny gave him a thumbs-up, understanding immediately.

It hurt Henry to up his pace, but he kept alongside Blackstone all the way out to her car. His next problem was actually getting into the little beast, which was a 1960s Mini Cooper that Blackstone had rebuilt and renovated from nothing but a body shell, a worn-out engine block and four wheels. She had done it during the dark months of her depression following the acid attack with no engineering or mechanical skills whatsoever. She was now the proud owner of a rare car that an enthusiast had recently offered her £50,000 for. She'd refused. The process of renovation had been one of her lifelines during that torrid phase of her existence, and she would never let it go.

Blackstone jumped into the front bucket racing seat behind the wheel while Henry eased himself in a little more slowly and inelegantly, but she caught him off guard as she fired up the finely tuned engine, slammed it into gear and set off before he'd finished lowering himself in or closing the door.

He was rammed back into the recess of the racing seat, and the door slammed shut by itself because of the forward momentum.

'Crikey!' he blurted. 'Old guy alert.'

'No time to waste,' Blackstone said, enjoying the surge of speed from zero while Henry grappled with his seat belt and gripped the inside door handle to brace himself for what he knew would be a short but exciting and probably vomit-inducing journey to Veronica's house. Blackstone always drove with a kind of wild abandon, but when he was alongside her, she always braked harder, later and sharper than necessary and took corners tighter and faster, just to wind him up.

The fact that he had been stabbed didn't make any difference to her.

'You think it's genuine?' Blackstone asked.

'It's the first time it's gone off,' Henry said. 'So, knowing her, it's genuine. Foot down, please.' He clung on even more desperately as Blackstone dropped a gear and took the next corner too quickly and had to over-correct coming out of it in order to avoid a collision with the car travelling in the opposite direction.

Lennox swerved the Mercedes out of the way of the Mini that skittered around the corner in front of him, almost wiping him out, but other than that he paid no heed to the little car as they zoomed past each other with probably less than four feet of fresh air between them. He was too busy ensuring that his passengers knew exactly what their jobs were in the coming minutes.

Ernest would be with his father, and Ella, Benny and Jimbo had their own specific instructions. The only extra part of this was how to deal with the cash in Henry's safe, the unexpected blindside that had thrown him initially. Then, thinking fast, he had seen the possibilities.

'No fucking hesitations, guys. I'm depending on you all to step up to the mark,' he said like some motivational team leader briefing his staff. 'As soon as I give you the word, it all fucking happens, OK? No arsing about, no hesitation. This is the real thing. OK?'

He got three muted yeses.

'Fuck was that response?' he demanded. 'Come *on*!' He took his hands off the wheel and shook his fists.

The next much louder shout of 'Yes' almost burst his eardrums, and he pounded the steering wheel in gritty appreciation. Underneath his ski mask, his face was a contorted, screwed-up tableau of hatred and concentration.

Moments later, he skidded to a chipping-spraying stop on The Tawny Owl car park alongside what he knew was Henry Christie's sporty Audi, the only other car parked up there now, which was the target for Ella to deal with initially. Lennox knew that apart from all the other outstanding criminal attributes that made her so special, Ella was also an excellent arsonist as shown, several years ago, when she burned her parents' house down. To be fair, Benny and Jimbo were also good fire starters, but Ella was more turned on by the act of arson and was still wanted for burning down a series of big, empty public buildings in Blackpool one night, fires that had caused major disruption to the resort and had gutted four historic buildings, which all had to be demolished.

'Place is closed,' Ernest said. 'You were right, Dad.'

Lennox had made a speculative, innocent-sounding and untraceable phone call earlier that night and discovered The Tawny Owl would be closing early after the fair, which would make things much simpler for *Lennox's revenge*, as he had started to refer in his head to what was about to happen.

'Front door's still open, though.' Lennox opened the car door and got out, wanting to get this done quick and smooth. 'You two – crates in the back,' he said to Benny and Jimbo, who scrambled out of the back seat and round to the rear of the car and opened the boot. Benny grabbed a twenty-compartment crate containing milk bottles all about two-thirds full of petrol with rags stuffed into their necks. Petrol bombs. Jimbo lifted out a twenty-litre steel Jerry can, also filled with fuel, and Ella, who had joined them, grabbed herself the remaining five-litre plastic petrol can.

Ella immediately got to work, splashing the contents over Henry's Audi, laughing maniacally as she did so. She wanted to get this job done quickly so she could be part of the proceedings about to take place within the pub itself.

Lennox jogged up the steps on to the terrace, Ernest following.

Both had handguns drawn, six-shot revolvers, held down to the outside of their thighs.

The other two lads followed, the bottles rattling in the crate being carried by Benny.

At Henry's car, Ella placed the petrol can down, coolly took out a disposable cigarette lighter with one hand, flicked it and set fire to a petrol-drenched rag she was holding in her other hand.

She waited for the flame to get going, then tossed the rag

underneath the Audi where it ignited the fuel that had dripped on to the ground. There was a tense pause, followed by a whooshing sound when a massive blue flame engulfed the car within moments, the heat of the fire making Ella step back and shade her eyes.

Lennox and Ernest barrelled through the front door of the pub ahead of Benny and Jimbo.

'I hope she's all right,' Ginny had said to Fred as they watched Blackstone gun the Mini off the car park. They were side by side at the front door, watching the car disappear into the distance.

When they could no longer hear the scream of the engine, Ginny said, 'I'll leave the door open for when they get back.'

Fred nodded. They turned back into the pub and, with their arms around each other, walked towards the door leading to the private accommodation. Since revealing their good news to Henry earlier in the day, they'd hardly had a chance to talk to each other. Both were exhausted and looking forward to a day off; even though there would be work to do, it could be done at a more leisurely pace. They pulled each other tight.

'You should ease back a bit now,' Fred said.

'I will when I feel the need to,' Ginny said, grinning as she thought what a superb husband this guy was going to make.

'OK, but don't do yourself in,' he said. 'Me and Henry will pick up all the slack . . . He was so pleased by the news, wasn't he?'

'Over the moon. It means a lot to him on a few different levels.'

They stopped. Fred angled sideways slightly and placed the palm of his hand on Ginny's tummy. 'I am so happy,' he told her. Tears formed in his eyes.

'God, you can be a bit of a blubberer,' Ginny said tenderly, touching his cheek. 'Such a softie.'

'I know! Can't help it. Gonna be a dad!'

'And I'm going to be a—' Ginny stopped mid-sentence before she could say 'mum', they both turned towards the pub door as they heard the sound of tyres crunching on the car park and saw the sweep of headlights across the windows, followed by the slamming of car doors. Together, they watched and waited, side by side, almost reflections of each other, a perfect couple if there was such a thing, looking back over their shoulders, until the partly open front door burst open and two men, followed by another pair, entered, all wearing ski masks.

Behind them, there was a sudden whoosh of flames in the car park.

Fred reacted, disengaging himself from Ginny, turning and stepping towards the intruders.

'What's going on?' were the only words he had the chance to say in challenge to the raid.

In fact, the words uttered by this young man, whom Lennox did not recognize, did not even register with him, so focused was he on what he was about to do.

As he strode forwards, his gun came up and, from a distance of eight feet, he fired twice into the man's face, soft-tipped bullets slamming into him and churning through his brain just above the bridge of his nose and right eye, exiting messily to leave a big, gaping, horrific hole at the back of his skull.

He died instantly, tipping backwards, not knowing anything.

Some of his blood and brain matter splattered across Ginny as though someone had flicked thick, congealed paint across her.

Even before she could react, Lennox was on her, grabbing her face in the cup of his hand between finger and thumb, squeezing hard while at the same time running her backwards into the wall where he pinned her and shoved the muzzle of his gun under the point of her jawbone.

'Where's fucking Henry Christie?' he snarled into her face, spittle spraying from his lips. 'Where is that out-and-out twat?'

'He . . . he's not here . . . Please, please,' she begged through distorted lips. Her eyes darted to Fred's body on the floor with huge gouts of blood gurgling out of the head wound. He was clearly dead.

This was the realization that made Ginny begin the battle for her survival. Being close enough to the man who was holding her, she brought her right knee up into his balls. Hard. As hard as she could, hoping to crush them and drive them up into his lower belly.

The move caught Lennox unexpectedly.

He screamed as the knee connected, released his grip on her face and took a few steps back, doubling over as he clutched his crotch with his left hand. A wave of agony seared up through him. He emitted a hiss of compressed air through his clenched teeth.

'Bitch!'

Ginny attempted to twist away, but before she could, Ernest

moved in and, with a hard, single blow, crashed his revolver across her face, knocking her sideways. She sank to her knees, spitting blood and crying.

Despite the pain, Lennox recovered quickly and moved to Ginny, shoving Ernest out of his way, going down on his knee by her, grabbing her blouse and shaking her while banging her head against the wall.

'You'll fuckin' pay for that,' he screamed.

By this time, Ginny had amassed a mouthful of blood and a section of broken tooth, which she spat into his face, and although this went on to the material of his mask, he reared away in disgust for a moment, but then came back quickly to smash his free hand across Ginny's cheek. It was a blow that took all the strength and willpower out of her. She went limp and sank down the wall, sobbing.

'Where is Christie?'

'He's just gone out.'

'*Just?* How long will he be?'

'Don't know, don't know. He's gone to help somebody,' she said, finding it hard not to slur her words through the blood.

'Shit.'

Lennox re-evaluated his plan.

'You're his daughter, aren't you?'

Ginny nodded. She never even considered denying this because it was how she felt.

'Good. In that case, the money. Where did Christie put the takings from the fair?'

'I don't know wh—'

Lennox dug her hard with his fist and leaned in close. 'I know it's here. Where is it? You don't tell me, I'll kill you, I promise.' He gasped with the throbbing agony in his lower belly.

Ginny did not respond.

Lennox glanced around. Benny and Jimbo were doing their bit. Benny was splashing petrol around the bar area from the Jerry can before going into the kitchens to continue – and to turn on the gas taps at the ovens.

Jimbo was in the entrance hall, calmly lighting each rag stuffed into the bottles in the crate.

Lennox came back to Ginny. 'I won't ask again. Where is the money?'

Ginny gave up, knowing she had an unborn baby to protect. 'A safe in the back office. The key's in a key safe on the wall behind the filing cabinet.'

'Code?'

'One-zero-one-zero.'

'Good girl.' Lennox tapped her head with the gun barrel and rose stiffly to his feet, his bollocks still in agony. Ella jogged in, danced around Jimbo in the vestibule. Outside, the flames rose from Henry's car.

'It'll blow soon,' she promised Lennox delightedly. 'What do you want me to do now?'

Behind his mask, Lennox smiled grimly, then gestured at the terrified Ginny and said, 'Deal with her how you see fit.'

Lennox could only guess at the expression of happiness on Ella's face behind her mask.

Father and son knelt in front of the safe as Lennox senior slid the key into the lock, turned it, hearing and feeling the levers fall with a muted clunk, then pulled the door open and rested back on his heels.

'Fuck me!' Ernest gasped.

Lennox had a moment of reverence before Ernest lurched forward and began to load the cash into the rucksack he had brought along for the purpose.

'Two birds,' Lennox said, watching the transfer of the money.

'What?'

'Weekend's cash takings from the fair and the pub. Jackpot! Get every last cent of it, lad.'

A minute later, they had finished. As they stepped back into the corridor, Benny came out of one of the bedrooms with the almost empty Jerry can in his hand.

'Done,' he said.

Lennox said, 'Go for it.'

Benny stepped back into the room, which happened to be the guest bedroom that Blackstone was currently living in. He'd splashed petrol over the bed. He struck a couple of matches and tossed them on to the mattress which ignited instantly.

By the time Lennox, Ernest and Benny stepped back into the bar area, Ella was standing over Ginny's unmoving body with a knife in her hand.

Jimbo was at the door leading into the kitchen, holding a lighted petrol bomb, waiting for the nod from Lennox, which he got.

He flung the bottle into the kitchen and shouted, 'We need to move!'

Ella tossed the knife on to Ginny's chest, and they all sprinted to the front door where each picked up another lit petrol bomb from the crate and flung them back in against the walls, against the bar, against the stone fireplace, ensuring they smashed and the fires started to spread immediately.

Then they turned and ran out, stopping to throw more petrol bombs against the outside of the pub and on to the picnic benches on the terrace before jumping into the Mercedes.

ELEVEN

'I'm all right . . . honestly,' Veronica Gough protested feebly as Henry and Blackstone finally managed to manoeuvre her from where they had found her on the floor, up on to her wheelchair, both talking to her in low voices. 'Nothing's broken. I'm OK. Honestly.'

'What happened? Did you fall?' Henry asked. 'Do we need an ambulance? I'm going to call an ambulance, get you checked over at A and E.'

'No, no.' She brushed away their hands and then looked despairingly at Henry. 'I'm so, so sorry.'

'What the hell for? Sorry for what? You've no need to be. That's what the panic button's for—'

The old lady held up a gnarled finger to shut him up. 'I told them, Henry, I told them. I had to,' she said desperately.

'Told who what?' he asked. He went down beside her to get to her eye level and she grabbed his sleeve. He suspected that the fall might have confused her and jangled her mind. 'What is it, Veronica?'

'They pointed a gun at me. They were going to kill me. I was terrified, Henry. That's why I wet myself.'

This stunned him. 'What are you talking about?'

'The gang, the gang that came in. I had to tell them. They wanted to know where the money was. I had to tell them. They would have killed me.' She started to weep.

'Veronica, what are you saying?' Blackstone crouched down on the opposite side of the wheelchair, taking Veronica's left hand between hers.

'The money?' Henry said. 'You mean the takings from the fair?'

Veronica's sobs rattled her body. She nodded.

Henry turned away, 'Fuck!' playing on his lips.

'You mean someone came here to your house wanting to steal the takings?' Blackstone asked, getting her head around the scenario.

Veronica grabbed Henry's T-shirt in both hands and dragged him towards her. 'Yes, I'm so sorry. I had to tell. They had guns.'

Henry looked across at Blackstone, realization dawning. In unison, they said, 'Ginny!'

In that moment, Veronica also understood the implications of what she had admitted with a gun in her face. 'Go, go now,' she told Henry and Blackstone. 'Don't worry about me, I'll be fine.'

They ran to the Mini. Henry had his phone out and was speed-dialling Ginny. As he dropped into the seat, jarring his whole being with a pain he ignored, the call went to voicemail.

Blackstone set off, reversing the small car off the driveway into the road, slewing it round in the right direction.

Henry redialled. Moments later, he swore.

Blackstone crunched into first gear and stamped on the accelerator, throwing them both back in their seats.

She said, 'What?'

'No reply. Voicemail.'

'Try again.'

'Am doing.' His thumb jumped on the keypad and he redialled. The call went through to voicemail again. 'Not happening.'

'Call the landline,' Blackstone said.

'Fuck d'you think I'm doing?' he responded unpleasantly, his stress level already at boiling point as he fumbled with his phone.

Blackstone let it go, not least because it was so unlike Henry.

'No answer, just ringing out,' he said. In the footwell, his right leg twitched with anxiety.

'Keep at it,' Blackstone said grimly, concentrating on getting the last ounces of power out of the 1275cc engine as she sped along the winding street through Kendleton, from one side of the village to the other, emerging seconds later on the opposite side, with The Tawny Owl less than a quarter of a mile distant.

'I am, I am,' Henry started to say, but didn't finish anything because the horrendous shock of what he was seeing hit him like a blow to the head and he moved the phone away from his ear.

'Oh no, no, no, no,' Blackstone uttered.

Henry said nothing as a sense of dread overwhelmed him.

In the car park, his Audi was burning ferociously.

And The Tawny Owl itself seemed to be consumed by a huge inferno. At the front, many of the picnic benches were ablaze, and flames poured out of the bay window where, only a short time before, he and Blackstone had sat chewing the fat. Those flames licked out and curved upwards as though from the eyes of a demon, literally melting the windows on the first floor belonging to guest bedrooms.

But that was nothing.

The front door of the pub was open, and as flames also poured from it, Henry was reminded of the gates of hell from mythical pictures he'd seen as a kid.

Blackstone swerved to a stop at the entrance to the car park at the exact moment Henry's Audi exploded with a massive boom of multicoloured flames, rocking the Mini Cooper with a shockwave and showering it with chunks of molten steel and burning plastic raining down from above, making both occupants recoil.

With a scream, Henry reacted. 'Ginny! Fucking hell!' He opened the door and swung himself up to his feet, instantly feeling the blistering heat encompassing him. Suddenly, all his own inner pain had gone and he reverted to autopilot as he sprinted towards the pub, giving his burning car a wide berth and no thought because that did not matter anymore. It was just a car, a machine, not a person. What was imperative now was getting to the pub, entering it and saving the lives of Ginny and Fred if they hadn't managed to evacuate themselves via the rear fire doors. There was no sign of them at this moment, which Henry knew instinctively was very bad. If they were safe, surely they would now be spectators to this terrible event.

He took the steps up from the car park on to the terrace, heading towards the front doors, having to veer away from the picnic tables which were blazing.

Even as he approached, he knew what he was doing was futile, yet even though part of him heard Blackstone screaming her lungs out behind him, 'Henry, no!' he forced himself to go on even as the heat intensified. He covered his lower face and nostrils with his left arm, already feeling his hair and eyebrows beginning to sizzle, as well as the skin on his forehead.

He had to slow down.

The extreme temperature made it physically impossible to go on. His run quickly became a walk, but he pushed himself on, holding both hands in front of his face now like shields, as though they would protect him.

'Henry, get back, come back,' Blackstone begged him.

Suddenly, he did not have a choice.

He heard a rumbling sound from within the belly of the building and he knew what would follow – an explosion – followed by a huge ball of flame that would roll through The Tawny Owl like a terrible, roaring demon, intent on destroying anyone and everything in its brutal path.

Henry stopped, spun and shouted to Blackstone, 'Get down, get down.'

He threw himself sideways on to a flower bed behind a low wall, hitting the soft flowers, inhaling their sweet aromas as he crushed them, a strange contrast to the fire. Less than a second later, the pub erupted and the roll of the explosion burst through the front doors, flinging glass and burning wood over a wide area, thudding down around Henry like burning arrows from a volley of medieval bowmen. The power of the blast rocketed out from within the building like a huge, amplified lion's roar.

Henry tried to keep as tight as he could to the low wall, hoping Blackstone had managed to do something similar, maybe using the terrace wall for protection; otherwise, she might have been a victim of the blast and maybe incinerated.

And then it was gone.

Its power and energy dispersed into the atmosphere, followed by a thick cloud of lung-clogging smoke spewing out of the pub doors, cloaking the whole of the terrace. Something heavy dropped on Henry as he started to get cautiously up on to one knee. He wasn't sure what, but he tried to peer through the acrid smoke, still hearing the flames crackling.

He got to his feet.

'Henry,' Blackstone called from behind.

He turned, seeing her emerge from the smoke, wafting it away with one hand, but with her other hand clamped to her face, covering a deep cut she'd received in her cheek from a flying shard of glass buried in her flesh.

Henry saw her but nothing registered. He turned back and his eyes took in The Tawny Owl, which was still fiercely ablaze. The fire had caught hold of the first floor properly now and was spreading fast towards the annexe where there were further bedrooms.

Once more, his instinct made him go towards it.

All he could think about: *Ginny and Fred.*

Blackstone caught up with him and grabbed his arm. 'No.'

He wrenched free of her grasp. 'I have to,' he said like a robot.

'No.' Blackstone took hold again and shook him. 'You'll never get in. The fire's too well established.'

'Round the back, then. I must try.'

But it was no good. There was no way in. Finally, Henry admitted failure, gave up, backed off and sank to his knees on the grass of the village green, unable to function, unable to think straight; all he could do was wait while the Fire and Rescue service arrived from Lancaster to deal with the atrocity.

It might have been a getaway car, but once Lennox had left the scene and was beyond the environs of the village, he reduced the speed, drove carefully and sensibly, adhering to the limits, so as not to draw attention.

He said nothing as his thoughts of a perfect revenge consumed him as he hoped and wished the blaze had consumed The Tawny Owl and death had consumed Christie's daughter and her boyfriend. So what if Henry Christie had not suffered directly? Yes, it would have been amazing to have killed him, but then it would all have been over.

Now it was even better.

Henry would now suffer – poor mite – *for the rest of his life.* He would mourn his loss forever – the daughter, the pub, the boyfriend, all destroyed, obliterated and with no way to pick up the pieces.

Lennox imagined Henry standing beside the smouldering embers of his life. And smirked.

Then, as he drove, Lennox thought through the events of the evening.

Had they done anything that could identify them and bring the police crashing through the doors?

He did not think so. The ski masks had been on all the time, so no one could ID them in that way, and when they got back to head-quarters, all clothing and weapons would be destroyed completely. He would make every one of the gang shower thoroughly to rid themselves of any evidence that could physically link them to the crime scenes.

Then they would hunker down, count the takings and keep a very low profile for a few months. At some point, they would need to make a run to Holyhead to unload the accumulated stolen property that had already been paid for upfront, which would then cross into southern Ireland and find its way into the established and sophistic-ated supply chain of stolen goods in the EU.

But that was just something normal. Something he and his gang did, just business that was the occupational hazard of being a thief. Even if that went wrong, what was important was that no connec-tion should ever be made to him and Christie and The Tawny Owl.

He glanced in the mirror.

Benny, Jimbo and Ella were in the back seat. Ernest was riding alongside him, twisted around and laughing with the two lads, but not with Ella who stayed silent, just looking out of the window at the passing countryside, deep in thought.

'Eh? Were good that bit, weren't it, Dad?' Ernest was saying, breaking into his father's reverie.

'What bit?'

'That old slag in the bath. God, that were hilarious,' he giggled, referring to their imprisonment and humiliation of Maude – including the theft of her dog which was now on Ella's lap. 'Rich bitch, weren't she, Dad?'

'Eh?' Lennox said. He hadn't quite been listening. 'Say that again.'

'Fucking cloth ears! I said she were a rich bitch, Dad.'

Lennox focused on that last word: *Dad.*

They arrived back unmolested and unchallenged at headquarters, pulling up into the driveway next to the bungalow.

Lennox turned around in the driver's seat so he could see them all. 'OK, this is how it goes,' he said. 'Ernie, you unload the stash and dump it on the dining-room table, OK? But that's it, nothing else – you don't touch it, you don't take owt, nothing, just leave it there. Then each of you go for a shower and bung all your clothes in a bin bag and I mean *all* your clothes, even your under-keks and knickers. This is serious. You must do that. The cops will be all over this like a rash, and if they get a whiff of us, we need to be clean. Which also means two more things: we need to get rid of Tony Owl's body and also' – here he looked at Ernest – 'think about how you're going to deal with that lass you kidnapped. Nothing good is going to come of her.'

Ernie took that in.

Lennox said, 'I know a guy who has a stone crusher. I'm probably going to slip him a wodge and he'll turn a blind eye. Get my drift?'

Ernest nodded but said, 'And Mum? Isn't it time she went, too?'

Lennox looked momentarily into space, then came back to Ernest. 'You could be right. Maybe it's time to deal with that. Anyway, first things first – showers, clothes, then we heat up that chilli we did earlier and count up our results from the night's work.'

Ella launched herself out of the back door. 'I'm in the shower first before you dirty gits use it.'

'Not too long,' Lennox called after her, knowing she was rarely in the shower for less than half an hour.

She jacked up a middle finger and disappeared into the bungalow with Manderley in her arms.

It took a good hour for everyone to get changed. The clothing had been bagged up and the guns had been put away, hidden under the sink for the moment. Now it was time for sustenance, and each of them had a bowl of chilli and rice, all sitting around the dining table which had been extended to accommodate the take.

At first, it was just a big pile of money and jewellery, and their eyes were fixed greedily on it, desperate to be given the go-ahead to begin counting and sorting it.

Lennox kept them on a tight leash, though, wanting them to get rid of the adrenaline in their systems, relax, come down from the job.

He had some words to say.

'You did good today, team. Better than good. The day was profitable and the night . . .' He wafted a hand across the table, not having to say a word as to how profitable the night had been. 'I had a job of my own to do, as you know, and although I didn't directly achieve what I wanted, I got a good second best, which will do. Now, what we need to do is count up and then decide how and where we're going to lie low. OK, everyone eaten up?'

They had. It had been a good chilli, excellent post-job fodder. A joint or two would be passed around later with beers, but for now they stacked their empty plates on the edge of the table and the boys looked meaningfully at Ella. She knew what they meant and said, 'You can eff off.'

'Come on, love, woman's work,' Lennox cooed.

'Fuck that.' There was no chance of Ella ever washing plates, or doing anything else for that matter, for men. She stood up with the dog in her arms and stalked out of the room.

Lennox took the pile of crockery and balanced it on her chair to make extra space on the table.

'Right.' His cold eyes surveyed the stacks of money and jewellery. 'Let us begin.'

TWELVE

Kendleton's village green was mostly flat, as village greens tend to be, but there was a corner of it that rose gently into a grassy hillock.

This was where Henry Christie sat on his backside, knees drawn up with his arms encircling them, staring, unfocused, across towards The Tawny Owl.

Although it wasn't in his nature to do so, he'd had to withdraw after some more heroic – or maybe stupid – attempts to enter the pub when he had realized there was absolutely nothing he could do other than impede the emergency services with his antics.

Reluctantly, he backed off, let them get on with it and watched from a distance.

The whole village had been woken by the explosion, which had rattled window panes for over a mile distant. Sleepy-eyed but horrified, many folks had gathered to gawk on the village green behind a cordon tape that the fire service had stretched out at a safe distance to keep people back while the blaze was dealt with.

Three fire tenders had arrived, plus an ambulance and a plethora of police cars from Lancaster. The fire service was still – over an hour and a half since arriving – trying to extinguish the fire, which Henry could see had spread rapidly through the ground floor and first floor of the main building and then, via the glass-covered walkway that linked the two parts of the property, to the bedrooms in the annexe. The flames had simply rushed along that corridor and taken hold in spite of the fire doors, gutting the annexe.

The view reminded Henry of a wartime bombing raid, smoke rising, flames crackling, firefighters emptying hosepipes into the ruins.

A figure was coming towards him. Debbie Blackstone trudged across the grass, up the rise of the hillock, then flopped down alongside him. The glass shard in her face had been carefully removed by a paramedic, the cut cleaned and dressed but not stitched. She had been told to get to A & E to be dealt with properly, but she didn't have time for that. She was still in her tracksuit bottoms and T-shirt because all changes of clothing were in the now non-existent Tawny Owl.

She sat down exactly like Henry, knees drawn up, then exhaled a long sigh and said, 'Damn!'

Henry didn't want to talk. He wasn't sure what he wanted. His mind was a mess, like a jumbled-up ball of steel wool.

Eventually, he asked, 'How is the cut?'

She touched her face delicately. 'Be OK.'

'Good.'

Another silence descended between them, although they could hear the sounds of the incident a couple of hundred yards away: the throb of the fire engines, the shouting of personnel, the murmur of the shocked onlookers from the village. Sounds Henry associated with his police career when attending similar incidents.

Now he was a player in such a thing, part of it, a victim, not the one who waded in and sorted it all out. 'Have they managed to enter at all?' he asked Blackstone.

'Not quite. Flames keep reigniting, but even when it's all under control, there will be a lot of dousing down after to control it.'

'Yeah, yeah.' Henry rubbed his face, which had a feel of sand-paper to it. 'Part of me thinks I'd be able to deal with this if I thought it was just a terrible accident. Wouldn't be easy, but it would be more acceptable. But it wasn't an accident, was it?'

Blackstone shook her head.

'My car was a bit of a giveaway.' He visualized his burning Audi, which was one thing the firefighters had dealt with quickly. It was now a charred shell, an engine block and four wheels but no tyres. 'That, the burning picnic benches and the reek of petrol.'

'Yep,' Blackstone agreed. 'Deliberate. Targeted.' There was little point trying to argue otherwise.

Henry hung his head and jammed it against his knees, began to rock back and forth slowly as it all began to overpower him.

Blackstone slid her arm across his shoulder in what she thought was a pretty useless gesture, but there was nothing more she could offer. No words, nothing.

And when Henry reached for her hand, she realized she was all he had in that moment and began to weep softly. But then she stiffened abruptly and said, 'What the hell?'

'We need to start getting the rest of the gear into the truck now, lads,' Lennox said with a clap to urge them on a bit. 'Got a long journey ahead, and the sooner we get moving, the sooner we'll be safe from prying eyes and cops.'

He had decided to get on the road with the box van; it seemed sensible to get out of the county for the time being, maybe even the country.

He had gathered the crew in the kitchen after they'd completed the count-up.

'You all still up for this?'

The general consensus was a yes, but all eyes were firmly fixed on the piles of money and jewellery on the dining-room table.

A big payday.

Lennox glanced at Ella who still cuddled Manderley in her arms. The dog licked her face, and she licked him back.

'He likes you,' Lennox said.

'He *loves* me,' she corrected him. 'And I love him and I want to keep him.'

Lennox agreed, too weary to argue.

'Yesss,' Ella said. She kissed the little dog on the nose, then raised him in her hands and shook him gently. 'You're mine.'

'What are you going to call him?'

Ella considered it, then declared, 'Mad Dog.'

'Mad Fucking Dog?' Benny laughed raucously. 'What sort of name is that, you daft bint?'

'It's an ironic name,' Ella said haughtily.

'Fuck's ironic mean?' Benny asked.

'It means the opposite of what I'm saying.'

'And where did you learn that?'

'In the only English lesson I ever went to,' she laughed and squeezed Manderley who, after the trauma of his kidnap, seemed to be revelling in the attention. 'I wuv you, Mad Dog. And,' she said to Benny, 'he's sort of named after us. We're like mad dogs, aren't we?'

'Well, we're definitely a pack,' Lennox said. 'With a leader.' He jabbed his finger in his own chest.

'Silly cow,' Ernest said of Ella.

'Right, whatever,' Lennox said, interrupting the chit-chat, eager to get the show on the road. 'Ella, you go check on the dogs, feed and water them, get them ready for the journey.'

At first – and Blackstone chided herself for this subsequently – she thought it was some attention-seeking stunt by Maude Crichton as she watched the woman stagger and stumble towards her and Henry on the hillock, and for a few moments she could not quite understand what Maude was blabbing on about. Initially, she thought that perhaps Maude had fallen at home and smashed her face, but when she calmed her down, it quickly became apparent that something much more sinister had happened. And terrifying.

'A gang . . . a gang,' Maude cried as Blackstone steadied her. 'Broke in, hit me, hit me in the face, tied me up . . .' At that point, everything poured out as she sobbed, 'They took my little dog, took Manderley, stole him . . . oh God . . . tied me up, stole my jewellery.'

'Jesus, Maude,' Blackstone said, looking at her smashed-up face.

Henry had watched the scene with a sense of detachment as though he was watching a blurred old film, but suddenly his senses seemed to kick in and he rose from his position and went over to the two women.

Maude was being supported by Blackstone with one hand while she was on her phone with the other, requesting one of the police officers at the scene of the fire to contact one of the paramedics and get them to come across to deal with Maude who, as Blackstone spoke, seemed to lose all use of her legs and slithered through Blackstone's grip to the grass.

'What's going on?' Henry asked.

'Maude's been attacked in her home and her dog's been stolen,' Blackstone said. 'Tied her up, too.'

'Henry, Henry,' Maude sobbed, looking desperately up at him

with her face covered in half-dried blood. She was wearing a plain white T-shirt and a pair of jogging bottoms. 'Please, Henry . . .' She reached up pitifully.

He did not react, but Blackstone glared at him and hissed, 'Henry, help her.'

He responded, stepped around Blackstone, took hold of Maude's outstretched hands and pulled her to her feet. From there she collapsed loosely against his chest, encircled his body with her arms and began to cry with huge, body-shuddering sobs. He patted her back half-heartedly.

'It's OK, it's OK,' he said quietly.

'What's going on, Henry? What's going on?' Maude twisted her face out of his chest and looked across at The Tawny Owl as if she was seeing it for the first time. 'Oh my God!'

'Someone's burned the pub down,' Blackstone told her.

'Is everyone all right?' Maude asked.

'No,' Henry said bluntly. He may not have known for sure at that moment, but his instinct told him that he *did* know. 'Everyone is not all right.'

Ella played with the newly named Mad Dog all the way from the bungalow to the unit at the far end of the track. She had fallen in love with the little pooch. He was so cute and lovable and playful. At one point in the journey, she lifted him up again and shook him affectionately. 'I'm going to look after you, Mr Mad Dog. You're mine and I'm going to make you so happy.'

Manderley – Mad Dog – licked Ella's little snub nose. He seemed to like her, too, even though he was confused by what was going on.

She cooed into his face a little longer, then dropped him back on to his feet and continued on her way up the track. She entered the building and went over to sacks containing dry dog food. She used a plastic scoop to gather enough food for the dogs in the kennels and walked down to them, calling out, 'Feeding time at the zoo. Food for my little animal friends, but not for you at the end. You'll have to beg for anything *you* want,' she said for Charlotte's benefit. She glanced along the enclosures but could not see Charlotte and envisioned her cowering out of sight in her kennel.

She slid back the bolt on the first kennel gate in which a meek, chained-up and muzzled springer spaniel watched her with wary eyes. She slid some of the dry food into its bowl, then reached for the dog, which tried to writhe out of her grasp. She grabbed it roughly by the nape of the neck, unfasted the muzzle and pushed the animal towards its bowl.

'Fraidy cat,' Ella sneered at the dog.

She stepped out and closed the gate, sliding the bolt back into place. It was then that Ella looked properly along the line of kennels to the one Charlotte was imprisoned in.

There was something not right about it.

She dashed to the enclosure. And swore.

Manderley had followed her on this short journey, tail wagging, but as Ella turned and ran, she tripped over the little dog, almost falling over. She kicked the dog out of the way, picked herself up and ran as fast as she could back to the bungalow.

Lennox spun around as she skidded into the kitchen. He and the lads were back at the dining table, sorting out the cash.

'What?'

In response, Ella strutted to Ernest and towered over him, red-faced, fists clenched. 'That bitch you kidnapped? You stupid twat!'

'What about her?'

Ella snarled and spat the next words into his face. 'She's gone. She's fucking escaped!'

THIRTEEN

It was an early dawn. The sun rose slowly but inexorably, molten gold into a clear sky, illuminating a scene of pure horror in front of Henry Christie's eyes as he surveyed the smouldering remains of The Tawny Owl jutting up from a mixture of smoke and early-morning mist like a medieval castle after a siege.

The walls of the main pub, slabs of locally hewn stone from the Pennines, had been in place for almost two hundred years ever since the pub was originally built as a coaching house on some long-forgotten route across the Bowland Forest. And, more or less, those walls still stood, resolute, challenging all comers, but everything else – ceilings, roofs, joists – had collapsed in on themselves like a badly made model. Burned and blackened beams jutted up like lumps of what they now were – charcoal.

The fire service was still damping down, having had to run their hoses from the village stream. Seats of fire continued to ignite sporadically in spite of the drenching. The other emergency services were still on site, one ambulance and many of the police cars. A temporary six-foot-high fence was being erected around the perimeter of the pub, which would also encircle the car park, and, ominously – as far as Henry was concerned – a low loader had driven into the village and was parked a little way down the road, the ominous part being that the load it carried was a brutally big bulldozer that looked capable of flattening the Houses of Parliament.

Henry understood its significance. He knew the local council's building inspector and health and safety officer were already on site and in discussions with the senior fire officer, and that meant a decision would soon be made, to which he would not be privy or be allowed to influence, about whether the whole pub and annexe should be bulldozed flat for the sake of public safety.

'Fucking brutal,' Henry had muttered at the prospect.

But he also knew that would only happen once the area had been cleared as a crime scene, which would take some time yet.

He had changed location now and was sitting on a bench on the village green close to the war memorial, mutedly observing proceedings in a detached, unreal way, feeling powerless and ineffective. He'd been plied with a succession of coffees from residents, who all gave their sympathies even though nothing had yet been confirmed. He had refused offers of food, knowing he wouldn't be able to keep anything down. He was even struggling with the coffee, and several cups had been emptied discreetly on the grass.

Blackstone walked to him and sat down.

He didn't acknowledge her. He had nothing to say.

She understood but needed to speak to him.

'Rik Dean's almost here,' she told him. 'Apparently, he's coming armed with Diane Daniels and DCI Wellhaven, also known as "The Lovers".'

The news didn't seem to impact Henry. He'd already taken a series of phone calls from Rik and his sister Lisa, Rik's wife, the latter particularly making him want to puke. It was far too early for Henry to be on the receiving end of sympathy.

Henry arched his eyebrows.

'Maude seems to be a bit better,' Blackstone told him. She'd handed her into the care of a couple of good detectives from

Lancaster who had slowly extracted her story, feeding it bit by bit back to Blackstone. 'She's gutted about Manderley being taken, not so much the cash and watches and jewels and such, although there were some treasured pieces among it all.'

'She doted on the little brute,' Henry murmured, coming to life a little. 'What does she say about the attackers?'

'Masks on all the time, no names, no pack drills,' Blackstone said. 'One girl, four adult males.'

Henry nodded.

'They stole oodles from her – I mean, thousands and thousands.'

'And it could all have been mine,' Henry quipped cynically, 'according to the son who probably stuck the knife in me.'

Blackstone smirked. 'You missed that boat, pal.'

Henry laughed, then asked seriously, 'Maude is OK, though?'

'She will be. Anyway, it sounds like they were the crew that went on to hit Veronica . . . actually, not sounds like – *is*, one hundred per cent,' Blackstone said firmly.

'Who then went on to do this,' Henry said, opening his arms in a gesture that encompassed the devastation in front of him. Then he clammed up, closed his lips tightly and got a firm grip of his feelings, which felt as though they were being stored up behind a dam that was about to burst. 'How's Veronica?'

'She's as tough as old boots.' Veronica was in the care of other detectives who were piecing her story together.

'They went to her house thinking the takings from the fair would be there, but weren't,' Blackstone said, 'so they came here.'

'Except they were going to come here anyway,' Henry said.

Blackstone agreed.

'And torch the place and kill whoever they found here, which should have been me. Instead . . .' His voice trailed off weakly.

Henry stared into the distance across to the thickly wooded area on the opposite side of the stream where, in the morning light, he thought he saw some movement in the trees. He focused. A moment later, an immense red deer stag stepped into view, sporting a huge, majestic set of antlers which the animal shook contemptuously. The beast's shoulders rippled with muscle, and a strange sensation made the pit of Henry's stomach turn over.

This, he knew, was the leader of the local herd, his position unchallenged for several years now. Henry had named him Horace.

'That is one hell of an animal,' Blackstone said appreciatively.

'I'd like to think he was my lucky charm,' Henry said wistfully. 'Maybe not so today.'

'You never know.'

Horace seemed to look across at Henry and make eye contact, even though Henry knew this to be preposterous.

Then, with another quiver of his muscular hindquarters, Horace turned and disappeared back into the woods, was gone.

He and Blackstone returned to silence again until Henry said, 'We must have passed the bastards on our way to Veronica's house.'

'I know.' Blackstone narrowed her eyes. 'I keep running the journey through my mind. I know we passed a couple of cars coming in the opposite direction, but I was concentrating on driving.'

'Yep.' Henry was replaying the same journey through his mind, but it was clogged up with too many things, and he had to force himself to concentrate. Nothing really came to him. 'Has anyone checked Veronica's security cameras yet?'

Blackstone hesitated. Henry said, 'What?'

Blackstone shook her head and closed her eyes.

'They're not working, are they?' Henry guessed.

She gave a helpless shrug.

'Unbelievable. Daft old bat was planning to have thousands of pounds in her house all weekend and her cameras aren't working.' Henry was suddenly furious, but then all the anger dissipated from him as quickly as it had built up, instantaneously. Much of his rage was because, so far, footage from the security cameras in The Tawny Owl had not yet been recovered and was unlikely to be because of the devastation. 'Silly cow!'

'You don't mean that.'

No, he didn't. In fact, he liked Veronica too damned much now. And what could he expect? There was little point in being annoyed with an old lady in a wheelchair who, totally unexpectedly, had become a good friend.

'The detectives with her tell me she's mortified,' Blackstone said.

Henry nodded. 'Anyway, no doubt a getaway car will turn up, burnt out sooner or later, probably stolen, or cloned or whatever, and there'll be a link to this.'

'Any lead would be nice.'

'These guys are all very forensically aware – masks, gloves, no names used, although having a girl along seems a bit unusual if you'll forgive my rampant sexism?'

'I'll let it pass. However, there was one slip of the tongue both at Maude's and at Veronica's: one called the other Dad.'

'Interesting,' Henry said, but his mind wandered a little, 'but nothing changed the end result, did it? This was always going to be, wasn't it?' He pointed to the pub.

'What do you mean?'

'Even after they stole all the money and jewellery from Maude's, and if they had managed to steal the cash from Veronica's – if it had been there – that wouldn't have been the end of their night, would it?' Henry speculated. 'They were always going to come here, weren't they? They came prepared to burn the place down and murder whoever was inside. Now, call me a suspicious guy, but I'm pretty damn certain they didn't come for Ginny or Fred – who I know we are going to find dead in there – because they didn't have enemies, not one!' Blackstone opened her mouth to say something, but Henry held up a finger. 'They came for me, Debs. Doesn't take a genius to put that together. If I'd been here, I would be dead now. Probably you would be, too. Collateral damage. I should have been here and taken what was coming to me, and I should have protected Ginny and Fred.'

'Don't do this to yourself, Henry. Whoever came to do this came to commit an atrocity armed with petrol bombs, knives and guns. You wouldn't have protected anyone. They came to kill and destroy, and that's what they did, and,' she added unconvincingly, 'we don't yet know if Ginny and Fred are in there.'

'Don't be a dick! Where do you think they are? On holiday? They're in there, they're dead – you know it, I know it – and us two, we're the lucky ones, because the killers didn't know about Veronica's panic button and we got out just in time. How very fortunate for us.'

'OK, OK.' Blackstone raised her palms.

Henry said, 'You know it's Lennox, don't you?'

Blackstone breathed out through her nose. 'I know it fits. A festering grudge, maybe for you putting him away all those years ago. A girl in the gang, maybe the one serving at the burger bar. Three lads, one of whom is Lennox's son, who might have called him Dad in front of witnesses.' She sighed. 'Do people hold grudges like that and kill because of them?' Off the withering look Henry then gave her, she said, 'OK, yep, we know people kill each other for a lot less – looking at somebody wrong in the pub, or maybe being called a dick!'

Henry let that go. 'The other thing is we've still got a missing girl who had a picture of Ernest Lennox on her phone, and I'm more inclined to believe it's highly likely that little creep snatched her, and we must not forget that. If she isn't already dead, there's a bloody good chance she will be after they've finished with her.'

'I haven't forgotten. Jeez, what a mess.'

'And Tony Owl, where is he?' Henry turned and looked at the actual Tawny Owl. 'My focus would be on Lennox at least to begin with.'

'Coincidences?' Blackstone asked.

'You bet.'

'Well?' Lennox demanded of the gang.

'She's not there, Dad.'

'You've searched everywhere – barns, outhouses, workshops, inside vehicles?'

They all nodded as he went through the list.

'No trace?'

'Nowt,' Ernest said.

'Shit,' Lennox said. 'That puts a different complexion on things.'

All three lads looked at him as though they didn't understand his meaning.

Responding to the expressions, Lennox said, 'We need to get things sorted, quick.' He jabbed his finger at Ernest. 'You, with me, now.' To the others, he said, 'Search again; she could be hiding.'

Lennox spun on his heels and jerked his head at Ernest. Both set off back to the bungalow. Strutting quickly.

'What you thinkin', Dad?'

'I'm thinking we don't want any baggage, is what I'm thinking.'

Henry and Blackstone sat on the bench and watched Rik Dean walk towards them. They'd spotted his arrival earlier, watched his heads-together with the senior fire officer, who was obviously explaining what had happened in terms of the fire, its causes, how it had spread. When that discussion was over, Rik had a long talk with a crime scene investigator and a woman Blackstone knew worked for the forensic service specializing in arson investigation. When those discussions were over, Rik looked across and began to walk over. Looked like a reluctant journey to Henry.

Blackstone said, 'Whatever happens, don't ever call me a dick again, OK?'

'I won't. I was just getting wound up. Sorry.'

'Apology accepted.'

Henry was leaning forward with his elbows on his knees. He angled his face to her and offered an apologetic smile, then he looked at Rik who was almost upon him.

The detective superintendent stopped in front of his old friend, his face showing deep sadness. He knew Ginny and Fred well.

'Henry, I'm so sorry.'

'Yeah, OK,' Henry said numbly.

'You feel up to telling me what happened from your perspective, how it all panned out?'

'Not really, but Debbie can.' He jerked his thumb at her. 'It was a shared experience.'

'No disrespect, Debbie, but I'd like to hear it from Henry.'

Henry raised his face. 'Even I spotted the disrespect in that,' he said bluntly. 'She's better equipped to tell you than I am.'

Rik's mouth puckered up.

'Suggestion,' Henry said. 'Why don't we both tell you?'

Rik conceded. Henry and Blackstone shuffled along the bench to make room for Rik. Henry patted the space, Rik sat down, and they began to retell the story. Henry actually knew this was a good thing for him because it helped to clear his brain fog. Finally, they reached the point where they were back at The Tawny Owl as it was about to explode.

'And Ginny and Fred were inside? You're certain?'

Henry tried not to get annoyed and give him a flippant answer, just said, 'I'm certain.'

'Anyone else?'

Henry shook his head.

By now, all three of them were leaning forward, elbows on knees, so all three watched the senior fire officer approach.

Rik stood up.

The guy nodded. 'Mr Christie, Superintendent Dean, Sergeant Blackstone . . . I just wanted to update you as to where we are. First, the building is in a very dangerous state and there is no way in which it can be saved. The annexe section has been completely gutted. Unfortunately, the whole building will have to be demolished.' He pointed to the huge bulldozer on the back of the low loader. 'The building inspector and I have agreed on that course of action, and I'm very sorry.' He looked at Henry, who nodded.

'However, that will wait until a full forensic examination has taken place, which will be quite a perilous task, but I know needs to be done.'

'How did it start?' Henry asked.

'My initial findings are that accelerant was thrown all over the building, including the kitchen where there is evidence that gas pipes have been compromised – broken – which would account for the huge explosion you described. There is much work to do on that, though.'

'Arson?' Henry said as though he hadn't been listening.

'Yes, arson,' the man said patiently.

'Bodies?' Henry asked.

The SFO looked at Rik for guidance.

'We need to get moving with that now, so I'll be going in with a team in the next half an hour or so if that's OK?' Rik said.

The SFO nodded assent.

Henry had listened to this while staring at the ground, had asked his questions that way, too. Once more, his ears began to pound a bass drumbeat as blood rushed through his skull like a tsunami.

Blackstone saw him shaking. She slid an arm around his shoulder, understanding what the full implications of all this meant to him: the final, absolute, incontrovertible truth that Ginny and Fred were somewhere in the burnt-out shell that only hours before had been a thriving home and business, Henry's home and business and his future, and it had all been taken away from him.

She could feel him shudder.

'Mr Christie . . . Mr Christie?' the SFO said, breaking into Henry's state of mind. He looked up and tried to focus on the man; it didn't seem to be working.

'Henry!' Rik barked sharply.

And Henry's pounding blood flow settled and he returned to the world.

'We're going to go in now,' Rik said.

'I heard.'

He and Blackstone watched both high-ranking officers walk towards the pub.

'Excuse me,' Henry said. He stood up, walked around to the back of the bench, sank on to all fours, retched and vomited.

*   *   *

'Yeah, me dad thinks it's a wise move,' Ernest said to Benny. 'It'll put the cops off the scent.'

Benny screwed up his nose as he tried to understand the logic. He had been told by Lennox to take the getaway car, the Mercedes constructed from two separate models, out over to Pilling Sands on the coast and set it on fire.

Ernest had followed him in one of the vans from the garage to help him and drive him back. The others at the garage were doing the last-minute loading of the van, getting as much in as possible, ready to hit the road when they got back.

So Benny and Ernest were now on an empty car park adjacent to Pilling Sands, a well-known beauty spot just to the north of the village of Pilling. It was a huge coastal area of salt marsh overlooking the estuary of the River Lune at the southern end of Morecambe Bay. It had dangerous, fast-moving tides and was notorious for sinking sands. The area inland was protected from flooding by a specially constructed rocky embankment, adjacent to which was the car park the two lads were on.

Ernest had brought along a can of petrol, and as soon as Benny had parked up the Merc, he began splashing the contents inside and on top of the car.

'Surely the cops are going to find this,' Benny reasoned, 'I'd've thought it would've been better being left in one of the garages at headquarters.'

'Nah,' Ernest said opening the front passenger door and sloshing some of the petrol on to the seat. 'Oh, hang on, mate,' he said and withdrew, pointing into the footwell. 'I must've left that in. Look, just under the seat, mate. Can you just get it for me?'

'What is it?'

'There, just stickin' out under . . . see it?'

Benny walked past Ernest, bending over and peering down at whatever his mate was trying to get him to see. Doing so exposed his backside to Ernest who took a step back, aimed his foot just right and booted Benny in his arse to send him sprawling into the car across the centre console and both front seats.

'Sorry, mate, needs must,' Ernest grunted.

Benny yelled and started to push himself out, by which time Ernest had placed the petrol can on the ground and drawn the revolver out of his waistband, where it had been tucked out of sight under his T-shirt. He fired two bullets into Benny's exposed backside.

Benny screamed in agony, writhed away and attempted to scramble across the seats toward the driver's door with his backside bleeding profusely, one bullet having entered his buttock and the other going right into his anus, ripping a ragged hole up into his lower stomach and bursting his prostate gland.

Smirking, Ernest casually strolled around the car.

Benny, who had survivable wounds at that point, was trying to get his fingers to pull open the door handle, but the pain in his bottom and lower abdomen was as if he'd had a red-hot, straight-out-of-the-fire branding iron thrust into him, and he could not somehow find the coordination in his fingers to grip the handle.

But the door opened for him.

Ernest stood there with the handgun resting against his outer thigh. 'Let me help you,' he said.

'Ern, Ern, what the fuck?' Benny appealed, and also displayed his utter confusion. What had he done wrong? He was beginning to fade.

Ernest shot him twice in the head, then slammed the door shut on him and went back around the passenger side from which Benny's still twitching feet jutted out. Ernest folded them inside the car and finished dousing both Benny and the car with petrol. Moments later, the car was ablaze.

The vomiting made Henry feel much better, even though most of what came out was the coffee he had consumed throughout the night. He was a great lover of coffee; it had kept him going on many occasions, but sometimes too much was too much.

'Sorry,' he apologized to Blackstone as he rose from behind the bench.

The noise had made her feel queasy, too, but she'd held it together. 'No worries.'

After that, they crossed to the newly erected fencing around the remains of The Tawny Owl to watch the forensic team kit up in PPE and then, accompanied by a couple of firefighters, walk in through the still erect front entrance into the muck and mulch at floor level beyond.

Henry had done things like this in his past – searched scenes of arson – and sometimes, depending on what was in the property to begin with, it could be like wading through the undergrowth of the

Everglades: thick, gloopy, unpleasant and very smelly, particularly if burnt flesh was in the miasma.

Henry put his nose up to the mesh of the fence and clung to it with his fingertips, waiting for the terrible news he knew would come.

The van was loaded by the time Ernest returned alone, and the remaining crew were ready to set off with Lennox at the wheel.

The driver's seat was separate, and there was a bench seat for the remaining three occupants of the cab.

Ernest shuffled in first so he would be next to his father. Ella then sat between him and Jimbo who was pushed against the door. Ella had Mad Dog on her lap, lifting him up, kissing his nose, enjoying him licking her lips and tongue.

They drove out of the garage and turned towards the A6.

Jimbo was slightly confused. 'So, what you're saying is that Benny didn't want to come with us?' he queried, trying to make sense of the unexpected non-reappearance of his mate.

'Yeah, that's exactly what I'm saying,' Ernest lied. 'His choice, but I said he could have the Merc and go back to Blackpool if he wanted, then sell it on for a couple of grand.'

'But all this money!' Jimbo exclaimed, referring to the riches they had just accumulated.

'Yeah, but the chances are we won't be coming back here for a while,' Ernest said, 'and he didn't seem to like that, being away. Y'never know, he might change his mind and join us, and he'd be welcome if he does – that's OK, innit, Dad?'

Lennox nodded and exchanged a knowing look with his son.

Jimbo frowned but sat back, then shrugged, quickly working out there was so much more money for him with Benny out of the picture. A lot more. 'What's the plan, then?' he asked, looking across Ella to Ernest and Lennox.

'Get the fuck out of here first,' Lennox told him.

'OK, whatev',' Jimbo said. He sat back, took out his mobile phone and started to play Candy Crush, which he'd been doing for several years now, having achieved level 252. He was a much better thief than Candy Crush player, which he had never really quite got the theory of.

As ever on a journey of any length, he remained engrossed on the screen of his phone, not looking up once, so when he heard

Ernest say, 'I need a piss, Dad,' that was the first time he raised his eyes in twenty minutes as Lennox pulled into a layby. Jimbo had no idea where he was, didn't even care.

They were, in fact, on the A6 just to the north of Carnforth, where the carriageway split for about a mile as the northbound dipped under a bridge, beyond which was the layby.

'You're always peeing.' Lennox laughed.

'I know,' Ernest chuckled, but instead of clambering over Ella and Jimbo to get out, he stayed where he was, and Ella handed Mad Dog to him. This should have set warning bells ringing loud to Jimbo, but it didn't, even when Ernest said to him, 'Hey, dick brain, you need to get out.'

'Uh, oh yeah.' Jimbo was a bit sluggish from his busy night. He leaned forward to slide his phone on to the dashboard and then looped the fingers of his left hand around the door handle, opened the door a crack and thereby exposed the whole of his right side to Ella.

She glanced at Lennox.

He nodded.

The switchblade Ella had been hiding in her waistband, now in her right fist, a classic Italian one, opened silently.

She did not hesitate.

She contorted and plunged the blade with controlled frenzy into Jimbo's side, puncturing his lung, his liver, driving it into his neck, severing the carotid artery. Then, even as the blood fountained out, she twisted the blade under Jimbo's windpipe and sliced it with a jerking motion, finally shoving him hard against the door which he had opened and watching him tumble out on to the layby, licking her lips and tasting the warm blood that had sprayed across her face.

Ernest and Lennox watched this, transfixed and enthralled.

Lennox took Mad Dog from Ernest who jumped out of the cab behind Ella, and they both dragged Jimbo across to the grass verge and over into the drainage channel beyond where Ella knifed him once more through the eye, skewering his brain, killing him for certain.

The whole process took maybe ninety seconds, and then they were back in the van, Ernest shouting, 'Go, go,' to his dad.

Lennox tossed the dog back into Ella's hands and set off. At the point where the lanes of the A6 carriageway rejoined each other, he swung the van around in a wide U-turn and drove south. Ernest grabbed Jimbo's phone from the dash, dismantled it, snapped the SIM card, then leaned across Ella and threw the pieces out of the window.

He turned to Lennox. 'No baggage, eh, Dad?'

'Correct, no baggage.'

Henry watched a fire service drone hover in the sky above The Tawny Owl like a huge insect from a sci-fi movie. Or it could have been a police drone.

He didn't know. Or care.

He was just waiting for the inevitable.

It was four hours later – four hours since the scientific teams had initially entered the remains of the building, still smouldering as the morning came properly, still being doused down, though with less water now.

The villagers had gathered again, looking on. Those who knew Henry could not find any words, and he had no desire to enter into conversation anyway.

And the flowers had started to arrive as rumour spread.

Henry wanted to kick them to hell and back.

And his phone had been ringing continually.

He picked and chose who to speak to. His long-standing American friend Karl Donaldson, who still worked for the FBI, currently seconded to the Washington office, had called, somehow having found out about the fire. It was a stilted conversation even between old friends, and Donaldson had the sense not to prolong it but offered what support he could, even though he was thousands of miles distant.

Henry's two daughters had called, having seen the TV news – it had made national broadcasts. Jenny and Leanne both lived in the south of England now with their own families, but both loved Ginny and were in bits. Both wanted to travel back straightaway, but Henry told them no. He would get back to them. Just to know they were thinking about him was enough.

A mobile police incident van arrived on the scene, setting up on the village green opposite the pub. Other specialist units descended.

Henry observed it all with detachment, but he did show a little bit of interest when a CSI Transit van turned up and what he knew to be a forensic tent was unloaded and carried un-erected into The

Tawny Owl. He knew what that was for. Because the roof and ceilings had collapsed and the ground floor was exposed to the elements, the tent would be put up to protect any evidence that had to be examined and collected.

Bodies, in this case.

Finally, Rik Dean stepped out together with one of the forensic investigators. The pair stood on the terrace for a while, and then, grim-faced, Rik pushed back the hood of his forensic suit and started to remove his nitrile gloves as he walked across the terrace, past the burnt-out wreck of Henry's car and stepped out through a gap in the fence.

Henry knew better than to have unreal expectations and yet he was a human being.

He knew bodies had been found, but he didn't want to believe it.

Rik Dean's face was beyond sad. He shook his head.

Blackstone was standing next to Henry, holding her breath, one arm around his shoulder.

Rik stopped a few feet away, folding his disposable gloves into one another.

'Henry,' he said, almost choking on the word, his eyes watery. He knew Ginny, he knew Fred. He had known Alison. He had married Henry's sister at The Tawny Owl, so it was an important place for him, too, and the people who lived there were valued and loved. 'Henry,' he said again, 'I'm so sorry.'

FOURTEEN

Henry went for a long walk to try to process everything – the deaths and the confirmed theft of money from the safe in The Tawny Owl, the destruction and the evil behind it all. It wasn't working particularly well, but at least it got him away from people. He needed some solitude provided by the woods on the opposite side of the stream, and he followed a well-worn trail that meandered through the trees – half hoping to see Horace the red stag again – until he finally worked his way through and stepped out on to the road a little further up than Maude's house. His short break hadn't worked well from a mental perspective, but it did help him realize he was now hungry and thirsty.

A couple of police cars were parked outside Maude's house, so he walked towards it, part of him wondering if he should apologize to her for his disinterest in her plight, which he now knew was intrinsically linked to everything else that had happened in Kendleton. Maude was probably fortunate to come out of it alive.

There was a cordon across her driveway, and a young PC with a clipboard stood guard at the gate, recording all comings and goings and discouraging gawkers.

Henry stopped, gawked.

The young cop approached him. 'Can I help you?'

Not even a 'sir', Henry thought. 'Is Mrs Crichton at home?'

'Who are you?'

'A friend, a concerned one.'

'She is, but she's busy with detectives.'

'OK,' Henry said.

The officer's brow furrowed. 'You're the guy with the pub, aren't you?'

'Yep.'

'I'm sorry.'

'Thank you.' Henry had turned to continue walking down the road when he spotted Maude at her front window. She waved and beckoned him to stop. She disappeared for a moment and then came down the drive, scurrying to catch him up.

He knew an embrace was inevitable and that maybe it wouldn't be such a bad thing.

The inevitable happened. Without a word, her arms wrapped gently around him. For a moment, he remained as stiff as a board, but then he allowed himself to relax. He slid his arms around her slender frame and pulled her tight to him.

And it did feel good.

Something he needed at that moment.

He closed his eyes and let himself go, right up to the moment they disentangled themselves.

'I'm sorry if I seemed off with you before.'

She shook her head. 'Doesn't matter.' Tears streamed down her swollen face. 'This is all so awful. You must be . . . Oh, I can't even think of a word to describe it.'

'I might need a thesaurus if I'm honest. Look,' he paused, 'I'm also so sorry for treating you the way I have been doing. So badly.'

'It's OK. If you don't want an *us*, I get it. I'm a big girl. And I get it if you still think it was Will who stabbed you.'

'Um, let's not spoil the moment,' Henry said.

Maude grinned. 'OK.'

'Anyway, are you all right?'

She blew out her cheeks. Her nose and face were swollen, bruised and purple, where she had been punched, and looked very painful. 'At least they didn't actually break my nose.' She touched it. 'Hurts like hell, though.'

'I can imagine.'

'And they stole loads.' She looked rueful. 'Silly me, eh? And Manderley,' she added. Her bottom lip quivered. 'I hope they look after him.'

'He could have been stolen to order. I presume he was chipped?'

'Yeah.' She swallowed and blinked rapidly but got a hold of herself. 'I'm just doing a list of the stolen stuff. I've got photos of most of it, so that's good, and most of it didn't mean anything to me as such, but they did take a watch that my husband gave me on my fiftieth, inscribed and everything.'

'Oh, that's sad.' Henry was losing interest now in spite of trying his best. 'You never know, it could turn up when they try to sell it on, which they probably will.'

'Let's hope. Er, what are you doing now?' she asked him hesitantly.

'Just wandering like a lost soul. I may or may not have to ID the bodies, depending how damaged they are by the fire.'

'Oh God, how awful.'

'So I'm trying to get my head around that, but at the moment they're still in The Tawny Owl and may not be moved for quite some time.'

'Henry, look, the police won't be here much longer,' Maude said, referring to her house. 'Please come around anytime. If you need somewhere to live . . . whatever, I don't know. No strings, I promise.'

'Thank you.'

They embraced again as a car drew up alongside – it was Blackstone in her rural crime SUV. She ran the passenger window down. She was now in uniform, having got one from her office in Lancaster, and she had managed to borrow handcuffs and a baton.

'Get in,' she said urgently to Henry.

'You two all loved up again?'

'Back off, I'm in a killing mood,' Henry warned her.

'Aren't we all?'

'Anyway, what's this about?' he asked as he fitted his seat belt. It clicked into place as Blackstone floored the accelerator and the car surged forwards.

'Keeping you occupied so you don't go on a killing spree.'

Henry allowed himself half a grin at that. On the surface, Blackstone was no respecter of emotions; underneath was a different matter, and the arm she had put around Henry's shoulders, an unusually tactile move for her, had been exactly what he had needed in those delicate moments.

'Ricky Boy told me to turn out to a job that has come up and take you along for the ride – if you want, that is? Not going to force you.'

'Depends what it is.'

'Bit of an odd one – bloke rang in claiming to have found two bodies in a freezer.'

'Well, on balance I suppose that could keep my mind occupied for a while.'

'One of my lads was first response, and Rik has told me to cover it, see what it's all about.'

'Is it genuine?'

'First, we thought it was a nut job, but it would seem kosher.'

Henry gripped his seat belt when Blackstone threw the large SUV around the bends on the narrow road out of Kendleton in the direction of Caton, which was situated east of Lancaster.

'Where are we headed?'

'A disused petrol station just off the A6 near Garstang.'

A few minutes later, she was heading south on the M6, leaving at the next junction and cutting towards Garstang but turning left a couple of miles north of that town, to Scorton. Henry was familiar with many of the locations around this area, as he knew the majority of Lancashire very well. Blackstone reached a junction, turned right and came to the forecourt of a rough-looking former petrol station with a bungalow and, it seemed, quite a bit of land at the back with various buildings on it. Henry recognized the place having passed it a few times over the years, but not so often recently. He had even once filled up his car here, years back when he'd been out for a day trip around the area, which was quite beautiful, with Kate. He had passed it since it had closed down and ceased trading as a garage, and he recalled seeing a lot of scrap vehicles of all descriptions on the forecourt, which had become nothing more than a junkyard.

'I know this place, but only because I know it,' he told Blackstone.

'Me, too. Been past it a few times but never gave it a second thought really.'

One of the rural crime vehicles, another SUV, was parked in a space on the forecourt in front of a petrol pump with an old *Shell* sign on it, giving its age away. A uniformed constable was talking to an older man. Henry and Blackstone climbed out of their car and strolled over.

'Hi, Gary,' Blackstone said to the officer. 'What have we got?'

The officer indicated the man. 'This is Mr Whitehouse and he lives in the house just opposite.' He pointed to a small, detached bungalow on the other side of the road. 'And he has found two bodies in a freezer.'

Blackstone turned to him. 'Mr Whitehouse, I'm Sergeant Blackstone, and this is Mr Christie, my associate. What's gone on, please?'

'I hope I'm not going to get in trouble for this,' he said nervously.

'From what I've heard so far, I'd say no,' Blackstone reassured him. 'So, go on . . .'

Whitehouse was a sturdy man in his fifties. 'Well,' he said, stretching out the syllable. 'This lot here' – he gestured at the bungalow – 'bunch o' shits if you ask me, but not really my business because I'm just about far enough away not to let them get on my wick.'

'Who are they?' Henry asked.

'Father's called, uh, Lenny summat – can't quite remember. He pulls that eyesore of a burger van up there.' Mr Whitehouse moved sideways and pointed up the drive past the bungalow. Just beyond the gable end of the building, almost out of sight, Henry could see the corner of a caravan. He moved back a few steps so he could see more of it and recognized it as the back of the van Lennox had been using to serve his burgers from at the fair over the weekend.

Henry mouthed the word 'Jesus' silently.

'Who else lives here?' Blackstone said. She was trying to contain her excitement, having also seen the burger van.

'Erm, one's his son – Ernie, I think – and there are another two lads and a lass who's bonny but looks like she'd slice a man's cock off given half a chance – excuse my French.'

Blackstone shrugged. 'Whatever. So, what went on?'

'I knew he'd been out with the burger van all weekend, don't know where, and the other vehicle they have – among many, I might add. It's a knackered old motorhome – that was out, too. Anyway, the motorhome came back yesterday afternoon before the burger van and drove straight up the track to that big warehouse-type unit at the back.' Whitehouse pointed up the driveway again. 'I was just sitting in my window, watching like I do, and I just thought, "They're up to no good, these fuckers" – pardon my French. They spun the motorhome around and reversed it right into the unit, which I just thought was odd.'

'What did you think they were up to?' Blackstone asked.

'They're all thieves, scallies, I reckon. Up to no good all the time, officer.'

'OK.'

'Anyway, I watched that all going on, but I don't have an uninterrupted view up the drive and I got a bit bored. Anyway, I was sat in the window later and Lennox lands back, pulling his burger van. Got that girl in with him. He pulled up at the side of the bungalow, then, I don't know, all the lot of 'em were looking inside the Transit van at something, all animated, like. Next, they unhook the Tranny and drive it up to that back unit again. I couldn't see much, but I did see that lass had a little white dog with her, which she didn't have when they went out a few days back.'

Arses twitched.

'Well, a bit later they all went out in a fancy car that'd been in the drive for a few days, and they came back a few hours later in it. Next thing I know, they left in a big old red van pretty early this morning. Used to be a Post Office van, I think. Seemed to be a lot of activity all of a sudden, and some of it just plain odd.'

'And when they'd gone, you went to investigate?' Blackstone asked him.

'I, er, did,' he said unsurely.

'Go on,' she encouraged him.

'Well, I snuck up the drive – concerned neighbour and all that – and I just had a look.'

'And what did you find?' Blackstone asked him.

'A body in a freezer.'

Blackstone looked at her constable who said, 'I can confirm that. Maybe two bodies, actually.'

Henry held Blackstone back. 'Let's just take our time . . . let's saunter.'

She had been about to rush off, but Henry gave her a *cool-it* signal, and she nodded and slowed down.

They both put on disposable gloves from Blackstone's vehicle, then started the walk up the long driveway. Past the bungalow first, trying the door handles, finding the property locked. Past the burger truck, which stank of grease. Then past a workshop, also locked, followed by a single-storey unit on the left with a closed shutter door and a personnel door next to it, which was unlocked.

Blackstone stepped inside and looked down the length of this unit. Her mouth popped open. 'Oh my God!'

Henry came in behind her and said, 'What?' as he ran the side of his hand down a bank of light switches. The fluorescent lights hanging on brackets from the roof pinged on one by one.

Open-mouthed, Blackstone walked down a row of ten all-terrain vehicles, ATVs, reversed neatly back to the wall, recognizing one she had actually pursued on a police ATV but which had outrun and outmanoeuvred her in the Forest of Bowland. 'I've been after these bastards. And, in fact, not five days ago I was chasing that one.' She pointed to it. 'I bloody knew it was an organized thing,' she muttered.

Henry looked along the row, seeing that all the bikes were very clean, obviously having been washed off and polished. 'Ready to go out to new customers is my guess.'

'And these!' Blackstone pointed to four scrambler bikes, propped up on stands, also looking very clean.

'Stolen, too,' Henry said with certainty.

'Yep.' Blackstone stood back and took a short video using her phone and added a commentary.

They left that unit and continued on their journey up the drive, which became a stony, rutted track the further they went. An open-sided barn on the right contained a variety of farming implements, probably also stolen, Henry guessed. Finally, they reached the unit at the far end.

Lennox's Ford Transit van was reversed up to the roller door on a flat, concrete apron, and next to the side door of this vehicle was what looked like quite a big smear of blood on the ground. Avoiding stepping in it, Blackstone opened the sliding side door and looked inside, where there was a larger pool of congealed blood on the van floor and a trail of it leading to the roller door, indicating that someone had been dragged from the van to the building.

She looked at Henry. 'That's a lot of blood,' Blackstone commented. 'You think Tony Owl was brought here in this?'

Henry nodded. 'Could have been.'

Blackstone backed off and went to the personnel door of the unit, opened it and stepped inside, followed by Henry. The motorhome described by Mr Whitehouse had been backed in through the roller door and was parked there with its side door open. The trail of blood from the Transit van continued around the back of the Hymer, but there was also another trail of blood, though less extensive, from the motorhome across the floor of the unit.

'More blood,' Blackstone said and swore as she tried to work it all out in her mind. She looked down the unit and saw the kennel enclosures, this trail of blood from the motorhome leading to the one at the far end of the line.

'Let's follow this one, first,' Henry said, pointing at the blood trail from the Transit van.

They did, going around the back of the vehicle, and found a large chest freezer against the wall. Blackstone went over to it, still avoiding the blood and said to Henry, 'Shall we?'

'Be my guest.'

She slowly raised the lid. Henry, standing just behind her, was reminded of the raising of a coffin lid in a cheap vampire film. Creepy, especially as the rusted hinges creaked from lack of lubricant.

Chilled air from within rose like steam as it met the warmer air, adding to the cinematic atmosphere.

Blackstone made a hissing noise – more special effects – as she looked inside, and said something under her breath, standing aside for Henry to get a view.

'Well, now we know what happened to Tony Owl,' Blackstone remarked. The falconer's body had been dumped face up in the freezer and the huge axe-inflicted wound to his skull was clearly visible.

'Damn, poor guy . . . decent guy,' Henry said. 'But what is he lying on?'

Blackstone leaned in. 'Looks like another body to me – well frozen, though.'

'I think we're getting a good sense of why Mr Lennox and his son aren't at home,' Henry speculated.

Blackstone stepped back and closed the freezer lid. She was about to say something but stopped before any word came out and frowned, having heard something. 'What was that?'

'What was what?'

'A scratching noise from down there.'

Henry listened but his tinnitus ruled out hearing any low-level noises such as scratching.

'Yep, scratching,' Blackstone insisted, 'and a whining noise, too. I smell dogs.'

She strode over the blood trail and headed towards the row of kennels, the first four out of the six having a dog tethered and muzzled in it. The last two were vacant.

As they got to the front of each kennel, the dog inside backed off timidly to the rear wall.

'Stolen dogs,' Henry said. 'A growing trade over the pandemic.' He walked along past the enclosures, noting how sturdily they had been constructed, hoping to see Manderley in there. But there was no sign of the Bichon Frise.

'If they have done a runner, as we suspect,' Blackstone said angrily 'then each one of these dogs would die of thirst and hunger.'

There was a small workbench just beyond the furthest kennel on top of which was a little pile of objects the size of rice grains that Henry recognized as microchips used for dog identification. There were traces of blood and dog hairs on the bench top, plus a scalpel and a glue gun.

'They removed these chips,' he said with disgust. 'I wonder how many dogs don't survive that little operation?' he pondered further, feeling ire rise in him. 'Looks like another facet to their business.' He knew that people like Lennox wouldn't care a jot how many dogs died from infections from the chip-removal process, which was probably done here with no thought to sterilization, cleanliness or care of the animals. The glue gun was probably used to seal up the wounds.

Blackstone had not responded to any of his musings.

He swivelled his head and looked at her. She had followed him down the line of kennels, looking angrily at the dogs trapped inside. But she stopped at the last kennel and was looking into an empty space. The door was open, and Henry could see it looked as if the lock had been forced off by a jemmy.

'What?' he asked.

Blackstone still did not respond. She ducked and stepped into the enclosure and crossed to the back wall into which a chunky chain with a thick leather collar had been bolted, probably for the larger or more vicious breeds of dog, Henry assumed. Blackstone picked up the collar and chain, holding it carefully in her gloved hands, and inspected it.

Puzzled, Henry watched her as she bent her knees and went down on to her haunches.

'This would hold a pit bull,' she said, voicing Henry's thoughts. 'And it can be padlocked.' She pointed to the ground on which was a small but sturdy-looking steel padlock. She did not touch it, but Henry could see it looked as though the hasp had been snipped by metal cutters.

'No dog, though,' Henry said.

'No,' she agreed. She grabbed her phone and took a few photographs of the inside of the kennel and the chain and the lock, mystifying Henry.

'Problem?' he asked.

He saw the back of Blackstone's head nod as she took more pictures, pivoting on her heels as she then made a short 360-degree video of the enclosure. This done, she then shuffled slightly to one side and pointed to the metal dog bowl. She slid her forefinger under it, tilted it up and dragged something that had been protruding slightly from underneath the bowl.

'She's a clever girl,' Blackstone said, impressed, but with a slight tremble in her voice.

Still Henry could not see what Blackstone was up to. Her back was towards him.

She looked over her shoulder and said, 'Charlotte was here. They were keeping her in here, tied up like a dog, shackled like a fucking medieval prisoner.' To make it absolutely clear what she meant, she lifted up the object she had found sticking out from under the dog bowl and let it dangle from the tip of her finger for Henry to see. 'Another bracelet. I recognize it from the photo of Charlotte.'

Henry's mouth went dry.

It swung there. 'They've taken her with them,' he said.

'Or worse,' Blackstone said. She held it up for Henry to see clearly. This one had a gold crescent moon affixed to it. Blackstone fiddled with her phone and took a few photographs of it, then laid it carefully down on the floor.

'That said,' Henry speculated, 'how come the padlock's been snipped? And why,' he added as he stepped back to inspect it, 'does this kennel door appear to have been jemmied open?' He was looking at where the hasp and staple had been forced off.

'In a rush? Key lost?' Blackstone suggested. 'Panicking?'

'Maybe.'

'Right, anyway, this all needs sealing off, and we need to get a search team in here, plus all the other circus acts,' Blackstone announced, alluding to forensic, CSI and SIO officers, as well as the Support Unit. 'And let's go and have a longer chat with Mr Whitehouse, the nosy neighbour who's done a very good thing – see what more information we can extract.'

'God love a nosy neighbour,' Henry agreed, but despite everything he and Blackstone had just found and which no doubt was linked to what had happened in Kendleton, all Henry wanted to do was get back there and wait for news of Ginny and Fred.

Blackstone went into every other kennel with a dog in it, filled up the water bowls from a tap on the wall, and after checking the loose skin around the shoulder blades of each animal to see if there was any sign that the microchips had been removed or otherwise, took the muzzles off each dog which either cowered away from her or growled a warning. She also removed their collars so they could move freely around their small compounds, then closed all the enclosure doors.

'These dogs haven't had the chips removed yet,' she told Henry. 'All being well, we should be able to trace the owners.'

'This whole place is a lair,' Henry said, recalling the time he had entered Lennox's basement flat in Blackpool all those years ago and described it using the exact same word. 'Lennox likes his lairs.'

They had another look at the gruesome find in the chest freezer before heading back down the track to the bungalow with Blackstone continually taking still photographs or short videos. She knew that when the crime scene folk arrived, they would do everything in more professional detail, but for the moment she wanted her own record.

Blackstone spoke to the PC who had arrived first and gave him instructions about protecting the scene before she and Henry went over the road to Mr Whitehouse's house – a dormer bungalow. He was hovering at his front window but greeted them at the front door before they knocked.

'Hello, Mr Whitehouse, how are you doing?' Blackstone asked. 'Are you OK? It must be pretty traumatic finding a body and all that, but I'd like to thank you and promise that if you require any form of support, I'll ensure you're looked after.'

He looked relieved. 'Thank you, that is so kind.'

'However, we will need to interview you in some depth about the goings-on across the road.'

'I understand. I'm just glad I could help. They really are a set of rogues over there.'

'Yes, that seems to be an emerging theme,' Blackstone said.

At that moment, Blackstone was called up on her PR. She backed out of earshot and answered, leaving Henry at the front door with Mr Whitehouse.

'You live in a pretty nice spot,' Henry said for want of anything else. If he had still been a cop, he would have been having a very different conversation with a witness. He glanced around the front garden, which consisted mainly of chippings, paving stones and a number of rose bushes in tubs, all blooming delightfully.

'I do, thanks,' Mr Whitehead said.

'Nice roses.'

'Cheers. They're my passion, as you can see.'

Blackstone finished her transmission and came back, drawing Henry to one side. 'Don't know if it's connected, but a car's been found burnt out near Pilling with a body inside . . .'

She was about to say more when Henry gripped her arm surreptitiously but urgently and pulled her towards him and said into her ear, 'This guy's got Charlotte,' between clenched teeth.

'What?'

'Whitehouse. He's got Charley. He's told us a pack of lies, or at least made up some facts to suit his own narrative and cover his tracks.'

'Henry, are you off your rocker?'

'Nope.' Gently, he turned Blackstone around and nodded down

to the path at the side of the house. Lying at the edge of it was a jemmy. 'See!'

'That's a big leap,' Blackstone said, rearing back slightly.

Henry released her. 'Come with me.' He turned and walked back down the path to the front gate with Blackstone in tow. He stopped and turned to face the house, and on his left was a row of pretty rose bushes in pots.

He pointed to the second bush along.

It was a gorgeous plant in full bloom, beautiful big crimson flowers with thorns that looked like scimitars.

At the base of the stem, lying on the soil, was a bracelet.

In synch, Blackstone and Henry turned their faces towards Mr Whitehouse at the front door.

It was almost comical how he looked at them, glanced down at the soil in the pot, saw the bracelet, looked back up, put two and two together, then realized he had been rumbled. He stepped smartly back into his hallway and slammed the door shut.

Except he didn't quite make it.

Blackstone had already started running towards him in a blur of speed and covered the dozen or so yards between her and him so quickly that he did not manage to get the door closed. Blackstone smashed it back into him. It hit him hard, sending him staggering back into the hallway with her on top of him. In an instant, she flipped him over on to his chest, yanked his arms behind his back and expertly applied her rigid handcuffs, stacking his arms.

She pinned him down with her hand on his neck and leaned forwards so that her mouth was next to his right ear. 'Where is she?'

Mr Whitehouse, with the breath knocked out of him, said nothing, but his eyes looked down the hallway. Blackstone followed the line of his sight towards the door of the cupboard underneath the stairs.

'Guess what,' she said to him, 'you're not going to get any support at all now.'

'I simply cannot thank you enough,' Melinda West said through the tears that drenched her face. 'You never gave up. You did everything right.'

'We're just glad you've got her back in one piece and, as far as we can tell, even though she's been through one hell of a traumatic experience, undamaged,' Blackstone said.

'Yes, thank God for that mercy.'

It was two hours later, and they were in the public foyer at Lancaster police station.

'We do need to interview her in depth,' Blackstone warned Melinda.

'I understand. All I ask is that you do it,' she requested of Blackstone.

'If you want, I will,' Blackstone promised. 'We have enough details to be going on with for the moment, but I would like to talk to her sooner rather than later, while everything's fresh in her mind.'

'Yes, yes, of course.'

'Maybe this evening?' Blackstone suggested. 'You and your husband take her home now, pamper her for a few hours, let her have a sleep, tell her how much you love her . . . you know where I'm coming from. We've got all the samples we need from her, and as she's adamant she hasn't been touched in any way sexually, we're OK with her showering and getting cleaned up.'

Melinda nodded and looked at Henry. 'Thank you, too. And I'm so sorry to hear what happened at the pub, so awful.'

'Thank you . . . by the way, that daughter of yours has got one cool head on her shoulders. If she hadn't done what she did with her bracelets, we might not have been so lucky. She led us to her.'

Melinda hugged Henry and Blackstone, then left the building and joined her husband and daughter who were waiting outside in the car. She got in, and they drove off.

'I can't fucking believe it,' Blackstone said.

'Believe what?'

'That I offered him support, counselling.'

'You weren't to know. We thought he was a member of the public doing his civic duty, grassing on his neighbours.'

'Phh! And all the while, he was just another pervert in waiting. I checked PNC, and he's got a list of previous convictions, all related to indecency, going back years. Must have thought that finding Charlotte was his lucky day. But why tell us about the body in the freezer?'

'Only he can answer that one. Just chancing his arm, as people do.'

'Mmm,' Blackstone said, troubled by it. 'Anyway, well spotted, Henry. You don't quite need glasses yet.'

Blackstone's mobile phone rang, and as she answered it, Henry walked out of the foyer on to the street. He wanted to get back to Kendleton.

FIFTEEN

Three months later

Steve Flynn had never really thought of himself as a vindictive or mean-spirited man, and certainly not one to bear a grudge – not one that he allowed to eat away at him, anyway. But sometimes there were things that needed doing, if only to make a point, even if the point being made might be lost on those it was targeted at, mainly because they were dead. Yet he still felt impelled to do it.

That was why he was secreted on a hill, hiding behind a rocky outcrop, looking down towards a luxury villa situated on the eastern edge of the Akamas National Park in Cyprus.

The villa was the property of a Russian crime clan known as the Lyubery, and until fairly recently had been the hideaway for a now-deceased Albanian crime lord called Viktor Bashkim. Steve Flynn, through no fault of his own, had aroused the ire of the Bashkim crime family who, over a period of time, had made his life a living hell, even though their intention had been to put Flynn into a dead hell.

They had not succeeded.

Flynn had taken them on and finally succeeded in bringing down the Bashkims with the assistance of FBI Agent Karl Donaldson. The end result – the death of Viktor Bashkim – had, ironically, been of natural causes, when the old man's aorta had split like an old inner tube and he had died a quick, painful death rather than the long, slow, agonizing one Flynn had planned for him.

Bashkim's death had occurred at the same time as those of his two heirs to the crime family, another thing Flynn felt a bit cheated by.

He had wanted to feel his hands encircling necks or putting bullets into brains, but no, all denied.

So Flynn was frustrated and could not settle, and just for the sheer hell of it, he decided to make one final parting gesture and have some fun at the same time, which is why he had returned to the villa in which Viktor had been secreted and protected by a Russian mob.

Some time had passed since the demise of the Bashkims, and Flynn had returned to the villa not certain what he would discover.

He had sailed across the Mediterranean to Cyprus in his sport-fishing boat, *Faye*, all the way from Gran Canaria, where he ran a fishing charter business out of the resort of Puerto Rico on the south coast of that island with his lady friend, former cop Molly Cartwright. That said, he had travelled alone on this journey because Molly refused to be a part of his childish, very dangerous retribution scheme. He knew she was right, but he also knew it was something he had to do; otherwise, he would never fully relax.

With the permission of the harbour master, he had managed to secure a berth in the tiny harbour of Agios Georgios, to the north of Paphos. He had kept in contact with Molly all the way, but as he got closer to Cyprus, she had literally and metaphorically become more distant until she finally told him to recontact her when his 'stupid mission' was over, done and dusted.

Flynn accepted her stance.

She had been involved with his fight against the Bashkims, knew what it was all about, knew the horrors he had been subjected to, but she wanted it all to be over now that Viktor was dead. She didn't want Flynn to keep putting the boot in, because he could not be certain that there weren't more tigers waiting in the long grass which, if prodded, might be even worse than the Bashkims.

Flynn knew all that, knew the risks, but had to take them.

He took his time, almost twelve weeks, crossing the Mediterranean on *Faye*, harbour hopping, and although he hated to admit it, he relished being alone – but not lonely – at sea. He spent beautiful nights in places he had never visited before, finally making the last leg to Cyprus where, once berthed in the tiny harbour, he had taken a long shower on board his boat. As evening came, he strolled up to the Sunset restaurant, ate a wonderful stifado, downed several beers, had an interesting chat with the friendly owners and wearily slogged back to *Faye* to collapse in a heap on the double bed and sleep for nine solid hours, no dreaming allowed.

He woke early the next day, changed into his khaki-coloured

summer gear, threw a rucksack over his shoulder and walked up to do a recce of the villa on the edge of the national park.

He had been in this vantage point before, but he had been discovered and escaped with his life – just – following a breakneck chase through a banana plantation.

Today, though, if what he had learned to his advantage last night at the Sunset was correct, there would be little chance of being seen, because the villa was unoccupied and seemed to have been abandoned.

It was surrounded by a high wall with an internal walkway, handy for protecting vulnerable guests – or, as Flynn knew them, gangsters. The double gate was open, the left one hanging loosely at an angle from its hinges.

Flynn settled behind the rocky outcrop, pulled the peak of his baseball cap down over his eyes, wriggled under the shade of an olive tree behind him and started to watch.

No one came or left. Four hours into his surveillance, nothing had moved.

He called it a day, crawled away to keep out of sight just in case and went back to *Faye* via the Sunset where he had a large lunch. He spent the remainder of that day sunbathing on the small beach by the harbour and swimming in the bay, even spotting a turtle in the sea which made him incredibly happy. He remained on *Faye* for the evening and started back to watch the villa again early the next morning.

This time he spent six hours watching.

There was no movement of any sort.

The next day, he left it until later in the afternoon and watched until midnight.

Still no movement.

He grinned all the way back to *Faye*. He woke early the next day but spent the morning killing time, swimming, eating at the tiny café at the back of the beach, leaving it until mid-afternoon before returning to his observation point, this time with his rucksack and a heavy sports bag.

Nothing had changed; even so, he waited an hour before moving.

He knew the villa belonged to Russians, which was why, he had learned, it was empty, seemingly abandoned. From his conversation with the owners of the Sunset, it seemed that Russians had been banned from entering Cyprus because of the war in Ukraine.

Russians did still come, usually by more circuitous routes, but their presence and money on the island had been reduced to a fraction of what they had been.

This made it much easier for Flynn to implement his plan, so when he was absolutely certain the villa was empty, he made his way cautiously to it from his hiding place and went in through the gates to the inner courtyard. He did a quick tour of the once elegant house, now beset by damp, it seemed, and also did a stroll around the inner walkway, working out how best to achieve his aims.

It took him an hour and then he left, never to return.

That evening, he had another fine meal at the Sunset, and a one-way conversation with a crane that stalked around like an undertaker in and out of the outside tables. He ate well and spoke briefly by phone to a frosty Molly, who didn't seem convinced when he told her his time in Cyprus was almost over.

At ten fifty-seven p.m., he got an unexpected phone call.

Puzzled, he answered, 'Flynn.'

'Steve, it's Karl Donaldson,' came the twangy American voice belonging to the FBI agent who had assisted Flynn in toppling the Bashkim regime. 'Where in hell are yuh?'

Flynn hesitated but thought it best to come clean.

'Hell yuh doin' there?'

'A bit of house cleaning, you could say.'

'Is that what I think you mean?'

Flynn checked his watch. It was an old analogue Timex, cheap and reliable. The second hand was just ticking past the thirty-second mark. In less than half a minute, it would be eleven p.m. exactly.

'It might do,' Flynn admitted. 'Put your phone on video call,' he told Donaldson. Flynn touched the icon on his phone as Donaldson did on his, and suddenly the two men were face to face.

'Hold on,' Flynn said. He stood up and crossed the road, looked in an easterly direction up to the hills below which the villa owned by the Russian mob nestled, maybe a mile and half away from the restaurant.

He checked his watch.

Five seconds before eleven.

'All being well, and if my skills are half what they once were . . .' he said to Donaldson, then turned his phone around so the American could see what Flynn was looking at in the distance.

The first firework, a rocket, went off at exactly eleven o'clock, Cyprus time. Flynn had no idea what time zone Donaldson was in.

Loudly, Flynn said, 'A magical memory for you.' With a bang, a huge Roman candle spat out a splattering of stars, then a shower of sparks high in the sky, followed by even more rockets bursting colourfully against the clear, black night, building up over a five-minute period to a loud, spectacular crescendo of bangs, crackles and stars.

It was a modest but brilliant firework display, from within the villa.

Flynn heard Donaldson say, 'You haven't?'

The display died down, the night returned to darkness and silence.

'I have,' Flynn said.

There was a pause before a massive explosion of blue and orange flame, lighting the sky, shaking the earth underfoot, sending a mushroom cloud of smoke and debris straight up as the explosives set by Flynn at strategic points around the villa reduced the building to a pile of rubble within seconds.

Flynn turned the phone back to face him. He had a huge grin on his face.

Donaldson looked stunned. 'Quite impressive,' he said as Flynn walked back across the road to the restaurant and retook his seat, smirking at the concerned chatter among the other guests. He picked up his beer and said, 'Couldn't resist.'

'OK, I understand.'

'Now then, what can I do for you, my Yankee mate?'

'Have you heard about Henry Christie?'

Suddenly, the possible implication of those words made all the euphoria Flynn felt about destroying the villa fade in an instant. 'No, should I?' he asked with trepidation.

It could never be said that Steve Flynn and Henry Christie were friends.

Both had been detectives, and at one point in Flynn's career, he had been suspected of stealing a million pounds from a drug dealer. Henry, who was temporarily seconded to the Professional Standards Unit at that time, had been one of the main players who essentially hounded Flynn out of the police, even though the accusation of theft was never proven, mainly because Flynn didn't steal the money; his partner did.

This, plus Flynn's messy divorce, had sent the former Special
Boat Service man scuttling to the Canary Islands where, through
a friend, he became skipper of a sportfishing boat. Since then, his
and Henry's paths had crossed several times, and their relationship,
while never quite blossoming into friendship, had become one of
mutual understanding and tolerance. Both of them knew Karl
Donaldson, who was really Henry's friend, not Flynn's.

'I've been at sea, and I don't generally look at online news,'
Flynn explained after he'd listened to Donaldson's explanation of
the events involving Henry and other people he knew, such as Ginny,
Fred and Blackstone.

It had been a hard listen.

'Thing is, pal,' Donaldson said, 'I'm stuck way over the pond
on some very hush-hush shit and cannot be released, and I'm
wondering – and I know this is a big ask – if you would go and
see Henry? Apparently, he's a complete mess and I don't know . . .
I just don't know,' Donaldson concluded helplessly in a tone Flynn
had never heard from him.

'Let me think about it. Not sure what I can do.'

He hung up, ordered a whisky sour and sat there ruminating a
while before setting off back to the harbour.

Once there, he did log on to the internet in the cabin, something
he rarely did other than for shipping and weather forecasts; other
stuff just wound him up, so he avoided it. He searched for the story
of The Tawny Owl, finally sitting back after rooting out a bottle of
Bell's whisky and pouring a generous measure, which he sipped
while lounging in the fighting chair on the rear deck. Then he
received another phone call, this time from Debbie Blackstone. He
didn't know her particularly well, but he knew she worked with and
was friends with Henry.

'You're not an easy person to track down,' she accused him.

'I don't like being tracked down. You never know who's doing
the tracking.'

'Karl Donaldson gave me your number.'

'I made that assumption.'

There was silence on the line. Then Blackstone said, 'Would
you? You know? What Karl asked?'

'People skills aren't my strength,' he admitted. 'I have no idea
what use I'd be.'

'I have. You get hold of Henry and drag him down to the Canary

Islands and get him working on that boat of yours. I know it's
out-of-the-box thinking and all that.'

'You serious?'

'As fuck.'

'Does he even have sea legs? Henry doesn't strike me as someone
who would be comfortable on a duck pond. We're talking Atlantic
Ocean here.'

'It's not about giving him a career, Steve; it's about getting him
out of himself, because if he doesn't . . . I . . . don't know what
will happen to him.' She went quiet again. 'He's broken, Steve. I
know you've been through shit, too – lost people close to you in
violent acts.'

'I'm a different kettle of fish. I take revenge. That's my therapy.'

'OK. Sorry for asking.'

She hung up.

Flynn looked into the sky. Inland, a thick pall of smoke hung
above the villa he had just destroyed. Coming and going in the light
breeze, he could hear the wail of sirens.

He tipped his Bell's back, glugged another measure into his
enamel mug. Neat. He took a mouthful, picked up his phone and
looked at the last number received, and called it.

Henry had not been allowed into the mortuary where the post-
mortems had taken place but had waited outside in Blackstone's
Mini Cooper, sitting in the bucket seat, his eyes fixed on the mortuary
doors, staring at a building full of death that he himself had been
into many times over the course of his police career. He knew the
layout well. The two rooms in which the actual post-mortems took
place. The room where there was a bank of fridges in which the
dead were kept chilled, just at the right temperature so they wouldn't
rot. For the life of him, he could not recall that temperature as much
as he tried. Then there was the viewing room into which relatives
of the dead were ushered with quiet voices while their loved
ones, or maybe the ones they had hated and killed, were wheeled in
on a trolley, their faces to be revealed if they were fit to see and not
mangled or burned beyond recognition, and their ID confirmed.

Henry hadn't even been given this.

Ginny's body, contrary to what he'd been told initially, was just
a blackened husk, as was Fred's, whose family was beyond consola-
tion. At one point, Fred's mother had beaten Henry's chest in a fit

of despair and grief, before the pounding fists lost their strength and the poor woman wilted to her knees in front of him, weeping inconsolably at the loss of her son.

Dental records, personal knowledge and the chain of evidence based on Henry's and Blackstone's movements on the night – having left Ginny and Fred at The Tawny Owl, then returned a short while later, and there being just the two bodies found in the premises – were all the ID required.

Then, despite Rik Dean recommending that Henry leave the scene for the sake of his mental health, he had stubbornly remained when eventually the two bodies were recovered from the rubble and taken to the mortuary at Royal Lancaster Infirmary. He had followed the hearse all the way and watched when the undertakers had carried the bodies into the mortuary and closed the doors behind them.

The post-mortems had taken place two days later, performed by a Home Office pathologist Henry knew well, a certain Professor Baines who had carried out many post-mortems on victims of Henry's police cases in the past.

The only good thing was that he knew Baines would treat Ginny and Fred with absolute dignity in a procedure that, by its very nature, was brutal, invasive but necessary.

And Henry had waited.

Eight hours later, the mortuary door had opened. Blackstone and Rik Dean emerged, their faces pale and shocked. They talked quietly to each other on the steps, looking occasionally over at Henry who remained seated in the Mini, not realizing he was gripping the steering wheel with all his might.

Finally, the two cops nodded and separated. Rik went back inside with a weak wave towards Henry. Blackstone, head down, approached him.

She sat in the car alongside him, reeking of smoke and death. She rubbed her face with her hands.

'It's done,' she said unnecessarily.

'Thank you. Thank you for being present.'

She nodded.

'Now tell me the result.'

Blackstone closed her eyes, braced herself, gathered herself, then told him.

*   *   *

Henry was kept at arm's length from the investigation. Word had come from on high, an order from the chief constable, not to allow him anywhere near. He was too close to the dead, it was far too personal, he couldn't be trusted not to act off the books, he might jeopardize the whole course of the inquiry . . . the list was endless. He needed time to grieve, his mind would be all over the place and he had other things to do.

All good, solid reasons, which Henry accepted.

His only insistence was that he be kept up to date with progress, but those bulletins became less and less frequent as the weeks went by.

But he was kept busy anyway.

The coroner released Ginny and Fred's bodies two weeks after the post-mortems and a very quick inquest simply to establish their identities. A full inquest would take place much later and would hinge on the police investigation which was wide-ranging and complex, and included two other murders, those bodies identified as the two young men who were part of Leonard Lennox's evil gang.

Then, of course, there were also the bodies in the freezer.

Jim Taylor, known as Tony Owl, and the other body, which, after two weeks of defrosting at room temperature, was identified as Jean Lennox, Leonard Lennox's wife, who had mysteriously left him and disappeared about fifteen years earlier and who had a broken neck. Add into the mix the robbery at Maude's and the attack on Veronica, and it was always going to be a complex investigation for the cops.

Meanwhile, Leonard Lennox, his son, Ernest, and a young girl identified as Cinderella Watkinson remained at large.

No one knew where they were. Rumour had it that they had fled abroad and were lying low in the company of like-minded criminal gangs, but no sightings had been received from any source as to their actual whereabouts since the day of the fire and Mr Whitehouse's poorly judged phone call.

It was exactly the sort of investigation that Henry had excelled at when he was a cop, but he wasn't given a look in, so he had to put his trust in the police murder team, under Rik Dean's direction, to get a result. From the forlorn look on Rik's face about three weeks into the job, Henry knew a result was not imminent.

Outfoxed by a toerag, was Henry's innermost thought, though he didn't share that gem.

He had plenty of his own crap to deal with, a joint funeral being one thing.

The turnout from the village was overwhelming as the hearse carrying both bodies made its stately way from outside the remnants of The Tawny Owl to the crematorium at Lancaster. It was a day Henry hated and wanted to forget, but he was touched by the reaction of the locals, many of whom had known Ginny for a long time. Many had also, a few years earlier, turned out for her stepmother Alison's funeral, to pay their respects.

After spending the required amount of time at a gathering in a pub in Lancaster after the service, hugging lots of people, including Fred's devastated parents, Henry had done a runner – but not before Fred's father had collared him.

Albert was a few years older than Henry, but recent events had made him look so much older.

'I hear you're not part of the investigation,' Albert had said. He knew Henry's background well.

'I'm not and rightly so,' Henry conceded. 'I'd spoil everything by taking my revenge on the suspects if they're ever caught.'

'More's the pity.'

'Why?'

'Because I want revenge, Henry, pure and simple. Neither of those kids deserved to die that way.' Albert almost choked on his words. 'All I'm saying is, if you get the chance, take revenge for them, for me, for Fred's mother, for you.'

Albert hugged him.

And Henry left, getting into the passenger seat of Blackstone's Mini Cooper, a car that still bore the scars of being pelted by burning debris raining down from the explosion at The Tawny Owl. She'd understood his prearranged nod and need to escape.

He spent the next few days holed up in a hotel in Lancaster, but when the remains of The Tawny Owl had been finished with as a crime scene, Henry fitted a green mesh to the inside of the fence that now surrounded the carnage to deter onlookers, bought a cheap, knackered static caravan, had it relocated behind the fence and moved in – out of sight, out of mind, he hoped.

Blackstone was co-opted on to the murder investigation, paired up with a DC she did not know and given actions to follow up. In reality, she was very much on the periphery of it all. She also had nowhere to live, pulled out of the sale of her flat in Preston, moved back into it and mostly lost contact with Henry, who became a hermit behind the fence.

For a while, few people saw him other than in mysterious glimpses of a bearded, thin-faced man who occasionally ventured out for supplies in an old rag-top Fiat Panda.

Blackstone and Rik did try to get to him, but he was lost to everyone, it seemed. His grief looked to be destroying him. Hence the last-ditch effort to get Steve Flynn on board following a long-distance conversation between Blackstone and Karl Donaldson. They had mentioned Flynn's name in passing but then both homed in on it as a possible solution – and the only one they could think of.

Blackstone picked up Flynn at Liverpool John Lennon Airport. She watched him make his way through the arrivals hall two weeks after their phone chat, with a rucksack slung over his shoulder, dressed in a ragged Keith Richards T-shirt and equally ragged three-quarter-length cargo pants, a pair of aviator-style sunglasses wrapped around his eyes, his greying hair cut short under his baseball cap, his complexion a deep walnut brown.

She thought he looked amazing. She had met him a few times before and always secretly fancied him. As her jaw dropped, she had to slurp up noisily when he spotted her and came towards her because she was actually drooling. This reaction annoyed her intensely because she didn't drool over men, ever . . . but Flynn, even though he was quite a bit older than her and the thought of them together was entirely preposterous, had an effect on her that she found incredibly difficult to keep under wraps. She knew it didn't help matters that she'd offered him the spare bedroom in her flat on the docks.

Would she, she thought dramatically, be able to prevent herself from kicking down the door and jumping on his bones? Probably not, she admitted.

'Oh, there you are, Steve,' she said, pretending she hadn't noticed his approach as he stood in front of her and peeled off his sunglasses in a way that reminded her of a certain *Top Gun* actor but with an extra foot of height. Blackstone pushed her hair back nervously. 'Didn't spot you,' she fibbed with a slight hoarseness to her voice.

He smiled.

God, did he use teeth whitener? Had he had his teeth straightened? They looked so perfect.

'Hi, Debs, thanks for picking me up.'

'No worries,' she said, flustered. 'No luggage?'

'Just what you see. I travel light.'

'Car . . . um . . . car's just outside,' she said, turning towards the exit so her back was towards him and she had a chance to blow out her cheeks and waft her flushed face with her hand like a fan.

By the time they reached the Mini, she had managed to recover her composure and was back in business mode while chastising herself for being so pathetic.

Flynn eased himself into the passenger seat and a few moments later they were on the road.

Even though he had read up on it, Flynn listened with growing anger as Blackstone regaled him with all the lurid up-close and personal details of that night at The Tawny Owl, especially when she mentioned Ginny's pregnancy, which hadn't been included in any of the online reports Flynn had read.

'So what do you think?' Blackstone asked finally. They were on the M6 northbound.

'I really don't know.'

'It's a big ask, nannying an old guy.'

'We are a bit chalk and cheese, so he might not want nannying.'

'And yet, according to Karl Donaldson, you and Henry have managed to work together a few times and get results.'

'Working together is a bit of a generous phrase. Thrown together kicking and screaming, making the best of bad shit, would be more accurate,' Flynn corrected her mildly.

Blackstone turned to him. This time not with lust in her eyes but tears. 'Look, I know I haven't known him as long as you have, and I know this really sounds soft arse, but I love him as a friend. I just do. And I don't know how to help him, so could you just try?'

Flynn grabbed the steering wheel and yanked it down to avoid a collision with the back of a fast-nearing truck.

'Oops!' Blackstone shouted, retaking control. 'Sorry, forgot I was driving.'

Flynn grinned. 'If we get there alive, I'll suck it and see. But no promises, OK?'

Flynn was shocked by the scene of devastation as he dragged open the gate of the fence and looked at what remained of The Tawny

Owl. Blackstone had given him a pretty full-on description, and he'd seen some photographs, but reality overshadowed everything, probably amplified by the fact that the whole scene had now been completely flattened and the place simply no longer existed. Flynn saw that the stone blocks from which the pub had been built originally had all been stacked at the rear of the site.

The scorched spot where Henry's Audi had been set alight was still visible on the car park, although the car itself had gone.

To the left was the static caravan Blackstone had described, the one in which Henry the hermit now lived, and parked next to it was the battered Fiat Panda, which Flynn quite liked the look of. Next to that was a very swish-looking Jaguar with personalized number plates, and standing in the middle of the area that was once his pub and country hotel was Henry Christie himself, holding a clipboard and talking to a man in a suit whom Flynn did not recognize, who also had a clipboard under his arm and was taking photographs of the site using a mobile phone.

Henry glanced over, noticed Flynn, and for the first time Flynn got a glimpse of Henry Christie's new gaunt look – his bearded face, his sunken eyes, his prominent cheeks – and thought, *Fuck me!*

Henry scowled on seeing Flynn and returned his attention to the man he was with, although it seemed their discussion was coming to a close with lots of nods and finally a handshake. The man gave a wave, then turned, walking past Flynn, nodding amiably at him, and went out through the gate.

Flynn went over to Henry, whose demeanour had changed from dealing with the man, whoever he was, to Flynn, and not for the better.

'OK, Steve,' Henry said cautiously.

Flynn held out his hand for shaking. Henry did not reciprocate. Instead, he demanded, 'What are you doing here?' But even as he asked, the answer dawned on him. 'Ahh, a last-ditch attempt to save my soul,' he said scathingly.

'Nah,' Flynn countered, 'you lost that a long time ago.'

SIXTEEN

Despite thinking it would be a complete waste of time all round, Henry surprised himself by agreeing to be steered down to Gran Canaria simply to placate his two friends who had become so damned worried about him and been at their wits' end; he thought the least he could do was show willing, even if he knew he'd rather be holed up in his grotty caravan.

There wasn't much he could be doing now anyway. The site clearance was being completed by a trustworthy local company, and plans for the future of The Tawny Owl were just in embryo stage, with an architect on board who he'd been meeting when Flynn turned up. One thing was certain: he was going to make sure the place would rise from the ashes like a phoenix and would be better than ever, a fitting memorial to Alison and Ginny and Fred. The old stone would be reused, but the whole place would be redesigned with both a nod to the past and a proper view of the future.

He explained all this to Flynn as they sat in a taxi taking them to the airport a day later, having politely declined a lift from Blackstone.

Flynn listened, then said, 'You actually seem to be on an even keel.'

Henry sniggered and said, 'Even keel – I see what you did there.'

Flynn didn't. Not immediately. Then he did.

'I won't lie,' he said when Flynn stopped laughing at his unintentional pun. 'I've been through the wringer, but so have others. Fred's parents – Blackstone, too. She was good mates with Ginny and was going to be a bridesmaid at the wedding. I was Ginny's only family as far as I know, and for me, living right on top of everything was tough, but I soldiered on like the trooper I am,' he said. 'I quite like the caravan life, actually. And the shitty car. And living behind the fence. All sort of suits my reclusive personality – what I've become, anyway. I realize it can't last, and maybe coming to chill with you for a while will do me good.'

'Chill?' Flynn said. 'Who said anything about chilling?'

*   *   *

The time spent with Flynn was relentless.

The fishing business for a good charter skipper – and Flynn was one of the best in the islands – never really had downtime, although there were parts of the seasons more bountiful than others.

Flynn's boat, *Faye*, was fully booked for the next six weeks.

That meant a normal day's fishing began at nine a.m., although preparation time – the rods, the bait, the food for the clients – started at seven; return to the harbour at Puerto Rico was at three p.m. if a full day had been booked, and most were.

Post-fishing duties included cleaning all equipment, washing down the boat, which all went on until five o'clock at least. Several of the charters were overnighters to the waters around El Hierro or La Palma where the fishing was abundant.

Evenings were usually spent eating paella on the beach and then falling into bed for a long, dreamless slumber.

Flynn chucked Henry right into the maelstrom of his lifestyle with little explanation or training, but with the tacit understanding that Henry was from a generation that got on with things, asked for help when necessary, but sank or swam otherwise.

Henry was determined to swim.

For someone still recovering from a knife attack and who was a tad weak physically, it was gruelling, particularly on the occasions when a big haul happened, and Flynn managed to hook a client into a big fish such as a marlin. The fish, unless it threw the hook, finally ended up alongside the boat to be photographed, videoed, tagged, then released. It was during these wild, physical contests of strength and willpower that Henry began to understand and respect Flynn. He was so fucking good that it really irked him.

Even though it was tough for Henry at first, there came a point about two and a half weeks into his 'secondment', as he called it, when the knife wounds began to hurt less, muscles seemed to be re-forming, his strength – inner and external – was growing; four weeks into it at six a.m. one morning before breakfast, Henry showered and looked at himself in the full-length mirror in his tiny bedroom and saw a very different person.

He'd shed more weight but replaced it with muscle. He was tanned all over, except for his intimate regions. His legs looked strong and his face, though still haggard (but now shaven), had lost the deep bags under his eyes. His eyes themselves had become sharp, found their blueness again, and his hair was close-cropped and neat and silver-grey.

Obviously, he was still a man in his early sixties, but he could probably have blagged his way to being ten years younger.

'Holy shit,' he said on his appraisal.

That was what hard graft, good food, a bit of drink and deep sleep did.

Flynn rapped on the bedroom door. 'You running?' he called through.

'Two minutes,' Henry replied, found his shorts and ragged T-shirt and pulled on a pair of decent trainers to get ready for another facet of his new existence: a morning jog with Flynn.

Henry had always run as part of his life but had let it slide over the last few years, and he had baulked initially when, on the first day in Puerto Rico, Flynn had rudely awoken him and announced that a run was part of the day's work. At first, Henry had been a sloth – everything hurt, ankles, knees, hips, and his lungs wanted to burst – but eventually he managed to build up to a thirty-minute run around town, finishing off with a swim across the bay.

Henry impressed even himself.

He came out of the bedroom into the lounge of the semi-detached villa that Flynn rented on the edge of the town park behind the beach. It was small but just about big enough to accommodate Henry and Flynn and Molly without Henry getting under their feet too much. Henry knew his time here was coming to an end, not least because work on rebuilding The Tawny Owl was due to commence. And Henry needed to be there.

Molly was still in bed as the two men set off for their run.

Then it was the usual sort of day on the boat, everything done and dusted by five p.m., with a decent enough catch to leave the client grinning from ear to ear. After long showers, the two men plus Molly strolled down to one of the restaurants at the back of the beach, ordered San Miguels and paella.

Finally replete, the three of them sat back with their chairs facing across the beach as the sun began to descend slowly, although the heat remained.

'I need to thank both of you,' Henry said. He looked at Flynn who shrugged and said, 'Whatev'.'

Molly smiled. 'You're welcome.'

'I think it's time for me to head back to my reality. I know it'll be tough, but I think I'm all right up here now.' He tapped his temple with the neck of his beer bottle, sat back, put his feet up on a low wall and pulled the peak of his cap down. 'You know, I never thought my nemesis would be a good-for-nothing shithouse like Lenny Lennox. A paedophile, a petty criminal. Albeit one who was pretty organized,' Henry said wistfully. 'I'd have thought the ghost from my past would have been some big-time crim harbouring a grudge from his prison cell, but no, the reality is that they are few and far between.'

'My nemesis was,' Flynn said proudly.

Henry nodded, knowing all about the Bashkims and the horrors Flynn had endured.

'But when a rat comes out of a drain,' Flynn said, 'sometimes it bites you on the arse.'

'True,' Henry said. He frowned. 'I wonder where the hell he is?'

Henry's phone rang. He checked the screen: Blackstone. 'Debs,' he answered.

'Henry, hi. How's it going?' she asked. She and Henry had kept in touch sporadically. She had not wanted to crowd him, just allowed him to recover his mojo in his own time.

'Good, yeah. Caught a marlin today . . . You should come out.'

'If only I didn't have a job to do.'

Henry sensed hesitation. 'What's up?' he asked. His eyes flickered to Flynn and Molly.

'It's Lennox . . . Henry, we think he's back.'

Henry and Flynn bagged the last two seats on a late-night flight back to Liverpool, both crushed into seats far too small for them, no legroom, too tight and separated by the length of the plane. Henry dropped his tray, rested his elbows on it and jammed his forehead on the seat in front, his head supported by his hands, and tried to sleep. He had four and a half hours of restlessness.

Blackstone met them in a plain car she had managed to snaffle from the headquarters pool.

'Tell all,' Henry said, flopping into the front passenger seat.

Flynn climbed in and stretched out across the rear seats.

'Better off showing you,' she said.

An hour later, after Blackstone had floored the rather tired car all the way from the airport, she showed the two men into a room at

Preston police station. A laptop had been set up with four chairs around it. She invited them to take a seat.

Then she nipped out and returned a minute or two later with Rik Dean.

'How're you doing, Henry?' he asked. He gave Flynn a cautious nod.

'All good. What have you got?' Henry didn't have any time for chit-chat.

Rik nodded to Blackstone who sat down next to Flynn after giving him a sly once-over, reached forward and tapped the computer's keyboard, bringing the screen to life. Rik took the final seat and said, 'A second-hand dealer on Downing Estate, just off New Hall Lane, Preston. A lot of legit stuff goes through this guy, but he also fences a lot of stolen goods for local toerags and is well known for his connections to the stolen jewellery and watch market. We have our tentacles into him and give him some slack in the name of the greater good, and he does have a bit of a conscience, oddly, mainly because he wants to keep operating. He deals a lot of precious metals, more than we know, obviously, but as long as he informs us of what we're really interested in, it works both ways, doesn't it?'

Henry understood. Sometimes it made sense to allow such people to operate within set boundaries, as Rik said, for the greater good.

Blackstone pressed another key and a fairly clear security camera image came up on the screen, a shot from quite high behind a shop counter protected by a toughened glass security screen, panning down the length of a shop to the front door.

The proprietor was sitting on a stool at the counter, and the image showed the back of his head. He was wearing a large pair of headphones and his head was bobbing to a beat.

'That's the owner of the joint,' Rik said.

'Terry Dootson,' Henry said immediately. He knew the guy. Dootson had been buying and selling stolen goods for as long as Henry could remember, had owned a number of shops in different locations around Preston over the years, and Henry had arrested him a couple of times and 'negotiated' with him on others. Dootson was a flexible kind of guy.

'You know him?' Rik said. 'I'm not surprised by that. Anyway, thing is, as you also know, Maude Crichton had photographs and descriptions of most of the jewellery stolen from her house, and we circulated these far and wide to dealers, shady and otherwise, with an accompanying hard word – i.e., that if someone turns up trying to sell any of the items, we want to know.'

Henry knew that dealers had no qualms in making money from items stolen in house burglaries because that was how they survived, but some had an unwritten code that if something came into their possession obtained through excessive violence or murder, it was worth contacting the police who might then be more lenient regarding other transactions. The way of the world was give and take.

Henry stared at the laptop screen. He saw Dootson look up, reach under the counter and press a button, then remove his headphones. The button was probably the release for the front door as it opened, and a young girl came in, the peak of a cap pulled down over her face, shadowing her face and keeping her features from the camera, which she must have known was there. A chill shimmered through Henry because the girl had a dog with her, which she lifted in her arms and walked the length of the shop. Henry focused on the dog, one with a short white coat and corkscrew curls. A Bichon Frise.

He hissed an enraged expletive because although he could not be certain, he pretty much knew this was Manderley, the dog that loved to shag his leg.

The girl kept her face tilted, and she reached the counter where she had a conversation with Dootson, silent because, frustratingly, the video had no sound.

Eventually, the girl slid her hand into her jeans pocket and drew out an item which she slid through the gap under the counter screen. As she lifted her hand away, Henry saw it was a watch, but it was too far away from the lens to be identified, plus Dootson was also obscuring it by leaning over.

'A Rolex Oyster Perpetual, for a woman with an inscription on the back of it,' Rik said. '"To Maude from Jeff with all my love, babe". Dated April 2012.'

'The one her husband gave her on her fiftieth,' Henry said. 'She told me about it.'

'That's the one,' Rik confirmed.

On the screen, Dootson sat back so it was possible to see him lift up the watch, turn it over a few times and inspect it. It was also clear he was having some sort of conversation with the girl.

'He asks her how she got it,' Rik explained, 'and she tells him it belonged to her recently dead mother, a present to her from her dad, also dead.'

'Cheeky cow,' Flynn said.

'What's he saying now?' Henry asked Rik.

'He's telling her it looks genuine, and if it is, it's worth good money, far beyond what he can lay his mitts on today,' Rik told him. Henry kept watching as Dootson slid the watch back across to the girl. 'Now he's telling her he knows someone who might be interested in buying it, but he will have to contact the guy. She wants to know how long that will take, and Dootson tells her he will make the call now if she wants to hang around.'

'He's going to spook her,' Flynn said and leaned towards the screen, brushing accidentally against Blackstone's arm, sending a very pleasant little shimmer down her.

Rik sighed. 'Yeah, she didn't want to stay, unsurprisingly, but she tells Dootson to contact this buyer, get a yes or a no, then she will arrange to meet him in person. She will call Dootson in a couple of days to see how it's all progressing. He asks for a phone number, but she refuses to give him one.'

'Clever girl,' Flynn said.

She then left the shop with the dog.

'When was this recorded?' Henry asked.

'Two days ago,' Blackstone said.

'Upshot?' Henry asked.

'Well, first of all, we're pretty sure this is the female called Cinderella – Cinderella Watkinson, known as Ella. She was involved in both house invasions, at Maude's and Veronica's. Charlotte, our missing girl, also identified her as the girl who held a knife to her throat.'

'And she's the one, we believe, who terrified Maude in the bath,' Blackstone added.

'Correct,' Rik said, then hesitated.

'What?' Henry asked suspiciously.

'We can't be a hundred per cent certain, obviously . . .' Rik said.

Henry could already guess what his old friend was about to reveal. Although Henry had been kept away from many details of the investigation, he obviously knew how Ginny and Fred had died. 'You think she's the one who cut Ginny's throat, don't you?' He shook his head as he said it but was once more calmed by Blackstone sliding an arm across his shoulder. It all came back, tumbling through his inner being like an avalanche. *Maybe I'm not as well as I thought I was*, he pondered.

'But yes,' Rik said quickly, 'she is likely to be the one who killed Ginny, and the lad whose body we found on the A6, who was knifed to death.'

'OK,' Henry said, holding it all in. 'Anything else I need to know?'

'Ballistics,' Rik said, 'confirm that the gun that killed Fred was the same one that killed the other young lad, the one found in a burnt-out car near Pilling Sands.'

'The two lads were baggage,' Henry said. 'Getting rid of dead wood, anyone who might be a weak link, ballast. Ruthless fuckers.'

There were a few moments of thought, then Flynn said, 'And the upshot of this is?' He tapped the computer screen.

'Dootson contacted us, and we've put an operation together.'

'The details of which are?' Flynn asked.

'He's going to wait for a phone call from the girl and set up a meeting with her, telling her he's found a buyer for the watch, no questions asked. But this buyer wants to see the watch before he parts with any money, so we've got a team on standby, one of whom will act as the buyer, the others being a plain-clothes, armed team that will move in when the buyer gives the nod and arrest her.'

They went silent as Henry ran this scenario through his mind. Eventually, he said, 'Have you thought about tailing her rather than arresting her there and then?'

'We've thought about a lot of things, Henry,' Rik said in a voice Henry considered to be verging on patronizing, 'not least of which was even telling you of this development, so really you don't have a say in anything, OK? So yep, many things can go wrong whatever we do, but the consensus is that we move in fast and lock her up – a bird in the hand and all that.'

Henry's nostrils flared, but he knew Rik was probably right. He'd run similar operations himself and decided to follow suspects, which was always dicey, sometimes ending up with them being lost, but he thought that if this Ella was followed and did lead them to Lennox, that was very appealing.

'She won't turn up alone,' Henry said. 'She'll have a lookout.'

'Likely as not, but also good. We can bag the lookout, too. Whatever happens, it'll be a fast-moving situation,' Rik said. 'We have to accept that.'

'If she actually comes back,' Flynn said.

Henry glanced at Flynn, a look caught by Rik who said quickly, 'I've seen that look before . . . Don't even think about it – just don't.'

But Henry had already thought of it.

'You can't,' Blackstone pleaded, clapping the palms of her hands over her ears and singing, 'Blah, blah, blah, I don't want to hear this.'

Gently, Henry peeled her hands away and said, 'Then don't listen.'

'You will get in so much trouble.'

Henry's wicked half smile told her getting into trouble was the thing that worried him least.

They had left the nick and were now down on Preston Docks having an early-morning flat white at Starbucks.

'We haven't seen the video, OK, whatever happens,' Flynn told her.

'What if you cock it up?' she demanded.

Henry placed his cup down on the saucer. 'Debs, Ginny is dead, Fred is dead, my home and future have been actually and metaphorically razed to the ground. Thousands of pounds have been stolen from my business and the Kendleton fair. Tony Owl had a fucking axe buried in his skull. A young lass was kidnapped. Maude's house was invaded, Veronica's house was invaded, and both of those ladies, if you ask me, are lucky to be alive. Add on two teenage lads horrifically murdered, and you think I'm worried about getting in trouble?'

Blackstone's right hand dithered as she picked up her coffee and tried to bring it up to her mouth. Flynn saw the problem, reached out and slid his hand underneath her cup to keep it steady just as she took a sip of the red-hot brew, an action that made it all the more likely she would spill it everywhere.

'OK, OK, what do you plan to do?' Blackstone asked. She couldn't help but smile at Flynn who guided her hand and cup back down to the saucer, not knowing that she now had a foamy milk moustache.

'Jump the queue,' Henry said.

Dootson ripped off his headphones. 'How the hell did you get in here?' he demanded, reaching down behind the counter for a baseball bat.

'Your back door seemed to be open,' Henry Christie said.

'It was never . . .'

A large, very fit-looking, muscular man appeared behind Henry, holding a crowbar in his right hand, tapping it menacingly into the palm of his left in a very evocative way.

Dootson let the bat slither out of his grip, having quickly weighed up the odds, and said weakly, 'I'm going to ring the police.'

'I wouldn't,' Henry warned him. 'Not if you wish to survive this little encounter.'

Dootson looked at Henry, then at Steve Flynn, who was the tough guy standing just behind him, and said to Henry, 'I know you, don't I?'

'You do, and I need a word.'

Henry and Flynn had managed to enter the shop via the back door simply because Henry remembered one thing about Dootson: he liked his music loud through his headphones, which put him at a disadvantage when someone wanted to sneak up on him. Henry even remembered that when he had once arrested him well over ten years ago, the rapid entry team had burst in through the same back door, making a huge amount of noise, crashing and bashing, and Dootson, who was busy reading *The Sun* at the counter with headphones on, music blaring directly into his ears, hadn't even heard their approach. So getting Flynn to jemmy open the door again (which still bore the scars of repair from that previous rapid entry) as quietly as possible would mean there was every chance of surprising the villain again.

Obviously, Dootson hadn't learned a lesson and almost leaped out of his saggy skin when Henry and his accomplice appeared through the door behind the counter.

Henry had not wanted to go any further into the shop, though.

He knew he couldn't enter via the front door or get too close to Dootson behind the counter either, because the security camera would pick him up, and even if he wore a cap, he would probably still be recognized, something he wanted to avoid.

Henry beckoned Dootson back into the office behind the counter with a crooked finger.

It was half a plan, which was better than no plan at all.

'But I've already told the cops,' Dootson whined.

'I don't know anything about that,' Henry lied. 'I just heard half a rumour from my contacts and decided to come and see you.'

'Why? What's it got to do with you?'

'I have a vested interest, shall we say.' Henry did not expand.

'But the cops . . .'

'Fuck the cops!'

'But you used to be one,' Dootson said. 'You locked me up more than once. It was a pleasure to be arrested by you. You were always so fair.'

Flynn snorted at that.

'You must have got me on a good day, pal,' Henry said, shooting a warning glance at Flynn.

They were in the office at the back of the shop, which had a desk and a chair but was also crammed full of goods, mainly laptops and printers.

'Look, this is dead easy,' Henry explained as if to a child. 'Do it and we will erase you from the story.'

'B–but . . .' Dootson stammered. He was sweating heavily.

'No buts,' Flynn told him and gave him one of those looks designed to strike terror into his soul. It worked.

'All you have to do is tell the police the girl never called back.'

'But what if that's not true?'

'You mean you've never lied to the police?' Henry asked incredulously.

'Yeah, well, fair enough,' Dootson said grudgingly, and then something came to him. 'I could also say the same to you, couldn't I? That she never called back.'

'You could,' Flynn said. He was still holding the crowbar and, for effect, he smacked it into the palm of his hand again. 'But I would come and ask you about it. In detail.'

'I didn't mean it.'

'Good man.' Henry tapped him patronizingly on the cheek.

'OK, OK, what's this plan, then?'

'Well, it'll have to be fluid. Chances are she will make contact with you, and you'll have to tell her you've found a buyer who's very interested, has cash in hand, but who wants to see the goods before purchase, which is fair dos, wouldn't you say?'

Dootson agreed with a nod.

'Plus, tell her that if she has anything more she'd like to sell, your buyer would be interested and would love to see it if possible.

But don't push it, don't overdo it, because we don't want to scare her off. But you also need to tell her your client will need a couple of hours' notice. See how she responds.'

Dootson was listening. Not liking it, but listening.

'Then you call us, not the cops,' Henry added.

'OK.' It was a very strained word. 'So who's going to play my buyer?'

Flynn smiled. 'That would be me.'

'And you are?

'The mysterious Mr Flynn.'

Dootson's phone rang, the ringtone being the theme tune for *Antiques Roadshow.*

'Expecting a call?' Henry asked.

'Not specially.'

'Put it on speaker,' Henry instructed him. 'Just in case.' There was no particular reason it would be Ella calling, but if it was, Henry wanted to be in on it.

Dootson took the phone and answered it, 'Dootson's Department Store, Terry speaking.'

'Well?' the curt voice of a young female asked. A dog yapped in the background.

'I'm sorry, "well" what?' Dootson asked politely.

'Well, have you spoken to your buyer?'

Henry swallowed on hearing the voice. Could this be the person who had murdered Ginny? He exchanged a look with Flynn who arched a single eyebrow.

'Are we talking about the Rolex?' Dootson asked.

'What else would we be talking about?' the girl snapped irritably. Behind her, the dog yapped again. 'Shut it, Mad Dog,' she said, 'you noisy bugger.'

'Ah, OK, well, yes,' Dootson said. His eyes flickered nervously from Henry to Flynn and back again. 'Yes, we're on, and I have, and he is very interested. And in anything else you might have to sell.'

'He must have a lot of money and a lot of connections.'

'He operates mainly in London, usually acting for Russians but more with Arabs now because of the war.'

'Eh? What war? Anyhow, we need a meet.'

'OK, the man is in the area.' Dootson looked at Henry, who nodded. 'But he'll need at least two hours' notice because he's up here doing other business. Shall I tell him you'll meet him here, in the shop?'

'No fucking way! Y'think I'm Dumbo?'

'No, no, not at all. This is where I do my business from.'

'And what if you're setting me up with the cops?'

'I assure you, miss,' Dootson said, adopting his most affronted tone of voice, 'I would do no such thing. I have a reputation to maintain – and not with the cops.'

'Whatever,' she said, unimpressed. 'But I'm not going back in the shop.'

'OK, that's fine. What do you have in mind?'

'Somewhere in the open, somewhere I can see all around me, somewhere I won't get ambushed.'

'Fair enough.'

'Will this guy have cash on him?'

Dootson looked at Flynn, who nodded.

'He will. He's loaded.'

'I'll get back to you,' she said.

The line went dead.

'Did I do well?' Dootson asked Henry and Flynn for approval.

'So-so,' Henry said.

Lennox had taken a chance.

He'd known that he and his very depleted little gang needed to move on quickly in the aftermath of the Kendleton Country Fair. With that in mind, once Jimbo's body had been rolled into the grass verge of the A6, he had looped back on the southbound M6, then cut down on to the M56 into North Wales, finally on to the A55 which he followed on to Anglesey, straight up to a small industrial park on the outskirts of Holyhead.

This was his usual run when he'd accumulated enough stolen property to make it viable. On Anglesey, he would unload the van into the hands of a man who then transported it for him via another 'legitimate' lorry over on the ferry to Dublin, where it was delivered to another buyer who had prepaid for the goods which usually consisted of catalytic convertors, stolen quad bikes, various items of farm machinery and occasionally a decent small car. Lennox didn't have any idea what happened to the goods from that point, but he didn't care because he'd been paid upfront and the end of the trail for him, usually, was Anglesey. It was a sophisticated, smoothly run set-up, one he'd been operating and expanding since the end of his jail sentence. It had proved lucrative and relatively safe from the cops.

Usually, though, there wasn't a trail of death in his wake, so on this trip something different was needed and that different thing was that the three of them – himself, Ernest and Ella – were to acquire a car and get on the ferry to Dublin where they went into hiding among the criminal underworld in that city which, beautiful though it was, was as rife with crime as any other big city the world over.

With his connections, lying low was pretty easy – for a while at least.

Between them, they had a decent stash of euros, which was swallowed up quickly, and then he began to exchange the dollars and sterling notes they had stolen from Maude's house.

While Lennox was fairly relaxed, the two youngsters did not settle to life in Ireland.

Initially, they were fine. Ella walked Mad Dog a lot, and Ernest fell in with a gang of lads who specialized in stealing from tourists around the Guinness factory, but both started to get restless, not least because, as well as their cash, they also had a huge haul of jewellery from Maude's that needed to be converted into cash. They wanted this extra money.

Lennox managed to sell a few unidentifiable gold chains and a diamond ring to dealers in Dublin, but then realized he had attracted the interest of a street crime gang who'd got word of his possible hoard and the whispers surrounding him.

And after selling another gold necklace, Lennox was on high alert. It didn't take much for him to realize he was being followed. He shook off the tail, quickly returned to the three rooms he'd rented and summoned Ernest and Ella to pack their cases: they were heading back to England!

Lennox had a plan to offload the remaining watches and jewellery through the network of dealers he knew across Lancashire. Then, when all the assets had been converted into cash, he wanted to head down to Spain and settle on the Costas for a couple of years, under the radar, to let everything blow over.

Sun, sea, sand and sangria was his mantra, and it didn't take much for Ernest and Ella to be convinced. They loved that idea.

But there needed to be some preparation. After the rush from Dublin, then slipping up into Northern Ireland, it was an easy ferry crossing to Stranraer where they dumped the car they'd acquired in Holyhead and picked up a new one from the guy who'd provided Lennox with the Mercedes getaway car previously. He delivered another Merc, probably the front and back of the previous car, and left it on a little-used car park near Dumfries.

Next, they travelled back down to Lancashire, just him in the front with the two youngsters and the dog slouched down low in the back seat, to some new accommodation he had arranged for them, which was pretty much out of sight, out of mind.

When they'd settled in, the next thing to arrange was the acquisition of three good-quality passports, which he knew would cost a fair amount of money, hence the approach to Terry Dootson. The dealer had a good reputation in the underworld, but Lennox knew to tread carefully by sending Ella in with an easily identifiable watch and judging Dootson's reaction. If Dootson seemed legit, the watch could be sold, then there would instantly be enough cash to pay for the passports and more.

The reaction from Dootson seemed cautious but positive, yet even though he did have a good reputation, you never could tell if the cops were watching or if he had become a grass. But such was the nature of these people and these transactions. Occasionally, they went bad, but mostly OK, and the one with Dootson went as expected.

The hesitation on Dootson's part. If there hadn't been any, it would be highly suspicious.

Then the promise to contact a buyer.

Then to arrange a meeting, not in the shop but somewhere safe for all parties, so Lennox could watch from all angles, check for cops, for other crims and for a rip-off.

All seemed to be a go.

What Lennox hadn't expected was a brilliant suggestion from Ella, which changed everything.

When the two intruders sat down in the office, Dootson knew they were here to stay and there was no way out for him. He was screwed. Royally.

They were going to wait for the next call whenever it came.

They cleared a stack of boxes containing stolen earphones off a tatty sofa in the office and settled down, even cheekily asking Dootson to put the kettle on. Coffee and biscuits were ordered.

As the ancient kettle heated up, his phone rang again with an unknown caller.

'On speaker,' Henry said before Dootson answered.

He nodded. 'Terry Dootson, can I help you?'

'It's me,' the girl cut in. 'I've got a meeting point. Two hours' time. You be there with your buyer and no one else. No fucking funny business or this will all go very, very bad on you.'

'There will be no funny business, as you put it.'

'The guy must have the money for the watch – twelve grand.'

'He'll have it, but you must have the watch.'

'I will have.'

'And you must be alone, too,' Dootson said. 'If this is a set-up on your part to rip me off or involve the cops, I won't be happy, and I know people – nasty people.' He looked at Flynn.

The girl laughed. 'Stupid cunt. No set-up; just you be there with your buyer.'

'OK – where?'

SEVENTEEN

Henry had to admit that it was a pretty good place for a meet and buy.

Broughton roundabout on the A6 just a few miles to the north of Preston city centre runs underneath the M55 and forms junction 1 of that motorway, giving fast access to it and, within a minute of travel, the north or southbound M6. As a 'getaway' location, it was one of the best. Within half an hour, a speeding car could be in Manchester or Cumbria or Blackpool. There was also the option of using the A6, either back into Preston or north towards Lancaster. So quite a few fast escape options.

In days gone by, the roundabout was used unofficially as a car park for people jumping into other vehicles and getting a lift to work, and the apron under the motorway carriageway, around the concrete supports, was always clogged with cars.

That was no longer the case as the whole of the inner circle of the roundabout was now blocked off with barriers preventing cars from driving on.

Currently, there was only one area of pavement on which a car could pull and that was on the footpath on the west side of the roundabout; parking there was illegal, but vehicles still pulled on occasionally.

Which is where the girl, Ella, had told Dootson to drive to with his buyer. Once there, he was to lift the bonnet of his car and pretend he'd broken down and was waiting for a recovery vehicle. Both men were told to be at the front of the car, looking at the engine. If all was good and safe, Dootson had been instructed to use his hazard warning lights, but if the lights were not flashing, the meet was off, and he would not see the Rolex or any other jewellery. Dootson, who knew the roundabout, also knew that it was a parking-up spot for police motorway patrols and asked what he should do if there was one parked in the police-only spot, which was under the motorway on the north side of the roundabout, or if one should turn up, as they often did.

'Game over,' he was told. 'You see a cop, it's no deal.'

Flynn knew the spot well, too, and could see its positives for a crim but, like Henry, the difficulties for a cop.

It was a problematic location to keep surveillance on, with nowhere to hide either a vehicle or a person. Anyone loitering around the concrete struts holding up the motorway would stand out. Also, a car continually looping the roundabout would be a giveaway – for that matter, so would one belonging to a crim.

'I know all that,' Henry said. He was on the phone to Flynn as he raced from Dootson's shop in Preston up the A6 in Blackstone's Mini Cooper which she had let him use under sufferance, saying she would deny everything if it all went, as she said colourfully, 'tits up'.

He didn't tell her anything that she would need to deny. All he was doing was borrowing her car because she was a friend.

'The plus point is that if the girl uses a car and, say, pulls on behind or in front of Dootson, then she'd have to be driving from south to north, unless she goes against the flow of traffic, which would be impossible really; if she's on foot, she can come from any direction but won't have the wheels to get away quick,' Henry was saying to Flynn. 'So at least we know how she'll approach the meet.'

This was only a rehash of the hurried conversation Flynn and Henry had been having in the minutes before Henry set off. Like most surveillance operations, there were so many permutations, so many imponderables, so much to go wrong.

'We're just going to have to suck it and see,' Henry admitted. There was also the realization that Lennox would probably have done a recce of the site and might even be there now, watching from some vantage point. Henry checked his watch.

He had an hour and a half to do his own recce, hope he wouldn't spook anyone, then, if possible, find a discreet spot and hope for the best.

Lennox, Ernest and Ella were in their current rented accommodation when she made the call to Dootson, giving him the location of the proposed meet with the buyer. They were on an old narrowboat on the Lancaster Canal just north of a garden centre on the A6 called Barton Grange, which was also a popular tourist destination not just because of its flowers and its cafés, but also because of the huge cinema and indoor sports complex adjacent to it.

Lennox had sourced the boat through the guy from the chop shop who had provided him with the Mercedes left for him in Stranraer. Moored on a quiet stretch of waterway at Ibbetson's Bridge, it provided an ideal place to keep low while things were sorted and all the stolen jewellery was disposed of. To be fair, it was a rusting old wreck, but it had running water and an electric hook-up, and for the short term it was manageable for the three of them.

Like Henry and Flynn at the other end, Lennox had also listened to the phone call on speaker, trying to judge the timbre of Dootson's voice to ascertain if he was telling the truth or otherwise. Lennox had put a few things his way in the past and found the guy to be pretty laconic and laid-back, and Lennox could not hear anything untoward in his voice over the phone.

When Ella ended the call after giving Dootson the location of the proposed meet and buy, she looked at Lennox and said, 'Well?'

'It's on,' Lennox confirmed. 'You know what you're doing?'

She nodded enthusiastically.

'Right, let's get moving and go through everything.'

Ella scooped up Mad Dog and said, 'He's coming with me. No one ever suspects a tart with a cuddly dog, do they?'

Northbound traffic on the A6 slowed Henry down a little; even so, he was driving down the incline towards Broughton roundabout less than ten minutes after leaving Dootson's, moving the Mini to the outside lane which directed him around to the M6, but from which he could also peel off and drive all the way around the roundabout, which he did, constantly looking, checking possible locations where he might hide. He circled twice, just in case the roundabout was already being watched, then on the third loop he split off on to the A6 north, then deviated sharp left at the start of the new dual carriageway to turn up towards the village of Broughton.

After a couple of hundred yards, he turned into the grounds of a large hotel and looped around their one-way system to re-emerge on to the road and drive back towards the A6, but then turned into a car park close to a school by the new road and reversed tight up in the far corner, using cover provided by another car and the shade of some overhanging branches to be in shadow. From here, if he craned his neck to see through a fence, he could just about see the footpath underneath the roundabout where the transaction was due to take place. He decided this was probably as good a spot as any, even though it did have its drawbacks. Sometimes compromises had to be made. Nowhere was ever perfect.

He switched off the engine, slithered down low as he could in the driver's seat and watched the world go by across the top of the steering wheel. He called Flynn to tell him where he was. Flynn told him he and Dootson were ready to move, but the dealer was getting jittery.

Lennox drove the three of them down to the roundabout, then around it a couple of times before picking up the lane towards Preston. From there, he took several local routes to bring him back to the roundabout slightly different ways although the final approach was always down the A6, trying to spot anything or anyone that might be out of place or unusual. He knew that, given the tight timescale of two hours, if Dootson was in the police's pocket, then unless there was a squad of some sort already on standby, the cops would have to move fucking sharpish to pull something together. All in all, though, Lennox thought Dootson was on the level. If he wasn't, then somewhere down the line there would be hell to pay.

Finally, after a few more loops around, he was pretty confident that, for the moment, everything was fine. No obvious traces of cops – or anyone else, because there was also always the chance that Dootson was setting him up to just move in and steal the watch with some of his criminal cronies.

Lennox smiled at that thought and checked his watch, which was one of the others stolen from Maude's house that evening. Not as valuable as the Rolex, but still worth a few grand on the black market.

An hour to go. He knew of a coffee shop on a small retail park quite close by and decided to go and wait there for a while.

From his position in the car park, Henry could see all the traffic approaching the roundabout from the direction of Lancaster where the dual carriageway split into several lanes, left for the M6 (north or south), straight on for the A6 up to Preston and right for the M55 to Blackpool, or to circle back round again. It was a complex, busy junction with just an occasional lull in traffic.

It was during one of these short lulls that he saw a black Mercedes saloon approach the roundabout from the north. There was a man at the wheel and, as the car passed him, Henry thought there was just that one occupant, but then – briefly – he caught a glimpse of another person in the passenger seat, too far away for him to see the features other than it was a male, and he also saw there was at least one other person in the rear, sitting behind the driver. He saw the top of a blonde head and assumed that was a female.

He had been concentrating his attention on the driver, just as he had been doing with every other car that went past.

For most drivers, all he saw was their silhouettes, but this one turned his face towards Henry fleetingly, then the guy faced forward again and the car was at the traffic lights.

Henry swore. Could he be certain? In years gone by, he had been highly skilled at recognizing people from just a moment. That had been part of the job when he'd been on what was the Regional Crime Squad back in the 1990s, chasing top-class villains all over the country and beyond, and when positive identifications on the hoof were often crucial to operations. He hadn't made any mistakes back then, and he was pretty sure he wasn't going to make one now.

Yes, he was certain: the guy at the wheel was Lennox, and a grim sensation made Henry feel sick.

Yet even though he had an urge to immediately go after him, Henry waited just to confirm it. There was still over an hour to go

before the meeting, which probably meant Lennox was doing exactly
what he and Flynn thought he might do: scope the location, check
for cops and maybe other robbers. If that was the case, and Henry
was right, he would see the car again.

His only problem was that if Lennox chose to come on to this
car park, then things would probably become very fluid indeed.

He waited tensely.

And the car did circle back twice, then headed towards Preston
away from Henry.

'Just sit tight,' he ordered himself.

The car appeared a few more times, creeping around the
roundabout until it finally disappeared.

It was him. And Ernest. And the blonde head in the back was
undoubtedly Ella. They would be back. Henry phoned Flynn.
'They're here, checking it out.'

'You sure?' Flynn asked.

'Yep.' He described the car and the glimpse he'd had of three
people on board and its antics.

'Then you sit tight, let this thing play out, OK?' Flynn cautioned
Henry, knowing what he was like.

Henry knew where Flynn was coming from. 'Gotcha. How is
Dootson?'

'Bricking it.'

'Right, girl, you ready?' Lennox said to Ella.

They had been sitting on the chairs outside the café from which
they could see and feel traffic thundering past on the M55 close by.

Lennox had parked the Mercedes at the back of the car park that
served the supermarket on the retail park, hoping he would be away
from the CCTV cameras. He was savvy enough to know that security
cameras were too numerous to avoid completely, but common
sense and basic precautions such as wearing pulled-down baseball
caps minimized the risk.

They'd finished their iced drinks, Lennox his Americano.

He had checked his watch before speaking to Ella. Five minutes
before the rendezvous.

'Phone Dootson,' Lennox told her.

She did. He answered, and she said, 'Well?'

'I'm just pulling on to the footpath under the motorway now.'

'Just you and the buyer?'

'Yep.'

'What's his name?'

'Flynn.'

'OK, you get out and do as you've been told, bonnet up, hazards on.'

'I will.'

'And I now want that buyer guy to lean on the passenger door so passing drivers can't see him properly – understood?'

'Yes.'

Ella hung up and looked at Lennox who said, 'Right, we get back in the car, do one more loop of the roundabout, and if I'm happy, I'll drop you off so you can walk down to it, cross the slip road entrance to the motorway using the pedestrian lights and then approach Dootson.'

The threesome walked up to their car and climbed in. Mad Dog was in the back seat, laid out asleep, and Ella picked him up and gave him a cuddle.

Lennox said, 'You can't take him. You're going to have to move quick, and he'll just trip you up or something. Leave him in the car and have him later.'

She pouted.

'Not happening,' Lennox said, reaching under the driver's seat for a revolver hidden beneath, covered by a rag. He handed it to Ella who took it with a smirk of joy. 'It's fully loaded and the safety catch is off, so if you have to use it, it's ready, but don't shoot yourself in the foot or the fanny, OK, and remember there's only six bullets in it. Hopefully you won't need to fire it; they'll shit 'emselves as soon as you point it at them, then all you have to do is shout up, and me and Ernest will be there in seconds, OK? We'll be parked just up the road where we drop you off.'

'I know.' She looked admiringly at the gun, which was a snub-nosed revolver, a .38 calibre that had seen much better days. It didn't look dangerous at all, but it was a deadly weapon. For a giggle, she pointed it at Ernest, liking to see him cower, then laughed loudly as she tucked it down the front of her jeans and covered the handle with her blouse. Then she inserted a Bluetooth earbud into her left ear; the other two did likewise and dialled up to connect their phones so each could talk to the other.

Lennox pulled another revolver from under the seat, again a .38 but with a four-inch barrel, checked the load and slid it into the driver's door compartment. That was his gun. Then he reached for and handed their third and final weapon to Ernest, another revolver, this time a .22, smaller calibre but still capable of killing. Ernest looked at it with disdain.

'OK, guys, we do a drive past, then if I think all's well, we go for it.'

'Yay!' Ella punched the air.

Ernest nodded seriously.

Lennox started up and manoeuvred out of the parking space, but in doing so caught and mounted a low kerb. It was nothing in the normal course of events, but Lennox frowned on hearing a quiet but unsettling creak somewhere in the car's bodywork that seemed slightly out of place. He shook his head; it was probably nothing.

A minute later, he was on the A6, dropping towards the round-about, pointing out the place on the pavement where he would drop Ella off, from where she would walk and where he would park while she conducted business.

Dootson's car was on the roundabout as promised, the hazard lights flashing, the bonnet up and Dootson himself looking into the engine compartment. The other guy, the buyer, was leaning against the passenger side door with his back to the road.

'Looks a big guy,' Ernest commented from his position low down in his seat, just peering over the door.

'Then he'll go down hard if necessary,' Ella said, patting her gun.

Lennox found himself in the wrong lane to go straight back around the roundabout, and as he couldn't afford to take the chance of cutting up other drivers, he went straight on, down the new stretch of bypass. He was now obliged to aim for the next roundabout along, loop around and head back to Broughton round-about from that direction. As he passed the school car park to his left, he quickly scanned the cars on it, quite a few, but none that gave him any cause for concern.

Moments later, he had gone back under the motorway, heading towards Preston, where he did a cheeky U-turn across the central reservation, mounted the kerb on to the pavement opposite and stopped.

'Ready?' he asked Ella. He looked at her through the rear-view mirror.

'Too right.'

She got out, leaving Mad Dog behind and closed the door, which took two hard slams to close properly, then set off on foot towards her meet-and-buy appointment. Her right hand rested on the butt of the revolver hidden in the waist of her jeans. It felt good, the cold metal against her lower belly. She hoped she was going to use it. She was certainly going to get it out and point it at someone, that was for sure.

'They've gone past and looped back around,' Henry said to Flynn over their phone connection. 'Old Merc, black, three on board; I'm sure it's them. They went back up under the motorway.'

'Spotted it,' Flynn said. 'Looks like game on.' He was feeling good about it, although it seemed as if Dootson was about to hyperventilate. 'You need to calm the shit down, fella,' Flynn warned him. 'Otherwise, you're going to explode.'

'I know,' he gasped.

'You give this game away too soon and I'll break both your legs,' Flynn warned.

'I know.' He was leaning under the bonnet, supporting himself on the bodywork, liable to fold at any moment.

Flynn leaned back against the nearside of the car, folded his arms, checked his watch as though irritated. Then he glanced sideways and saw a blonde-haired girl crossing the motorway slip road. He pushed himself upright.

'She's here,' Flynn said to Henry.

'Roger that. Watch out, she's dangerous.'

Lennox watched Ella walk away from the car. In the back seat, Mad Dog yapped plaintively on seeing her go. From where he had parked on the footpath maybe fifty yards north of the roundabout, the angle meant he could not quite see the paved area underneath the motorway.

As he watched her, Lennox's mind re-ran the last recce, seeing Dootson and the buyer at Dootson's VW car, then because he was stuck in the wrong lane, having to go straight on to the bypass in order to come back around that first roundabout.

Something, just something.

His eyes narrowed and he re-scanned that school car park again. Maybe a dozen cars on it, not full by any means.

Something . . .

Over the Bluetooth connection, he heard Ella say, 'You the buyer?'

*   *   *

'I am,' Flynn responded.

Behind him, still staring, transfixed, at the engine, Dootson looked as though he was going to expire, but the girl's attention was on Flynn.

'OK, good,' she said. 'No small talk. You got the money?'

Flynn nodded. 'Twelve big ones. Do you have the goods?'

'I do.'

'You show me yours, I show you mine,' Flynn said. 'Fair's fair.'

The reality was that, unbeknownst to Flynn, Henry and Dootson – even though none had discounted this as a possibility – Lennox and Ella had decided that they were going to keep the Rolex *and* steal all the money from the buyer who was so stupid as to turn up with the dosh in his pocket.

Ella tucked her left hand into her jeans pocket and took out the watch, which she tilted to show to Flynn.

Flynn pulled a thick envelope out of his back pocket and smiled at her.

'In fifties,' he said.

Something.

When Lennox heard the buyer say, 'In fifties,' he realized what he had seen and what was troubling him.

The car in that car park. Tucked up tight in the back corner in the shadow of the trees. A red Mini with a Union Jack roof and a Ban the Bomb logo on the bonnet; not necessarily uncommon but not seen too often on the roads.

And he had seen this one before.

That day he had driven out of Kendleton with Tony Owl's body in the back of his van. The traffic had been slow to painful, and he had seen Henry Christie on the front terrace of The Tawny Owl talking to the couple who died in the pub. Henry's car, the Audi (that Ella had so spectacularly dealt with later) was on the pub car park. And next to it was a Mini Cooper. With a Union Jack on the roof and the logo on the bonnet.

Unlike Henry Christie, Lennox did not like coincidences, because they always meant trouble for criminals like him.

'*Ella, Ella, Ella,*' Lennox cut in urgently. 'It's a set-up. Just shoot the bastard and grab the money and I'll be with you in seconds.'

'What?'

'Just do as I say!' Even as he was talking, Lennox slammed the Mercedes into gear and drove off the pavement.

Flynn saw the sudden frown on the girl's face. He knew she was wearing an earbud because he could see it protruding from her left ear. He knew something had been said to her.

Flynn continued the charade with the envelope, running his forefinger under the flap, knowing it was stuffed with fifty-pound-note-sized newspaper.

But then things changed as the girl began to fumble for something tucked down her waistband at the same time as putting the watch back into her pocket.

'Tell you what, just give me the money,' she said to Flynn, trying to keep him looking into her eyes and not at what she was doing with her right hand.

Out of the corner of his eye, Flynn saw the black Mercedes accelerate through the traffic lights.

'Gone bollocks here, Henry,' he said for Henry's benefit and flung the money envelope like a frisbee into Ella's throat, catching her unawares; she stepped backwards but before she could properly grip the handle of the gun, Flynn grabbed her forearm and, in one easy, fast movement, twisted her elbow back and drove her down to her knees. Again easily, he forced the gun out of her hand, then, mercilessly, smashed her across the side of the head with it. This sent shockwaves through Ella and put her into a stupor. Flynn let her slump to the ground.

'They're on to us, Henry,' Flynn said. He grabbed Dootson and pulled him down to his knees on the nearside of the car for cover just as the Merc jerked to a chassis-jarring halt in the road and Ernest leaned out of the passenger window, pointing his pistol in Flynn's direction.

He fired off two shots.

Flynn dragged Dootson to the ground behind the engine block. From bitter past experience, Flynn knew that cars did not provide much protection from bullets, but the two shots that Ernest fired from the .22 did prove to be ineffective, both going into the front wing.

Ernest knew things hadn't gone well when Flynn rolled out from cover with Ella's gun and fired two shots back with the .38, both of which he aimed deliberately high and missed, although Ernest wasn't to know it was deliberate shooting because it was a pretty scary thing having someone shoot back.

Lennox swore, jammed his foot down and gunned the car away from the side of the road.

'What about Ella?'

'Leave her. Baggage,' Lennox said, his face tight with anger.

On the back seat, Mad Dog barked wildly, trying to keep his balance on the leather upholstery, but he could not prevent himself from sliding off into the footwell and howling with pain.

Lennox jumped the lights at the junction where the eastbound M55 slip road joined the roundabout and accelerated up the bypass, causing a couple of cars to slam on and swerve into each other.

Henry sped across the car park just as the black Mercedes hurtled past. It was gone like a shot, and the Mini skidded out in its wake on to the bypass, Henry fighting to control the steering. He corrected course and put his foot down.

'Behind him,' he shouted into the phone.

'Yep,' he heard Flynn respond. 'Be with you ASAP.'

Lennox saw the Mini hurtle out from the side road and get on his tail.

He just knew – *knew* – it was Christie at the wheel and that the bastard had been setting him up all along with Dootson and a false buyer.

'Ernest – him, behind – in the Mini: shoot the bastard!'

Ernest swivelled to look over his left shoulder, saw the Mini and twisted around, hung out of the passenger door window, raised the gun, took aim and fired at Henry.

Henry ducked instinctively, hearing the bullet skim off the roof of the Mini and took his foot off the accelerator, wondering how this was now going to pan out.

'Flynn, they're shooting at me!'

'Duck, then.'

'Cheers for that.'

Ella was coming around, slurring swear words that Flynn could not quite work out. He picked her up bodily like a sack and heaved her across the back seat of Dootson's car but not before – and it pained him to hit a woman – he had given her another punch in the head which made her swoon. Flynn knew how hard to hit people, and this was only a tap, just to keep control of her. A moment later, he had also zip-tied her ankles together and her wrists behind her back.

Dootson, kneeling, watched, blinking.

'Keys,' Flynn said, waggling his fingers.

'Eh, why? What about me? Where are you going? This is my car?'

'Jump in,' Flynn offered, 'if you want to keep a role in this; otherwise, we'll write you out.'

Dootson handed him the keys and said, 'Write me out.'

Flynn nodded, slammed down the bonnet and jumped in behind the wheel to drive off in Dootson's ramshackle VW Golf.

In spite of the forty-mph speed limit along the new bypass, Lennox was touching eighty when he approached the next roundabout.

Henry was keeping back because Ernest was still hanging out of the window, firing wildly at him.

Another bullet skimmed off the Mini roof, but Henry had no idea where the other bullets went; he just hoped that no innocent bystander got hit.

Ahead, he saw the brake lights on the Mercedes as Lennox reached the roundabout, slammed on and tried to negotiate it. Somehow, he did just that, pulled it straight and sped down the next section of road towards the next roundabout. Henry still hung back, hopefully out of range.

Lennox hit the next one at speed also, then managed to skid around it and leave at the three o'clock exit and head north towards Garstang.

It looked as though he wasn't going to stop.

'Current location?' Flynn piped up on the phone.

Henry told him, northbound on the A6. 'OK,' Flynn said, 'I'm in Dootson's car and I've got the girl and a gun.'

'Roger that,' Henry said. 'I've got a call to make.'

'Understood.'

Henry disconnected from Flynn and put a call through to Blackstone.

'Hey, Debs! You won't believe this.'

'I probably won't, but go ahead.' She sounded entirely miffed.

'Well, thing is, to cut a long story short,' Henry ad-libbed, 'just by pure chance, I spotted Lennox and his crew near Broughton. Next thing, the guy's shooting at me and Flynn . . . Anyway, the result is, I'm behind Lennox and Ernest who are haring up the A6 bloody well firing at me . . . so y'know, if you want to turn out the helicopter and a whole bunch of other fast patrols, I'm just driving past the Pickled Goose, and Lennox is way ahead, almost going over the railway bridge at Barton.'

'You fucker!'

'Honest, me and Flynn were just . . . anyway, we can bullshit you later, but for now, A6 north, going very fast, being shot at and I'm not going to let him go. Over and out.'

Henry ended the call and reconnected with Flynn.

'Authorities informed,' Henry said. He put his foot down as the Mercedes went over the bridge he had referred to, which was just a little further on than Barton village hall. 'Where are you?'

'Bit of a slug this, but not too far behind.'

'Keep up.'

Lennox hit the bridge at ninety. It was only just a bit flatter than a humpback bridge, and, spanning the West Coast railway line, it was much more modest than it should have been. The Mercedes seemed to lift all four wheels into the air, and Lennox had to brawl with the steering wheel to bring the heavy vehicle back on track and not swerve off the road.

As the car slammed down on its suspension, he heard that strange creaking noise from the bodywork again, like a metallic tearing sound, and the fact that this was a car from a chop shop played heavily on his mind.

The last thing he needed was for the thing to split in half like some prop from a James Bond film.

However, it was still in one piece, and there was now a long, straight stretch of road ahead, so he pushed his right foot down hard. The engine soared and the speed nudged a hundred, leaving Christie well behind.

In his mind's eye, he had hoped to abandon the car somewhere in the region of where the narrowboat was berthed on the canal, then do a quick collection of any valuable items from the boat and steal a car from a second-hand dealership he knew on the main road to the north.

He checked his mirror.

Christie was back there, in the distance, having sped over the bridge.

Lennox's face flinched.

'Fire at him again!' he shouted at Ernest.

Ernest looked behind and shouted, 'He's too far away, Dad.'

'Lean out, fire at him, scare the fucker!'

'OK, Dad, OK.'

Ernest leaned out of the window, having pivoted backwards, balancing slightly precariously on the sill.

Lennox looked at him, made the judgement and pushed his son out of the window. He went out screaming, like a kid going down a water chute at a swimming pool, legs up in the air and disappearing from view.

Grimly, Lennox glanced in the door mirror and saw Ernest rolling in the roadway.

'Baggage,' he growled.

Henry wasn't close enough to have to swerve wildly to avoid Ernest's tumbling body, but he did see it all happen.

'Flynn, I think he chucked the kid out on to the road. Jeez! You'll see, just after the railway bridge. You stop, sort him, will you? I'm well after the bastard now.'

'Yep, leave it with me,' Flynn said coolly.

Henry tried to get more speed out of the Mini, now knowing there would be no good end to this.

The speed limit through the village of Bilsborrow, which straddled either side of the A6, some five miles north of Preston, was thirty mph. The road was narrow, with cycle lanes on either side, central bollards at various points in the middle of the road and parked vehicles. It was a busy, bustling little place hemmed in by the M6 to the east and the Lancaster Canal to the west. A nice village.

Lennox entered it at eighty, immediately activating the speed camera at the entrance to the village, then being forced to swerve to the opposite side of the road because of a large lorry parked outside the village shop, causing oncoming traffic to anchor on and veer out of his path.

But he did not slow down, kept his right foot pressed on the accelerator pedal, having an unwavering belief in himself that he would somehow get free and that all the money from The Tawny Owl and the cash from the sale of the remaining jewellery would now be his.

That spurred him on. The possibility of perhaps having just killed his son wasn't even in his mind. Ernest was the product of a terrible marriage and, if anything, an encumbrance; he'd never particularly liked him, certainly hadn't loved him, definitely wouldn't miss him. Lennox knew he would probably have murdered him at some time in the future anyway.

All Lennox had to do now was look after number one.

With that, he tried to squeeze more power out of the Mercedes.

The built-up portion of Bilsborrow stretched for perhaps just over a mile from start to finish, so within a matter of seconds, Lennox had reached the northern side, crossing the road bridge over the River Brock and speeding down the slight incline to the roundabout at the entrance to Barton Grange Garden Centre.

This is where his first real misjudgement occurred.

The roundabout was a proper one, with a raised central feature consisting of a circle of chippings, and had big *keep left* chevrons, so it had to be driven around. Speeding towards it, now just in excess of seventy mph, Lennox needed perfect conditions if he was going to make it, which included no other vehicles using the roundabout.

But there were other vehicles. Coming in the opposite direction were three cars, all signalling to turn into the garden centre and having the right of way to cross the path of anything going north, as Lennox was. Lennox knew he'd completely screwed it up as the Mercedes hurtled towards the roundabout and there was no way for him to avoid a collision either with the cars turning into the garden centre or, instead, by mounting the kerb and smashing into a wall.

The line of least resistance was to power into one of the cars, which he did.

He hit the front wing of the middle car of the three, but his speed and the angle at which the collision occurred flipped the Mercedes on to its roof and sent it spinning up to the point where it crashed into the gatepost of the garden centre and came to a stop.

Lennox found himself crumpled up on the inner roof of the car, dazed and knowing that he had been injured. His left leg hurt terribly – he wasn't sure if it was broken – and he could feel the run of hot blood down his face on to his shoulder.

But he was alive.

Nothing happened for a moment other than complete silence. Then the terrible, unprofessional welding that had been used to seal two halves of two different cars together failed miserably after the stress of the last ten minutes and the Mercedes simply came apart as the chassis split in two.

Henry was on the scene seconds later.

He pulled up, flicked on the hazard warning lights of the Mini and jumped out, assessing the damage quickly: the car that Lennox had barrelled into smashed against the roundabout, and the Mercedes lying split into two halves at the gates to the garden centre.

A man, who Henry assumed was the driver of the damaged car, was standing looking at what was undoubtedly a write-off.

Henry hurried to him. 'You OK?'

He was an oldish guy. He said, 'Yep, but what just happened?' He seemed confused.

Henry pointed to the Mercedes. 'Where's the driver of that?'

'There! There!' The man pointed to a figure limping up the road over the canal bridge.

Henry set off after Lennox.

Less than two miles back down the road, Flynn stopped by the body on the edge of the road and activated the hazard warning lights on Dootson's car. On the back seat, Ella stirred as she came round from the blows to her head that Flynn had delivered.

He considered giving her another dig but decided not to tempt fate. As good as he was at packing just the right amount of power in a punch to knock someone senseless, he didn't want to chance giving her a third in case she didn't come round.

He got out and walked to the unmoving form of Ernest Lennox.

Flynn had seen enough bodies in his life to know when he was looking at a dead one.

Lennox left a trail of blood behind, quite thick gouts of it, so even when he disappeared from view Henry had no problem following him over the bridge and then sharp left on to a track leading down steps on to the canal towpath.

Lennox had gone under the bridge and was heading north up the canal.

Henry followed the blood.

The canal curved beyond the bridge, and the towpath became narrow, just wide enough for one person. In spite of whatever his injuries were, Lennox seemed to have made good progress and was moving quite quickly ahead of Henry, who adopted a slow jog, certain he would catch up with him in the next few minutes at most. He did not want to be out of breath for that encounter. There was every chance Lennox would be armed, but that did not deter Henry.

'Henry?' Flynn said over the phone connection. 'The lad's dead, just so you know. I've got the girl, Ella – she isn't going anywhere.'

'Understood. Lennox has done a runner along the canal. I'm going after him.'

'Take care.'

Around the next curve of the canal, he found Lennox on his knees with a gun raised in his hand, waiting for Henry to appear.

Henry stopped.

The two men looked at each other.

Henry could see blood cascading down from Lennox's skull, drenching his shirt. He hoped he had been very badly injured.

'You never give up, do you?' Lennox said.

'That's a bit rich coming from you.'

'You took ten years from me, left me with a broken nose. Screwed the best ten years of my life.'

'You would have taken everything from that little girl you abducted,' Henry said. 'You got off light, believe me. Now I wish I'd held your head down the toilet.'

'But you didn't, did you?' Lennox sneered. He wiped blood from around his eyes. 'And I made you pay, didn't I?' He pointed the gun at Henry. Although it wavered in his hand, Henry knew that if he fired, there would be every chance he would get shot in the chest from that distance. 'And still it continues.'

Henry swallowed.

'Actually, I wanted to leave it at that. I thought about coming for you again, but I thought no, what I'd done would ensure you suffered for the rest of your *fuckin' life*! I fucking ruined you, big style, didn't I?'

'You know you've just killed your son, don't you? A crime I witnessed,' Henry said as calmly as he could. 'He's dead on the road back there.'

Lennox blinked, then shrugged. 'He was a waste of fucking space – just baggage.'

At that moment, Henry could not believe that his hatred for this man had grown even more intense than he knew was possible, like a raging bull inside him.

'I'm looking at the waste of space, Lenny.' Henry pointed sharply at him. 'You . . . *you.*'

Lennox raised the gun again, but suddenly it seemed heavy in his hand and it wobbled. He brought up his left hand to support the weight.

Henry saw the moment of inattention and charged, aiming low as he dived down at an angle towards Lennox's guts while parrying the gun sideways.

It went off close to Henry's ear, but he had connected solidly with Lennox, and both men rolled back on to the stony towpath, Henry banging his head on something hard, but still keeping hold, not allowing anything to distract him as he went for Lennox's right wrist, grabbing it and slamming it down on the ground repeatedly until the man's fingers opened and the gun came out of his grip.

Lennox punched Henry, who encircled Lennox's body with his arms in a bearhug while the two men writhed and fought, rolling into the reedbed and over into the ferociously cold, murky water of the canal, which went over their heads as they slid underneath the surface.

The shock of submersion made them separate.

Henry kicked up, surfaced, gasping for air and spluttering having swallowed more than a mouthful of the horrible-tasting water. He twisted, trying to see Lennox, but there was no sign of the man, and Henry pushed himself to the bank and hauled himself back on to the towpath through the reeds, crawling completely drenched on all fours.

He spotted the gun Lennox had brandished and picked it up, then rose unsteadily to his feet. Further along the bank, he heard a groan and saw Lennox fighting his way out of the water through the reeds and finally flopping on to the towpath, rolling on to his back and looking up to the sky – but only for a few seconds because then Henry loomed over him, blocking his view and pointing the gun into his face.

'You wouldn't fucking dare!' Lennox challenged him.

Henry winked and looked at the gun. It was a revolver, double

action, meaning he could cock the hammer by thumbing it back
into place. It would then only need a few ounces of pressure for
his forefinger to pull the trigger back and fire.

He cocked it, slid his fingertip over the trigger and pointed the
weapon down into Lennox's face. The man's mouth opened in terror.

'Could go off by accident,' Henry teased nastily with a smile
simmering on his lips. 'Could blow your head off.' He looked
around, then back at Lennox. 'No witnesses here, pal . . . but the
thing is, that would be me doing you a favour. And I'm not inclined
to do that. If being in jail for ten years in your twenties made you
hold a grudge for the rest of your life, imagine how you're going
to feel when the next judge you see tells you you're going to die
in prison? That is something I'm going to witness and enjoy.'

Henry eased the hammer back into place.

After telling Blackstone where he could be found, Henry backed
off and left the carnage on the road to the police. He walked, still
in drenched clothing but with a blanket around his shoulders, into
the foyer of the Flower Bowl Entertainment Centre, went up to the
ice cream parlour and bought a cone with a double scoop of salted
honey and almond, then went outside to sit on a bench by the canal
and began to lick it. It tasted wonderful and got rid of the taste of
the canal.

He wasn't sure how he felt. Part of him wondered if he should
simply have shot Lennox and screw the consequences, and although
he did want revenge for Ginny and Fred's deaths, he knew that was
not the way, even if Fred's dad would have wanted it – although
Henry suspected that he wouldn't really have wanted it and had
been speaking from grief. Deep down, Henry knew this was the
best way. Lennox had been arrested and, once he'd been treated in
hospital, would likely never set foot outside a police station or prison
ever again. He would die behind bars and that, for Henry, was the
true cold dish of revenge – always had been.

The course of justice, flawed as it was, was something he believed
in, even if many people did not these days.

He licked his ice cream.

The best form of revenge, he decided, would be to carry on, put
his life back together, rebuild The Tawny Owl and honour the dead.

Suddenly, something was being dangled in front of his eyes.

'Look what we recovered,' Blackstone said. She had sneaked up on him, stood behind him and now held a Rolex watch on her fingertip. Henry took it from her and looked at the inscription on the back of it.

'That's brilliant,' he said.

'And this,' Blackstone said.

Henry felt his ear being licked and something cold and moist snuffling into it.

'Jeez!' He jerked sideways, turned and saw he was looking into a pair of big black eyes. Manderley was in Blackstone's arms. The little dog barked into his face and started to lick him excitedly.

'Found him uninjured in the wreckage of Lennox's Merc,' Blackstone said, plonking down alongside Henry on the bench, taking the ice cream from his grasp and letting the dog scramble over on to his lap, jump up and continue slurping Henry's face, who, stunned and overwhelmed, did not even try to stop the slavering assault. Blackstone licked the ice cream, laughed delightedly and said, 'See, he loves you, Henry. Maybe you should love him back?'